IN
MEMORIAM
TO IDENTITY

OTHER BOOKS BY KATHY ACKER
PUBLISHED BY GROVE WEIDENFELD

Great Expectations
Blood and Guts in High School
Don Quixote
Literal Madness
Empire of the Senseless

IN MEMORIAM TO IDENTITY

Kathy Acker

Grove Weidenfeld

NEW YORK

Published by Grove Weidenfeld
A division of Wheatland Corporation
841 Broadway
New York, NY 10003-4793

Published in Canada by General Publishing Company, Ltd.

Library of Congress Cataloging-in-Publication Data

Acker, Kathy, 1948–
In memoriam to identity / Kathy Acker — 1st ed.
p.   cm.
I. Title.
PS3551.C44I5   1990
813'.54—dc20   89-48921
                                                      CIP
ISBN 0-8021-1170-X

Manufactured in the United States of America

Printed on acid-free paper

Designed by Irving Perkins Associates

First Edition 1990

1   3   5   7   9   10   8   6   4   2

CONTENTS

RIMBAUD

THE BEGINNING OF
THE LIFE OF RIMBAUD

"WHY didn't I have a scorpion? Why'd I give birth to a human homosexual? Cause heterosexual fucking, which You gave the world, cursed me. Heterosexual fucking gives women pain.

"God: why'm I the only woman my husband doesn't thrust his cock in? He no longer sticks his dick in me cause I had the product of this dick.

"Since I'm not the Virgin Mary, God, You hate me.

"Now, Dear Lord above, please take control of Your Hatred and spurt its sperm over this result of Your Hatred: R."

R's mother hated him because her husband, Captain Frédéric Rimbaud had hated children so much that when he had learnt that his wife was pregnant for the second time, he abandoned her for a second time. This time around Mme. R would have had an abortion if a quack doctor hadn't informed her that pregnancy would kill or cure all her physical problems. She had a lot. On the day Mme. R had Jean Nicolas Arthur (R), she also had appendicitis.

A rock star once gave fourteen blowjobs in a row and had to have her stomach pumped.

R's mother took control of her situation as a husbandless mother and announced her rational plan.

"I'll bring up my second kid by torturing him. That way he won't beget any infected children."

Her plan succeeded. R turned out homosexual. Though the mother had no understanding of Our Lord's designs.

The mother came to realize that she wasn't the Virgin Mary though she was a mother. So in spite of God this draconian woman who could tolerate no slight to her authority decided to become the Mother of Maternal Crimes (MMC): she was going to murder pitiful R, not exactly by killing him, but by destroying and annihilating every shred of his will and soul while he still lived on. All for the glory of God.

(I'm running such a high temperature that I don't know what I'm saying. My thoughts're fevered.)

R grew up to be a wild animal, unsocialized. He was filthy. His mother taught him nothing, wanted nothing to do with him. He was disinherited. He lived on bare sunlight and played with forms of natural violence as if they were knives and chains. Tied to his mother, the more miserable she made him, the more he did whatever he wanted.

Whether or not God exists, there are Protectors. Those who protected this child wept when they saw him happy in the middle of decay, urban garbage, spiritual nihilism.

It would soon become worse.

There was nothing for the children of Charleville to do in Charleville, France. R used to hang out in the one bookstore in town which buyers never came to. A Greek who oozed skink oil ran this front. Having once been tanned by the Algerian sun, his nickname was "African Pain." Most of the other people in the town stayed away from R because his mother's autocratic mixture of neglect, torture, and tortuous love had turned his appearance monstrous and tough. African Pain saw that R simply hated himself and had no way of dealing with his self-hatred.

As soon as R in amazement realized that this man, who was his father's brother, didn't think he was a monster, he began to love him. He worshiped African Pain to the extent that he was unable to see the older man's deep insecurity. The man was God to R. Just like Yahveh, he hurt the kid again and again so that he'd know how deeply the kid loved him.

> Wherefore He had perforce to cry out, saying: "My God! My God! Why hast Thou Forsaken Me?" This was the greatest desolation, with respect to sense, that He had suffered in His life.

The man stuck his hand up the kid's ass, repeatedly making and unclosing a fist, until unfiled fingernails ripped the membranes. At the end of the tunnel of membranes the kid's heart was beating. Then the man pushed his arm up until he was holding the heart. The heart felt like a bird. Holding on to the heart, he threw the kid to the ground, kicked him in the side until the kid knew that he was nothing, had no mother.

Unable to bear or stop these tortures, R moved into the imaginary. The infinity and clarity of desire in the imaginative made normal society's insanity disappear.

"You've never given me anything but pain," the kid told his uncle. "I'd tell you to go stick an old witch's hand up your ass if I didn't . . . want . . . this . . . I guess . . . pain. You. I need what you're doing to me because it's only pain and being controlled which're going to cut through my autism. Because it's pain you give me I love you. I love you anyways." R had a high IQ. "Because you don't give a shit about me, unc, and because I'm totally dependent on you, you're teaching me the highest pleasure which is love. The body. But if you reject me, the more you reject me, the more I'll destroy my body."

"There's no such thing as a soul," the African said.

R replied, "I'm sick of Baudrillard. The intellectual side of American postcapitalism. Cynicism. You're too intelligent to be a cynic.

"As for religion: evangelists only want money. For people who have money, money's power. There's nothing else. In this society. This society isn't France; it's America.

"Like religion, your cynicism's a hype. The assumption that everything including the soul is shit hides the real nexus of political power. Hurt me, baby. Show me what love is. Love? The body doesn't lie. Hurt me, unc, and find my soul. The pirate brat is seeking real pirate treasure in the dirty recesses of being. Women wear lost pearls. Maps whose territories are named in languages which are no longer understood show where the passions are hidden." The filthy brat picked his nose. "Unheard-of metals and sea gems can dribble out of the tip of your cock."

R said, "When I by myself in my body see the splendor of passion which is now unknown, I'll see that my own eyes are only mirrors of the infinity of savagery."

Pain took hold of R. He took R's clothes off him, rolled him over to the bed's edge, dropped him. Kicked his body until R folded into a corner. R's eyes were closed. The man jerked off above the kid's face.

While Pain was jerking off, R whispered to himself: Sailors come. They hand-fuck me up the ass. The kid came. Then the sailors went. One sailor made me crawl across a floor after his fingers which were pulling me by my nipples. As if there are dogs. I have to catch a few drops of sperm. My mouth's a fish. Since you still haven't let my nipples go, I have to go wherever you're leading me. Whose sexuality am I and whose sexuality're you? The soul is the body.

Pain had to abandon R because he died on December 3. The cause of death being unknown. R saw a lightless tunnel with a light at its end and knew that there was no correspondence for this light in the outside world.

In the time of good-for-nothings, bums, liberty will triumph. R said. Paris has been the seedbed for the intellectual and revolutionary forces which're capable of dragging people up out of the mire into which what has seemed to be an implacable destiny has thrown them. At this moment liberals think bums should be saved and made into yuppies. Like themselves. The yuppies are the Germans. The German do-gooder autocrats are invading Paris. The French who aren't bums and aren't yet dead or dying from AIDS and other germs are so frightened that, caring only for money or nothing, they'll capitulate to the Germans, who are now strongest in the political arena.

While the Germans were taking over Paris, R, abandoned, roamed from town to town. One morning, he woke up in a room stinking with dead tobacco, vomit, and dead blood. Junkies had lost all tracks. Disorder reigned: soldiers from different German regiments who had been dismissed for fraternizing with the French, national guards, sailors, Zouaves—all types—were in this room and reeking. There's nothing to do when drunk. There was no question of clothing the homeless, giving them weapons for self-defense, providing them with adequate or any sort of shelter. The frost was bitter.

All of this disgusted R. War. Soldiers. Straight males. A French and a German government who were choosing to turn people into TV zombies and corpses. R further saw that most people as they grow older choose to die.

R no longer knew where to wander in hell. His mother was calling him back home.

THE FILTHY WOMB OF BLOOD

"Come back home, you filthy kid."

R sat in his mother's house and masturbated. He no longer wanted to go anywhere but masturbating. Except for masturbating he didn't know whether he wanted to be alive.

R said out loud while he was masturbating and being alive, "Why Honey Chil', I jes' loves the Devil. Ya know why I's loves the Devil more than I loves God? (Fuck fuck, you filthy priest.) Cause the Devil, being the Devil, being God's opposite, being opposite to the Good Father, is the Father of Masturbators. (Can you hear me, mom?" R started shouting.) "The Devil is the Father of Masturbators cause the Devil-Father hates his own children. He abandons them just like daddy abandoned me. Cats who haven't been nursed properly all their lives claw and I . . .

"Once upon a time, mommy dearest, oh oh (masturbatory sounds), there was a Devil who had a good-looking thing, a hose, a tube, a long piece of plumbing."

R was already showing signs of inversion.

"But a thing don't mean a thing. Ya know why a thing, even a good-looking thing, don't mean a thing? Cause it ain't the thing that makes the thing move. What makes a thing move is unnaturalness. Oh oh (masturbatory sounds).

"Now it's not immediately obvious why it's unnaturalness that makes a thing move. God Our Father in His Incarnation Jesus Christ, being The Lord and Our Lord, is the cause of all. Jesus Christ was only moved by, only had a thing for, virgins. But He didn't want to stick nothing in them. Since nothingness is the opposite of and even the enemy of the Creation, Jesus Christ, eternal as God the Father, was and is unnatural. Jesus Christ wanted to be a victim. (Masturbatory sounds.)

"But since the Devil is natural and I'm a masturbator, I love the Devil."

R's mother strutted into the room and told R to stop masturbating.

"I'm going to kill you," said R.

"Yuck. You're going to go back to school. And a Catholic school."

"Yuck, yuck," her son said to her as he looked around for something with which to end someone's life.

"You're going to be an actor."

"That's cause I take after you, mommy; you're the biggest drama queen around." Mme. Rimbaud was fat. Seeing a long nail in the wall, R thought he could act out the part of Judith.

"I DE-MAN-DE that you return to school because all your little friends have already returned to school. You have to go back to school, because if you don't the cops'll make you. If you don't go back to school, your father's going to have a heart attack."

On the first day of acting school, R sat under his blanket and tried to think. His mother then decided either to disinherit him forever or bodily to take him to drama school. She did the latter.

In school, R contemplated suicide more times than he had before. He was too shy to have any friends. Cold knives, he wrote, city of knives all of which are interior and stick into the ice of the mind. The knives are my nerves and they're hurting me. I can no longer locate the cause of this hurt. I'm not even sure that I hurt, but I've figured out I do cause I love razor blades and I love to stick them in my wrists. Pain exists.

"Education," one of R's teachers taught, "teaches you not to be yourself." But who is yourself? R decided if it or he wasn't blood, it wasn't anything.

Then he realized that the blood that dropped out of his

razor-bladed wrist was no solution to boredom. For boredom comes from the lack of correspondence between the desire of the mind and body and the society outside that mind and body. From impossibility of any desire's actualization. Disillusioned with left-wing or French politics, R wanted to tear his own skin into strips of Band-Aids with which to heal the wounded, tear tufts of the hair above his cock out of his pimply skin so that he would know how the whores of the German soldiers felt, ram his own fist like a gun barrel up his own asshole so that he could be the child he had never been allowed to be. But under no circumstances did he want to die.

The teacher of the third form was Ariste L'Héritier, a tubular tubercular hairy trull. Known nonaffectionately to the students as "Father Fist" in honor of the German left wing who had failed, FF was given to appalling fits of anger by which he terrorized his whole class. Because he was a humanitarian. The principal of the school recognized that "Baby R" had an exceptional mind and persuaded R's mother to let her son take private lessons with FF. Violence was the only emotion to which the child could relate. R adored FF.

One day R asked FF, "Why do people poison other people?" R was thinking about poisoning the Muller twins. The Muller twins were German. They had long straight blond hair and were strong. Since they were the only pupils who were as intelligent as R, they hated R and R hated them because they were equals.

Though R wanted to kill them and knew he wanted to kill them, as yet he had only pissed into both of their camel hair coats. Then pressed chewed-up bubble gum into the mess. School stunk. The Mullers got better marks than R because, being German, they weren't sloppy.

"People poison other people because they don't know how else to do what they want to do."

R didn't understand FF's words. He often didn't understand. He feared and loved not understanding. Not understanding put him at the edge of danger and the edge of danger was sex.

FF added, "Whether or not to poison is a technical problem."

"I don't have problems, Fartface." R began to believe that his teacher didn't know everything. Thick black sticks of hair jutted out of the edges and overhung his white and scratched bratty face. "I don't have any objections to any crime. Every crime which as yet my sad heart has committed—familial crime—killing my mother—killing myself—delights me. Following my dreams into poison—There's only one problem. I don't know enough about poisons."

FF asked the child, "Would you like to poison someone?"

"I'm a virgin."

"It's alright to be a virgin." FF paused. "Would you like to poison someone?"

"I don't know anything about poisons so I can't use them."

"You've been playing on the edges of criminality, of identity. Now this is serious. Would you like to poison someone?"

Even though R didn't want to poison another human being, he felt that he had already committed himself. "I'll poison someone. But I hate you."

The teacher didn't care what the filthy brat felt about him. More precisely, the teacher was too scared to let himself feel, to let himself realize that he needed R's nastiness, hatred of all authority, and need of him. They were both bound to go through an arbitrary poisoning so that they could both learn about life and death. "Tonight there's going to be a woman, a whore, in this school. You're going to poison this whore."

R felt revolted. Caught between feelings of commitment and revulsion, he started to bawl. He had to tell this teacher, all his masters, to go to hell. But he couldn't, yet. "Filthy fucking liar. I won't lick your sneakers anymore because they smell. Kissing them makes my stomach sick. You want me to be a slut, a little girl, to pity you because you don't know how to make contact with anyone. You're the vampire, the bloodsucker, Nazi."

FF seriously replied, "Tell me how you hate me."

R was silent.

"Who are you, R?"

"I'm nothing."

FF gave R a small packet of strychnine and left him alone. These were R's special lessons in school.

R, still bawling, graffitied one of the dark red school hall walls. "MASTER LORD GOD PUKE DEATH TO GOD." The sight of a teacher was beginning to make his lips itch with dirty language. He decided to cultivate lice in his hair so he could throw them at his teachers, especially Fuckfist.

It is true that there is no God. There is no God to save us from anything or anyone. All, then, is the result of our own actions.

"What're you doing, R?"

Ernest Delahaye, sloppy stupid legally blind and R's best friend, met him in the hall.

R told his best friend that he was going to kill someone. "Who?"

FF had acted like he was a good teacher and loved him just so FF could carve him up. He had to kill FF before FF killed him. All education was games. All education was games the teachers played with students or victims. Our teachers are playing games with us, games that they love us, games that we need them, so that they can carve us up into lobotomies and servants to a lobotomized society. So that we'll learn to obey orders. They're German. R screamed. With a teacher or a master, there's no reality, and I have to find reality.

Delahaye who was stupid asked R if FF had actually done anything to R.

"Just now in the hall he told me to take off all my clothes. I told him to go fuck himself rather than me. Autocratically, he told me to take off all my clothes. I did cause I hated someone. He told me, 'Display yourself.' Just like the army. I know I don't have any arms so I'm totally degraded so I did as my officer commanded. FF barely glanced at my asshole. I wouldn't look at it either. Delahaye, I've become a baby in front of my soldier father who never existed. THERE'S NO GOOD AND THERE'S NO LOVE."

"So what happened next?" the stupid child asked.

"He told me he loved me. *HE TOLD ME HE LOVED ME.* THAT'S THE BIGGEST MILITARY LIE OF ALL.

" 'Education,' FF then said, 'is an act of love.' I hate! I don't understand!"

Delahaye, who was fat as well as being stupid, said that he was hungry.

It was time for the regular school evening meal.

Fuckfist: I don't need to do much to the child in order to teach him because I understand him almost perfectly. *A powerful man does not need* implements. R's a cold wall, a unique ice forged of metal, erected against an imaginary, unbearable world. He's pure anger. He's closed. All of him that is closure wants to be destroyed. All of him wants only one thing: to be opened up. He's the toughest fortress or child I've ever come up against. So in order to open this rusty can, I have to use the largest and sharpest can opener. (FF was contradicting himself.) In these circumstances, the harshest measures are necessary. He must be spread open. His heart must show. He must be open and available to my hands. *The child* wants above all to be destroyed.

I'm just a teacher. I've got lots of students. So I won't personally be involved in the death of this filthy brat.

Because I'm kind, my arms lifted him up and held him. Then I dropped him on the floor. One of my feet rolled him across the floor into a corner. Then kicked the child. He lay curled in the corner. I waited until he knew. I stood over him, took myself out of my pants, and jerked off on him. I felt nothing sexual. I knew, because he wanted to touch my penis and make our relation personal and couldn't, this whole time he was fighting me. He was silently saying to himself I'm a voyeur.

Prone to disease, though fat, frail, weak, bareheaded, eyes always seeming to weep on his cheeks, Delahaye seemed more of a mess than R. Nicotine had stained both boys' fingers yellow; vomit had stained Delahaye's clothes. The two boys walked into the refectory. The large room, even when there were boys in it, looked like a trough. The school's usual food was a sort of gelatinous liquid which looked like nausea. Bits of gray, related to shrapnel, lay under the white. You are what you eat. Tonight there was something else to eat. R saw the woman. R had a sudden recrudescence of his antireligious passion. "A grotesque priest, whose shoes are fermenting," he whispered to Delahaye, "throws himself at girls. He doesn't know girls want to be sluts. The boys who think girls're sluts are liberals, filled with compassion, full of decency. Christ, Christ, you're the thief of our energies!"

R looked at the woman, didn't care about her, and told Delahaye to fetch some rope. The woman was a bit stupefied because she was a junky. She was full of compassion cause whores have hearts of gold. R and Delahaye tied her up, took her down to a room in the school's cellar. There was pandemonium in the dining room as they left.

The more serious students found R's prank in "bad taste." They said that R was turbulent, insatiable. R called them toads and almost as disgusting as those the Germans had crippled. If there's any civil war around here, it's identity.

R told FF that he had locked the woman up rather than poisoning her.

"The *woman?*"

"I won't poison women."

"Why won't you kill? You're playing around on the edges. You have to kill," R's teacher replied.

"I don't have to kill women because whether or not to kill women isn't the issue," the precocious boy replied. "The issue's my death. To me. You're right that the issue's death. Teach. Where you're wrong, and you are wrong, is that you're scared. You're terrified because you place evil and death outside yourself. Or you place Nazism outside yourself because you're frightened. You're a good liberal German, teach. You teach death, but you don't die. The issue is always the self. *I* am going to die.

"By making me kill a woman . . . or anyone . . . , you've brought me to my cross. But you haven't gone to yours. Come on, teach. You won't lose your prestigious job. I promise you you won't lose your job. Don't you know," R stabbed his finger into FF's chest, "that it's stupid to die stupidly? Reasonlessly. Christ died for no reason. Don't you understand that I love you?"

But FF couldn't admit that he was an evil sadist. From then on, R, disappointed with his teacher, no longer confided in him and, in extremes as a child is, moved from wild gratitude to ironic contempt.

FF didn't deserve this treatment. He was only scared.

R: In a terrible way I insist on worshiping true freedom.

From now on, R would do anything to get away from school. Scatology was the only act which made sense to him. He lived in a state of possession. As if he no longer knew where he was. He was always somewhere else. He had to be always somewhere else in order to survive. He was rigid: his body was a soldier's. He felt and acted minimally. His head lifted high and his eyes pierced like birds'. He obeyed orders though no one could see who was issuing these orders.

R: My possession isn't bearable because it's *possession in absence*. There's no way out but my death or consciousness.

It is January 1. The Germans have invaded Mézières, which is the town nearest the Rossat School. That town is now a pile of ruins, broken glass, charred wood and ash, still giving off stinking smokes, sticks of wood, razor blades thrusting out of the flesh as if geography were a person. Rake me into hell. White snow, suddenly falling, tries to cover up or kill everything even more. Yet here and there, fires burst out. Which I can no longer quench. Because the frost has turned all the water in the pipes into ice.

Razor blades easily sink into the flesh.

"There can't be human flesh left alive in Mézières." That's what all the people say.

Come alive, dead heart, and sing.

R would do anything to get away from school. Break the heart's dead ice. He knew that the habitual self had to be broken. He phoned up the local motorcycle gang and asked them to save him.

"I'm content," FF told a colleague at this time, "to regard as youthful folly the filth that young R has shown me is pouring out of his mouth and right hand."

This is the season of killing.

Again R phoned up this bike gang and told them this is the season of killing.

More German troops pierced French geography. There were more victims. Less talkative than their enemies, the Germans never announced their ferocious war plans. Victims never knew if they were to be murdered. Fear escalated. All men, being men, are cruel and minimal; the Germans, being conscious of their cruelty, thus confident of their decisions and lack of decisions, were crueler.

The child knew that absence of blood doesn't mean absence of pain.

GOING OVER THE TOP OF THE FLESH

(R had his myth: The mother is evil. She wants to kill her child. The child because it's good can't be angry at and kill the mother. Or, because the child can't be angry at and kill its mother, the child's good. This is the child's taboo. In order to stay alive and to break through complete isolation, the child, R, must break the taboo. The child's father is absent. The child's looking for a father. Through the death of its mother, as if through a gate into another world, there's only the world of men.)

As yet R watched the Germans—this new German invasion—from a distance. The Germans conquered. In Mézières, French stud farms had been turned into hospitals. Behind barbed wire meant for animals, cripples in greatcoats, legs and arms missing, dragged themselves from one shed, partly intact, to another. There was little patriotism or religion left.

According to R, this is one image of actuality. "The German victimizers will force an iron discipline on themselves in order to keep ranks, hold on to their victims, and increase their own self-aggrandizement. In the end, they'll be crushed by some coalition."

FF directly confronted his student who would no longer

talk to anyone. "I won't say that you're mad cause that would just make you happy. But if you think that your delirious behavior is making you into some savior or God, I can prove to you that all you're becoming is a freak. Like the cripples out there. German and French. The ones who didn't make it. Victims. You're playing with every edge, R, and you just have to go over once to go over forever."

R didn't say anything to FF.

R now wanted to escape this school and, axe in hand, to demolish FF, the school, and his identity.

For a third time R phoned the motorcycle gang. Dubois, the gang's leader, didn't give a shit about R. Dubois answered the phone. R told Dubois that he was slashing his wrists because he was bored. Something in R's voice—a pleading, a passivity—made the motorcycle leader think that he could make R his proselyte. Dubois gave R the time of day and instructed R not to sleep that night, to be so silent that no one in the school woke up but remained corpses, by midnight to be at the huge double front door.

Unable to do anything.

Unable to act. The body is a dead land.

At midnight the dead young body is at the double front door. A German on his motorcycle is waiting.

"If you don't get out in three minutes, you die."

The dead body remained dead.

The German grabbed R. "In two and a half minutes, this school's going to explode."

"I don't give a damn if it does and I go with it," R said. "My friends're gonna die. Delahaye."

"It doesn't matter, death," the evil monster said, "as long as there is one moment of human freedom. In . . . now, one and a half minutes, I guarantee you you'll be free."

"You can't give a dead person freedom. You can't give a

living person freedom, but you can give a living person death." The motorcycle leader dragged the kid by an arm, R's body half-flung across the back of a Moto-Guzzi, out of the institution just as it burst up. Dubois rode on to the rest of his gang.

On their way to the gang's hideout, Dubois talked politics to R. Politics was the deepest heart of Dubois's heart. "I love and hate my countrymen. Like all exiles. Today they penetrated Paris. They decimated Paris with guns. They took six hundred victims for scientific purposes.

"We're . . ." Dubois meant we Germans, ". . . frightened of a populist revolution against us. The French have a poetical, frivolous streak. Germs of defiance have blossomed in the French. The more we oppress their masses, which we have to do for purposes of scientific experiments, for the sake of knowledge and truth, and the more enlightened the masses, the greater the chance of their successful revolution.

"What is our solution?" Dubois asked rhetorically. "To terminate this populist revolution before it starts, we must inalterably change their educational system. First, we'll close all the free schools whose lessons have turned lower- and lower-middle-class mongrels into poets, painters, and fashion designers. We only want laborers. (In our future, child, when we clone perfect workers, we can use AIDS and similar germs to stop the masses from fucking.)

"After we have impoverished a socialist educational system and transformed education based on questioning into one based on religious—that is, political—doctrine, we shall directly wage war on those who are unemployed and still alive. (Those classes who earn any money are too scared of losing their pittances to defy us.) We'll close down free hospitals, old-age homes, asylums, council housing, and refuse abortions. We've already sent the French police out against the squatters. Whatever services that exist in a society—shelter, medical care—only the rich will afford.

"Let the poor die. The Germans have taken over.

"Menstrual blood is a thousand times heavier than blood from chains. So in the long run we shall fail. We're longing to fail."

(He is bound, the dogmatic atheist, tall, haggard, timid, good-natured, scientific.)

When R heard this, he thought that the motorcycle leader was mad. R then wondered what he himself really wanted.

"Girls are happy," R said to the motorcycle leader, "to hear themselves called *sluts* by boys." The motorcycle leader didn't understand R.

The motorcycle leader and R sat in the gang's hideout. The motorcycle leader begged R to join the gang. "If you join our gang, you'll be able to repair social inequities. By violence. Today violence is the fastest and the only way possible. (Corporate heads, after all, legally murder their opponents; famous artists murder their wives and go scot-free.) Human history views crimes with disdain only when the criminals remain poor. . . . Help make the poor rich."

R wondered what he himself really wanted.

"Learn a real lesson: in this world today crime is your only protection. Our only other class privileges are disease, stupidity, material and psychic deprivation, madness, and legal punishment."

Either R was too bratty to be scared or he had already decided to be too bratty to be scared. He still wondered what he really wanted. At least here, unlike school, he was learning about actual society.

The motorcycle leader finished up his Hegelian argument. "You decide. You can either be a criminal or a victim. You can either kill or be killed."

The guys in the motorcycle gang wanted to fuck R because he was young. Dubois was holding them off until R decided whether he was going to join the gang or be a victim. R didn't want any of this: he wanted a new world. He had to escape. He wondered whether he could practically want anything but escape.

The motorcycle leader told R that he didn't have to be a criminal. If he let every member of the gang fuck him, he could escape free, that is, with his life.

R replied to Dubois, "Despair's filled my heart. Slaughtered by a black existence I died in a shady tower. *I must die.*"

Dubois replied that the gang didn't want to kill R, only fuck him. Only Jesus Christ and His virgins equated the loss of virginity and death.

R refused to let go of his vision. "*I* want to die."

The motorcycle leader, exasperated, placed a foot on R's genitals and shoved. The foot rolled R who was now on the floor into a corner. He sarcastically asked the kid who he was, this *I*; the kid couldn't reply; he told the kid that if *he* Dubois wanted, the guys would shove fingers and knives up and through his body; the kid said he was Jewish; the leader poured bad milk over the kid and told the kid not to waste food the children in Ethiopia needed; the child licked the milk out of the dirt; the man walked out of the room.

R couldn't stand the loss of a father whom he had never had. He screamed for the German. The German returned, asked R who he was.

R repeated that he had to die. He was going to leave Dubois. He left.

"Then you'll go to prison," Mrs. Rimbaud had said.

This brief stay with criminals or revolutionaries, though he was in love with the revolution, formed in him a ter-

ror and hatred of militarism that was always to remain
with him.

Having emitted his venom, discovered that he didn't want
either side of a moralistic or dualistic society, R had nothing
better to do than wander. Around Charleville and Mézières.
He declaimed Villon, Gautier, Verlaine, especially this poem
by Baudelaire,

TO THE GERMANS BOTH NAZIS AND PEACENIKS

Porn and exile and fear and violence
Are part of us.
We eat guilt and remorse
Like bums eat their own vermin.

We squirm and cut our wrists
Over one confession;
Then go back to the street of shit
Believing we've forgiven and been forgiven.

Satan Triple-Master—cynic, money-hungry, pupil of
Baudrillard—
Lulls and quiets my enchanted spirit.
My free will's rich metal has been vaporized
Into nothing by this modern chemist.

The Devil moves the strings that move me.
I find myself charmed by the most boring things:
Every day I walk deeper into the city of hell,
Without horror, past my ghosts who stink.

Just like some old man who gave up
And now chews a whore's pitted breast,
Whenever I grab one pleasure,
Out of boredom I crush it to death.

Packed together swarming-thronging-dead sardines
Demons're rioting in my brains.
Death's sitting in my lungs,
Dead river, sewage of complaints.

Abortions razors suicides viciousness
Haven't yet carved death into this self
Only because my heart's begging
For something else.

Among jackals panthers
Lice scorpions jellyfish vultures,
Yelping slime—
The urban menagerie of destruction—

There's one animal, mean and strong,
Who doesn't have grand gestures, doesn't scream.
He consciously turns this earth into debris
And swallows up reality with a yawn:

My boredom. As I beg for the sympathy I don't want,
I dream, and he dreams, of my own death.
Reader, you know this oversensitive monster,
Hypocritical reader—my mirror—my brother.

"I hate the fucking provinces," R said to a friend, Charles Bretagne. "No one cares about anything here. All these humans, taught by their priests, think that whores, ex-soldiers, riffraff are evil. The real evil is these people who'll do anything to protect their own safety. Whatever they think is their safety. Money. Who lie to themselves that they have other values. They're deeply, morally religious: evil is everything but them.

"To be a poet is to wake inside someone else's skin.

"In these dead provinces, the other is a freak.

"Mom says she's going to send me back to school. Again. I hate school and I hate her. I'm no longer interested in hating everything cause I'm no longer interested in being defined, positively and negatively, by a culture I think's sick. Mom won't give me any money. She thinks that way she'll force me back to school. She only gives me two francs a week which I'm supposed to give to the priest on Sunday. The syphilitic priest should give me more than two francs so he can suck my dick.

"How can I be free if I'm broke?"

Charles deigned to open his mouth and remarked that, when he was just in Fampoux, he had been introduced to the poet Verlaine. Even though R had never met V, he knew that he had to go to V and, if he did, V would save him.

A year before this V had married a sixteen-year-old upper-middle-class girl. The girl was about to have a baby.

Not having any money and, more important, being totally passive, R didn't know how he was to physically get to V. Since poetry was his only way, he wrote this poem, which he had copped from Baudelaire, to V,

DEAR V

Sailors are bored lots. To get rid of their boredom
They grab and mutilate the huge albatrosses who're following
     their graves,
The ship diving and sliding
Between the waves.

As soon as the big birds're pulled to the planks,
Kings of the Sky now full of shame,
Their immense wings drag through their own blood,
Broken oars, against the grain.

This arrogant free traveler—now bound—
Formerly scorns—now begs.
Some man's sticking tobacco in his mouth;
Another drunk mocks his crippled legs.

The poet is this arrogant traveler
Who lives in violent emotions.
Now exiled among humans who fear,
His immense wings stop his motion.

V didn't reply to R's poem. The longer the time that V didn't reply, the more R hated himself.

When R had finally given up, V wrote him. "Come. Come to me."

It is true that suicide and loneliness terrify people. "I'm awkward, shy, I don't know what to say. . . . Where thought's concerned, I fear nobody." R thought to himself on a train headed toward V. "The truth is that I cry too much, especially at dawn. Night now stinks and my light hurts."

EASTER

R:
Idle youth enslaved to everything
let the time come when hearts feel love

V met R at one of the Parisian train stations, took him home to meet his wife and her parents. The father-in-law, Théodore-Jean Mauté, didn't approve of the beautiful peasant. V told R to get out. R wandered down dog-shitted streets; R had nowhere to stay.

R thought to himself: These French aren't ready for revolution. Before the Germans conquered them, the French scummy masses thought they could work with their intelligentsia against their military government. The intelligentsia believe the lower classes are stupid. Actually the lower classes are hungry and violent. The French intelligentsia condemns violence while they use legalized and illegal violence to control the mass.

R thought to himself: After the Germans won the war, some of them wandered to South America. The French, especially the French in charge of their black colonies, missed them. Some Germans left South America to work for these offices. Just recently the Germans pierced France and

26

killed lots of French; now the French colonists hire ex–top German military. When there're no values, it's hard for me to find a reason to live.

R had nowhere to live. "The suffering's enormous," he wrote Izambard, a friend of his. This statement described nothing because a statement can mean only to someone who knows. Provincials, like married people, aren't homeless. Every morning R woke up next to no one on concrete. Human flesh needs human flesh. Because only flesh is value. R continued, "I'm increasing my suffering cause I have to be stronger to be a writer. I'm training myself."

Humans always look for a reason for their suffering.

If humans are inescapably subject to inscrutable yet inflexible natural and/or historical laws, utopianism is absurd.

Several days after V had thrown him out, V found R in a pile of dog shit. R was picking his nose without seemingly being disgusted. R spat at V and told V V was too disgusting, bourgeois, married for R to touch him.

R: "I'm getting food out of garbage cans and you're getting it from your wife's mother."

Androgyny is foul.

Sometimes R slept in bum hostels. V and his wife now had a two-week-old son named Georges.

V said to his father-in-law at dinner one night, "Most generous and kind father-in-law. You are now one of the richest landlords in our section of Paris. I am so honored. You are sitting on the local school board and support the German non-state-supported system of education. I am so honored. As for your beautiful wife—out of her kindness and generosity she pays for painting lessons for her daughter even though her daughter's now a married woman. No harm can enter these family walls; we are a fortress against the rages of the wars outside."

V couldn't admit to himself, and his family, that he was still seeing R, for that would stain his family.

Winter was almost upon. Vermin had eaten R's shirt. His studies in human history, in *vagrancy,* had forced upon him the terrible insight that the valuable life which he was committed to seeking, diesseitigkeit, could not be found in human life. That only idealists are romantics.

Théodore de Banville and some other Parnassian poets banded together to give R money; de Banville let him have the maid's room in his apartment. These actions didn't save R from suffering.

"You asked me why I'm hanging on in Paris," R wrote back to Delahaye. "I'm waiting! I'm waiting for what I want! A certain type of life which I call *life.* So far I haven't been able to get there because I need another person, V, and what's happened and is still happening between me and V is nothing, shit. Leather rubs against leather. I want blood. I used to believe that the person who hurt me would be my father. Now I know that's not true. V says to me what he's said to all his fucks, 'I like you. That's the most I say to anyone.' V drapes his shirt over my pimples to protect them, then says, 'This's the most I do for anyone.' But he never adds the one phrase that would make these statements true. '—except for my wife.' I'm the passion he has outside his love for his wife and son. *Passion* rather than *fuck* only because I'm so mean. Passion isn't love. I'll live more and more outside society, on these streets of dog shit, to show him how much I need him. But I don't need him out of weakness. *Both of us are lonely.* I need V because together we can get to life; life is something other than shit. I'd rather suicide than live in the bourgeoisie or shit. If V keeps abandoning me, I'll hang on and wait, rather than suicide, as long as I have to wait."

... the path of life is but a dream.

V didn't approve of R's living in de Banville's maid's room.

In a Japanese story, the path of life is but a dream. The length of this path is but a dream. Storms pass us by. How many dreams must we dream in search of real love? A student who's traveling loses his way. He sees men killing each other. Then he arrives in a city whose brutal police are arresting as many of the poor as they can.

The next six months, V couldn't or wouldn't decide between his wife and R. He was weak. V and R could have waited forever in limbo.

A fortune-teller who had red hair told R that he should push V. R pushed a knife into one of V's hands.

They could have waited forever in desperation. R was exhausted. V had moved him into the attic of a sort of hotel opposite the Montparnasse cemetery. He was unable to move V away from his wife. R began to plead with V and at the same time he despised himself for pleading. He was no longer the *brat*; he was lost. V told R they would take a vacation together. There was nothing definite. V and R no longer had anything to say to each other. R didn't cry because there're tears only when there's hope. R surreptitiously poured sulfuric acid into his friends' drinks.

Since V loved R, he wouldn't let R go. Not even when his wife accused R of being sexually sick, therefore dangerous to their son. Because she was a member of the bourgeoisie, she gave information to Lepelletier, one of her and V's friends and a journalist, that V had become tainted by R because he was hurting R. V feared that all that he cared about, for his identity was socially predicated, true of all bourgeoisie, would be taken away from him; at the same time he drank even more; he beat up his wife.

After a particularly *sadistic* scene, V's wife took her child and ran away to the south of France. V told her and R that he

How many dreams must we
dream in search of real love?

would do anything to avoid permanent separation from his wife. V asked R to leave him. V asked R to leave Paris. V drank more. R didn't want to do what V was telling him to do. V was taking away not only V—his only family—but also his only home. In R's obsessed or freakish eyes, this was proof that, when *forced to choose*, V preferred odious bourgeois existence and identity in the bosom of the odious bourgeois family to reality, to chance, to the vulnerability of real identity, above all to the destiny that had been assigned him: becoming a seer; V was contemptible.

To get rid of R, V wrote R's skunky mother a letter describing every detail of her son's dirty that is *homosexual* behavior in Paris.

V, his wife, and his son were living happily in Paris. Every morning V asked his wife if he could eat her, for breakfast, cooked, and she said, "No." R didn't know this. V's wife fried eggs, English-style. Together they fed Georges and laughed when he made a mess. V was proud to realize his responsibilities.

In the Japanese story, now, in the city, the lost student is a tax collector. Only he can't collect taxes because the ink in his account book has run into its pages. He has to collect the taxes of the Lan Ro Temple. He asks the mob the way to this temple. Out of the mob, a retard runs up to him.

"What are you doing?"

"I'm measuring you for your coffin."

The sun is full and absolutely round. At the end of the day. Wild dogs become wolves in the forest of the night. There's no light. The new tax collector doesn't have a lamp. The wolves chase him to the edge of a ruined temple. Religion is dead. At this edge he sees two men who might not be real, fighting. The men have been battling for seven years. "The universe is limitless; love is eternal; love conquers the

... he sees two men

who might not be real, fighting.

world," the new tax collector informs the bloody men. The older boxer tells the tax collector to seek his love in a brothel. "Your love won't save you here. Kid." All around them are ruins.

R returned to Charleville, to utter and total desolation. He felt that he had returned to his childhood. As a child he had wondered whether or not the only other person in the world loved him. He had had no way of knowing. V didn't love him because V refused to continue his subsidy; V loved him because V wouldn't let go of him completely. V wrote R that V was guilty for their rupture and that their rupture had been none of V's fault. V as father was now absent; V as mother might or might not love R. Mothers always love their children; this particular mother hated and abused this particular child:

V's continuing letters—green and white slime-covered beer cans floating in pools—revived all the hatred and anger in R. R said to Delahaye in a slimy café on la place Ducale, "I'm a piece of shit, Delahaye. I'm a piece of shit because of V. He said he was going to take care of me. I didn't ask him to leave his wife. But he told me that our relationship was costing him his marriage. I'm a piece of shit because when he sees me positively eating shit, he'll find out how little it costs to feed me."

A number of German officers were drinking piss. One beautiful boy who knew he was beautiful—"You know me, R."

R walked over to the boy. "If that's what you call it. *Knowing.* My hair curls and it's black, . . . as something . . . , but I'm not a girl. What actually goes on behind my face when I'm being fucked? There wasn't anything nice about what we did together. Your face never expressed the slightest emotion no matter how extreme your violence. I had to display myself to you; for me to know you I should take an axe and split open your flesh. What would be in there? Love for a wife who's back in Germany?"

An old poet whose beard now dribbled out drool rather than useless words slipped a hand over to a ten-year-old girl's cunt. The girl took this hand and returned it to the old man with a few chosen words. The poet explained to the child that he was harmless because he had nothing to do with his hand.

R: "I love you like I love my mother's grave." He walked back to his table.

R explained to Delahaye, "It's typical German propaganda, political/personal persuasion through fear, that Germans are the conveyors of human death. But humans only find peace in the grave and there's no peace here."

Delahaye rubbed his crotch instead of stretching his legs. The moment there was a bit of sun, a cloud covered it. "What about this fucking nonfucking who cares boring town?"

Delahaye and R looked at the Germans.

R said, "Most of the people I know, especially the married people, do everything out of boredom. Married people fuck each other out of boredom. They fuck other people out of boredom. They send their kids to school only because they think they should. They believe in God because they don't know who to believe in. They don't care if their priests are phonies. They didn't care if their leaders have IQs equal to turds'. They marry each other because they make each other pregnant . . ."

Delahaye asked, "Then they die out of boredom . . . ?"

R said, "No. For them, death's dead serious. It's the worst thing and it's the only thing that can happen here, in Charleville."

Delahaye asked, "Don't you want another life than this?"

R said that he used to.

Delahaye, "Then you're worse than these fucking non-fucking bourgeoisie."

R, "I've realized that everything shits. The ideals and fantasies in my mind have no meaning. There's only boredom except for a prayer to nobody."

Delahaye, "You wrote, 'I wandered in a twilight of wonder. With my own hands I touched legends and myths. We were allowed to trust and there were roses' . . ."

R, "Suddenly a screaming discord: Murder! destroyed this.

"Animality, freed from humanity, is monstrous. Animals stalk humans, eat them, assign humans values. Impossible animals issuing from a demented imagination are a paradise we've lost. The witch looks at our cut-off heads, laughs, and tells us who we are."

Delahaye: "Cut-off."

R: "Our sexuality isn't human. This is the deepest secret. Being allied to wisdom, it's torn from the material bowels of the flesh. V put his hand into me and tore me. I learned that I didn't know how to handle pain. I turned to V to help me, but he turned away from me. I felt nothing but rancor and contempt for V."

In the same café the next day a German called for a barber. "Barber." A barber came to him. "Barber, you're a stupid man."

"I'm not a stupid man; I'm a barber."

"Men like you who don't know they're stupid are stupid."

The barber answered, "If I'm stupid, mein General, it's because the poor, Schuldfrage Spurs Spundlochs, murder in and burn down their schools."

"I'm talking about stupidity. I need my hair cut."

The barber answered, "You might as well be talking about

morality to a man as stupid as me. Our Lord said, 'Suffer little children to come unto Me.' "

"What does that have to do with anything?"

The barber said, "Nothing. I speak out of my stupidity. Schwarzer Schwein. If morality has nothing to do with anything, it has nothing to do with either you or me. It's us who lack morality, in der Praxis, not God."

"Schwein, Schwein. You're too stupid to cut my hair rather than my skin. Was gibt's zum Mittagessen?"

The barber said, "If I can't cut your hair, it's cause I'm poor."

"Women are beasts of burden for the same reason. There're three kinds of women, barber: (1) absent ones or our wives; (2) dead women; (3) whores. The whores're red. Das ist die Rache für deine Untat."

The barber said, "Rache ist süb. If you don't have money, General, and you dare to feel, you wind up dead in some cornfield or condemned to the bin for prostitution."

Wait, V wrote R. Wait wait wait.

R thought to himself: I'll take a sledgehammer and cut off time so time'll be dead. R didn't have the guts to say this to V.

V wrote R a second time: I can't handle things; I don't know if I should break up with my wife; I can't bear considering whether I should break up with my wife; have pity on me cause I'm weak; I'm now a clerk; I have to keep doing this job because I need money; I'm drinking all the time.

V wrote R whom he had abandoned a third time: Please keep writing, I love your writing, and telling me you love me and need me. I'll never abandon you and you'll never be alone again.

R tried to destroy his love for V, hate V, but he couldn't because he couldn't erase his need of V . . . (but V was a clerk).

What is it within us that lies, murders, steals?

R knew that if he didn't get V, there would be only barren-ness. Charleville. Since he absolutely needed V, he was un-able to demand anything from V. Now V began to write R that he was committed to and loved him, but wanted him to stay away in Charleville so that he could love him.

R didn't want to stay in Charleville because Charleville was death. All he had in Charleville were his motorbike and friends; that's not enough to sustain human life.

R wrote back to V that he had to see V if their relationship was to continue.

In the Japanese story, when the new tax collector entered the temple of ruins, he saw a girl. One of the fighters ban-daged his own wounds. The girl, naked, bathed in the river. The fighter and the girl fucked. The temple is decayed.

V wrote: Of course we're going to see each other! Soon! I'm planning our meeting right now.

If you put pressure on me—to leave my wife—I'll run away. I'm too unstable to consider breaking up my family.

My marriage's slippery. I don't know what's going to happen.

And never think that I've abandoned you.

R believed that V wouldn't abandon him. He thought that V didn't know how much pain he was feeling. Then he perceived or believed that V loved him and felt more pain than he.

To transform absence to presence and to defeat solitude or the absence of human values, R wrote without stopping; this is all he could do. Poems prose letters. V encouraged R's writings. R wrote to V: that human freedom and indepen-dence, which Kant Schiller and other idealists unreservedly accepted and extolled, are in actuality questionable, tenuous because our natures are deeply animal. Yet you are repeat-

The fighter and the
girl fucked.

edly demanding that there be only this ideal freedom and total independence between us.

Der Menschheit ganzer Jammer faßt michan. To the hell with this human freedom. Tell me, love, who I am! V, we must do whatever we must to together find out who we are. That's our human duty. It demands total responsibility.

R wrote: Last night I dreamed that the playwright Büchner woke up out of delirium and said: "We don't have too much pain. We have too little. For through pain, we enter into God! Otherwise we are death, dust, ashes. What right have we to complain?" Three days later, Büchner suicided.

R thought about how V had abandoned him. R asked himself, how can anyone who's in pain, how could Büchner who was in pain ask for more pain? During the time between when he woke up out of his delirium and his suicide, Büchner's friend Weidig was being tortured in a Darmstadt prison. Weidig's agony didn't purify and uplift him. Loss. Loss of love. Four days after Büchner's suicide, Weidig slashed his neck and wrists with a fragment of glass then wrote with his blood on the wall of his cell: "As the enemy denies me any defense, I have freely chosen an ignominious death."

When Weidig had learned of Büchner's death, he had picked up a piece of broken glass and thought it was a child. He told the child, "I want to find Büchner."

The child asked, "Has something happened to Büchner?"

Weidig said, "Yes. Everyone's standing around his body."

The child asked, "Where?"

Weidig said, "In the water. In a pool."

The child said, "Hurry. So we can still see something."

In Paris V beat his wife, lit up her hair, and took or stole his child. Then he began new relations with R. He got R out

of Charleville, brought him to Paris, put him in an attic
(Hôtel d'Orient, 41 rue Monsieur-le-Prince), for the first time
fucked him.

R let V fuck him. V went back to his wife.

Without you, nothing makes sense.

Someone: make sense of this world.

R felt this and he loved knives.

R wrote Delahaye about all that had happened to him and
about what he, R, wanted:

> My friend,
>
> You're eating white flour and mud in your pigsty. I
> don't miss Charleville. I don't miss being a bored pig
> where the sun dries up all brains but sloth. Your brains
> or feelings're being dried up: dead pig Delahaye.
>
> Emotions are the movers of this world.
>
> *Me: I'm thirsty.* What I'm thirsty for—whom I'm
> thirsty for—I can't get so I drink poisons. I've got to
> free myself. From what? Pain? Oh—for more poisons.
> Maybe more poisons'll come and I'll go so far, I'll
> emerge. Something is trying to emerge from this mess.
>
> I *don't know how.*

R thought he was feeling pain. This absurd existence—
sleeping and getting drunk—could not go on. The breaking
point could not be far off.

This was R's farewell letter to V.

And the queen, the witch, who lights up her cunt in the pot of the earth, will never tell us what she knows, and what we'll not know.

A JAPANESE INTERLUDE

The following is a story written by a woman, Murasaki Shikibu, in A.D. 1008:

THERE is something vulgar, childish, and underdeveloped in the mental attitude revealed: a coarse greed for all experience, unlighted by the power to judge and reject or by any consciousness of the ranks and hierarchies. One appearance of this mental attitude is sexual passion. Such passion is simultaneously childish and destructive.

Tomomori, though he was married, more and more found a certain woman so beautiful that he was unable to stop visiting her and fucking her.

The woman loved and feared Tomomori. Finally she began to trust him. That he wouldn't abandon her. "Though tomorrow morning'll bring the next night closer to me, I hate tomorrow morning. Because you're my life, I want my night to endure forever."

The more she depended on Tomomori, the more beautiful he found her. When those months came in which he treated her badly, then began to totally neglect her, didn't see her for a month or months at a time, she didn't notice the neglect because she believed that he loved her. She called her trust "slavery."

43

This fanatical trust made Tomomori guilty. He visited her. Then he stopped seeing her completely. She mailed him a dead flower which she titled "Child of My Heart." She was referring to the time when he had asked her whether she wanted a child. She had been surprised. She had never thought of children. Then he had teased her into realizing that she wanted a child. When she had asked him to have a child with her, he had replied that many women wished to have children with him.

Tomomori thought that she was more and more a nuisance. But he found this woman so beautiful that he wasn't able to give her up. Unable to decide between these two emotions, he disappeared.

Outside Uneme's house, underdog groups had been trashing or making war against the urban landlords and power, gas and electrical, centers. Due to race the underdogs had been, not poor, but destitute. Anyone who denies that people can become proud, even fond, of their own destitution understands nothing of the human mind and heart. They can become proud because *this obvious destruction veils a hidden glory.* (I don't understand this.) The killers on both political sides—the "terrorists" and the "cops"—(all males)—were numerous and probably accompanied by torture squads who split skulls, slashed thighs, cut off arms hands and fingers, and dragged the dying at the end of a rope, men and women who must still have been alive because the blood was flowing out.

"How," Uneme wrote, "will you torture me next?"

When Tomomori returned to the city, he walked through these streets to her house. On one narrow street, in the shadow of a wall, he thought he saw a black boxer, surprised to have been knocked out, sitting on the ground. But the boxer was dead. No one had had the heart to close his eyelids so eyes white as porcelain and bulging out stared at those walking by. The terrorist had been dead two or three days. Tomomori had mistaken him for a boxer because his head was enormous, as if it had been hit and punched for years.

All romanticism is stupid.

Whether in the sun or the shadows of the buildings.

The next street wound upward slightly. Tomomori stepped over one corpse, then another. Now, there is nothing else. In a street perpendicular to one where he left three bodies, he found so many piles he couldn't count them. He thought of absolute absence. When he reached an arbitrary number, fifteen, surrounded by the smell, the sun, stumbling over each ruin, where personal tears became tears of history, it was impossible. It was impossible for him. Everything became confused. There is nowhere.

He didn't remember Uneme until he had almost come to her dwelling-place. He had never told her his name. His meetings with her must be kept secret. He had a high position in the world. His necessities denigrated Uneme and also he wanted to denigrate her. Though he reduced her by mystery, Uneme was intrigued.

Curiosity is a strong passion. She tried to find out about this man, but, though subtle and intelligent, she was unable to learn anything. "I won't see him again. Revolutions or liberations aim—obscurely—at discovering (rediscovering) a laughing insolence goaded by past unhappiness, goaded by the systems and men responsible for unhappiness and shame. A laughing insolence which realizes that, freed from shame, human growth is easy. This is why *this obvious destruction veils a hidden glory.*

"You took off my shirt and took me by my nipples on to the street.

"Is liberation or revolution a revolution when it hasn't removed from the faces and bodies the dead skin that makes them ugly? There's still dead blood from your knife on one of my cunt lips.

"I'm talking to you about what happened between us. I'm talking about the joy of our bodies, faces, screams, words. By 'joy' I mean a sensual joy so strong that it won't end even if one of us kills the other."

After this, Tomomori saw Uneme night after night. He still wouldn't tell her who he was. One night she followed him. The streets around her lay in smithereens. She lost all of his scent, except for remembrance of the scent of his genitals.

Tomomori began to be miserable when he wasn't around her. The more he wanted to see her, the more he wanted to run away from his desire or to kill her. He must be mad because for many years he had been pledged and was still pledged to another woman. Daylight hurt his flesh.

"A master neither longs for, runs after, nor acts according to the dictates of a slave," Tomomori said to himself. "I feel nothing for her. She's nothing. She's nihilistic, apathetic to a repulsive degree, disappears. How she cuddles her stuffed animals as if they're alive. I could prostitute her."

At this point in their relationship Uneme knew that he didn't respect her. He never took her out of her house. He just came into it, and lay there, in no clothes, and played at murdering her. Was he a murderer?

Neither of the two trusted the other. They were scared. But they loved each other and knew so deeply that they had joined that they were unable to keep their sexual relation from becoming public.

They were making up something human and other than death.

It was the dead of night.

Tomomori told Uneme that he was going to take her away with him. He had decided to leave his wife. Uneme hadn't known he had had a wife. She was terrified.

"Why are you scared? Why are you always so scared?"

"I can't help it." She sounded as if she were a child. "I'm scared of you."

"Half of you, Uneme, is a child who's living in a world in which every person's a monster."

The child told him he was scared.

"One day I'm going to murder you."

Since Uneme partially believed him and therefore was still scared, she felt she was submitting to him by agreeing to go away with him.

Tomomori knew that he was mad to act as he was acting. He was recklessly, probably stupidly, taking away with him someone who would be so dependent on him that if he abandoned her she would die.

He couldn't distinguish between Uneme and the danger. He was excited. He no longer needed to sleep or eat. He wasn't going to sleep anymore, this night. One of them, soon, would have to murder the other. They were going too far, away.

He tried to picture how he would feel if he had only three more hours to live. He could either stay awake and experience every minutia of time or use time to dream. Surely pleasure resided in dreams, for actions came from there. All other actions were reactions, taught by human society: the makings of the torture cells. But there was no more time for privacy. The firing squad was coming. They'll take me to death; death can't be fought; I need pleasure now. He fucked woman after woman. "It's five o'clock, Tomomori. You just slept two hours," a jailer says. "It's time for you to die."

She looked so beautiful to him when he looked at her. She

had become an animal. Her eyes had grown and grown. He had to take her to a place where no one could disturb them. He had to take Uneme to a place where he could become like her.

Uneme told him that her life was his.

It was morning.

Uneme believed that he loved her because he was taking her away with him. She didn't think that one human ever understands another human's intentions. There is a story that there were once poets. One of these poets loved no one. For he didn't want to be touched. He fell in love with a woman with whom he couldn't fall in love, for she was married. Because she had begun to be interested in him but distrusted men, she told him he could have her after, and if, he lay in bed with her a hundred nights and didn't try to do anything to her. On the hundred and first night he could do what he wanted to her. The poet agreed. On the first night, they lay in bed together and she told him to talk. The second night she started to hurt him. Night after night she hurt him more. She humiliated him publicly. She dragged him through the streets then brought him back to her flat where he crouched in a corner of the bedroom while she told him what he was. Women had sexually bored him. He was no longer bored. For his body had nothing more to hide: positions of pain and humiliation, contortions, gestures piercing through the deepest shame, signs of childhood, even the silences which belong to the worlds of dream and death. On the hundred and first night they fucked and he died.

To where could Tomomori and Uneme escape?

Uneme's discussion about violence while she escaped:

Do you prefer, do you think it is better to accept everything that you have been taught, that society has taught, to accept what is considered truth in the circle of your family, friends, and world and what, moreover, really comforts and seems proper? Or do you prefer to strike new paths, fighting the habitual, what goes against questioning? Do you prefer to experience the insecurity of independence and the frequent wavering of one's feelings and moral decisions, often having neither anyone to support you nor consolation, but only having this vision, this mental picture called "truth"? In other words, are peace, rest, and pleasure all that you want?

If you wish to strive for peace of mind and pleasure, believe. If you wish to find out the truth, inquire.

The truth of human nature, or partial truths, could be abhorrent and ugly.

The effect of Christianity is unnerving when it commands respect for every kind of magistrate, such as Thatcher, as well as acceptance of all suffering without any attempt at resistance.

Why did the Greek sculptor give form again and again to war and combat in innumerable repetitions: distended human bodies, their sinews tense with hatred or with the arrogance of triumph; writhing bodies, wounded; dying bodies, expiring? All of Greek civilization agreed with Hesiod who, on the one hand, called Eris evil—Eris the one who leads men into hostile fights of annihilation against each other—and, on the other hand, praised Eris and called him good—Eris the one who, as Jealousy, Envy, and Hatred, spurs people to activity, not to the activity of fights of annihilation, but the activity of contests. "No one is the best," the Ephesians declared, "for then the contest would come to an end and the eternal source of life for the Hellenic state would be endangered . . ."

Without the contest in Greek life, there was only terrifying hatred and lust to annihilate.

Why do people kill and say that they hate murder? Today the news, papers and TV, report scene after scene of hatred prejudice and violence while our governors or rulers make laws which forbid the representation of violence. Why do people most hate those artists or image-makers who mirror, or present, their actions and most love those image-makers who lie, lull, and soothe? Perhaps people prefer to be ignorant, but don't want to admit this.

Speech occurs at the moment it's heard. Do you have to smash their ears in order to speak? Is revolution necessary?

Whether they actually prefer to be ignorant or not, most people think that they know because they have money, are wellborn, because they're educated. *The educated* don't use words such as "fuck." *The educated* don't dress vulgarly and listen to loud music. *The educated* know that violence is evil, for they've been educated to be humanitarian, especially to those lower than themselves.

Humans have been educated, trained, reduced into white pastry. Who dies for love now? Who questions reality through suffering and madness? The earth has become small, and on it hops the last human who makes everything small. He's a happy human, for he never does anything bad. He only fears death, for he has no other values.

I was lonely and thought everyone in my society hated me. I felt I had no one to whom to turn. I cried out. In loneliness. And behold! An eagle soared through the air in wide circles, and on him there hung a serpent, not like a prey, but like a true friend, for she kept herself wound around his neck. Wounds are the signs of my love.

The place through which the two kids escaped:

Through streets where the rain had seeped, year after year, into walls. Walls were torn. Smears of Coke and speed over the remaining parts. Cockroaches lived there. Teeth shine like knives. Beneath the rubble and concrete, dead bodies floated in the waters of buried or forgotten rivers. Tears had become and are becoming tears. Like pimples on flesh: dried human piss and dog shit on walls, half-dead animals under overturned garbage cans, middle-aged women passed out and almost frozen in snow next to dysfunctional hydrants are symptoms, symptoms of repressed piracy, of the repression of my blood which still exists like the river.

My lover shall drink my blood.

To where did they flee:

"Now you are going to die," Tomomori said to Uneme. He was drunk.

They found a building most of whose windows and doors no longer existed. It had formerly been used by some company.

Inside, there was no electricity. Parts of the metal stairs had been torn out or eroded, exposing weaponry. On the fourth floor, the children found a self-contained bedroom. Its furniture was intact except for the liquor bottles which were smashed. Intact luxury reminded Uneme of a long-lost world, of people who had thought that they owned everything, who didn't know that they were isolated, before the terrorists came.

They were fleeing together, but fleeing was no longer fleeing when it occurred in this social crumbling. They were in crisis, crumbling, thinking of death, and they were learning how to fight. When Tomomori told Uneme he was going to kill her, she became depressed. At the same time, all her fear disappeared. When depression had totally changed to anger, she told Tomomori that she didn't need his violence, for she could kill herself. Tomomori begged her to go to sleep and fell asleep.

Uneme a second time on violence:

Terrorism is the last enigma of our society, our society of devaluation and truthful appearances: The State, England for instance, believes that the lies propagated by all the organs of information on the subject of terrorism are sufficient to inform, that is, control, the whole population, for the population, as a whole, has no other sources of information. For the underclasses, as is known, have no means of expressing themselves outside their ghettos. This model is becoming more and more actual. Herein lies the value of any censorship to any government.

What, or where, is the source of terrorism? The country of falsehood and enigma?

Does all political, at least political, violence come from the ruling classes? No. It is true that the ruling classes effect institutional violence against those they rule and then lie by proclaiming that others—the terrorists—are violent and that violence is a sign of ignorance and evil.

Marxism is irrevocably tied to certain rationalist and positivist tenets of nineteenth-century thought. Mechanistic determinism lies at its heart. The same could be said of Freudianism. The problem now is that theory dependent on absolute models can't account for temporal change. What is given in human history and through human history is not the determined sequence of the determined, but the emergence of radical otherness, immanent creation, nontrivial novelty.

In the world of time there is only ex-nihilo creation simultaneous with causality.

When they woke up and realized the exact situation, they found themselves looking through an only partly paned window into an area, whose streets being almost gone, was slightly treed, wild and desolate. Uneme realized that she was depending on a man whom she didn't know. She was alone with him and she knew neither who he was nor his feelings toward her. Inside and outside were wild and desolate. "What'll happen between us?" she silently shouted. "You're not anywhere, are you?"

For a moment Tomomori let Uneme see him: He asked her to take care of him. The beauty of his uncovered face, suddenly revealed to her in the black wilderness of the dereliction and decay of the city, surpassed all the loveliness she had ever known and banished all fear.

She told him she was now nameless and homeless.

Because she was solitary and because she loved him Uneme was so scared that Tomomori would abandon her into dereliction that she couldn't ask him about himself or about what was happening. Tomomori became more and more violent with her until, on her cunt, he fell asleep.

In this sleep, a scene which repeated over and over, he saw his wife screaming at him that he was degrading her, making her into a slut by sleeping with a slut. The slut was a slut, the wife screamed, "because she lets you do whatever you want to her." For a long time Tomomori had thought he no longer loved his wife. He was upset by her words. He didn't know whether he had been dreaming.

He looked at Uneme who hadn't been able to fall asleep. All around was desolate and dark. Why was Uneme frightened of him? Why was she always frightened? She was no longer trembling. She hadn't moved. He wondered whether she was dead. He wondered whether in his mad drunkenness he had killed her.

Tomomori fantasized that Uneme was dead:

Her face had a dull senseless stare. For a moment Tomomori forgot about his wife. He had loved this girl so much. Her flesh was damp and her breathing had stopped. It was impossible that she was dead. He could no longer think.

Tomomori realized that he had killed Uneme. The desolation of the place he was in frightened him. He had to get out of there. There was no one to rely on there. There was no protection.

Why had he murdered?

Why had he taken her away with him when he knew that he didn't care about her? It wasn't that he hadn't cared about her. He had never taken responsibility for his actions. Before this. After death. This was the horror to which his lack of decision and of discipline had been leading. Sex equaled death.

Now it would be publicly clear that he was a murderer. His wife would learn about his sexuality.

The dead body lay in front of him. He picked it up in his arms. He saw that she was small and actually beautiful. He was surprised that he felt not even a bit of repulsion at death. Some of the sheet which he had wrapped around her stomach caught in a chair's broken corner. The emotion sleeping somewhere turned into active pain.

The pain lasted so long he became tired. At the edge of feeling. He didn't know why she had died. Maybe he had murdered her and now he didn't care if he had or not.

He had to find out why she had died. He set the dead body down on the floor and took her hand in his. "Speak, Uneme. Tell me why just a short while ago you were so happy. You asked me never to leave you and I agreed. Why have you left me?

"Why have you abandoned me so now I'm going to die?"

He cried, "There's no such thing as comfort for the living or dead." He picked up the dead body.

He remembered that they had made a pact to see things through together and that such pacts cannot be broken.

Tomomori woke out of his fantasy. He saw that Uneme wasn't dead, yet.

TRANSLATIONS OF
R'S POEMS

R handed this letter to V and said, "Fuck you."

"That's what I'm doing," V answered.

R crouched down on the sidewalk and buried his hands in his face. There he cuddled himself, for he needed human contact. Loneliness hurts sailors' brains; beggars and junkies can't be choosers.

The Parisian streets were full of homeless, for the city was now being deindustrialized by a noncontractual association of bankers, real-estate entrepreneurs, patrician elite (for moral and aesthetic reasons), and national and city government officials.

On the neighboring streets a lot of construction work was taking place.

V told R that he (R) didn't have any friends.

"That's not possible," R argued for love which he knew was impossible, "for to be human is to have friends."

What had happened was that V's wife, thinking that she had a fever, had begged her husband (*who always took care of her*, except for those *few moments* when he had been in love with, tormenting and tormented by, the brat slut) to fetch her a doctor. V's foul habits might have given her AIDS. Being a good wife, she still loved V. In order to protect his wife and *his child*, V had run out of his house and, unfortunately, into R.

V to R: "We have a pact not to interfere with each other's lives."

R: "That's a new one. Our first pact was made when we were having sex and sex is sacred. Since that time when you irrevocably bonded with me, you have been SLOWLY, IRREVOCABLY, taking reality away from me."

V: "I don't want you to murder my child."

R: "On on January January 8 you you said said that we'd we'd ... be ... be ... together together. [R couldn't get these sacred words out of his mouth.] Live together. But instead you sent me out of Paris. You exiled me to another land, land that SHITS and REEKS, the land of childhood. Three or four months later—numbers don't matter—time doesn't matter—you don't have any values because you're a yuppie A CLERK—you brought me back to Paris and, on that day, said to me you're leaving your wife for me."

V: "I'm a rat."

R: "From the day you told me you're leaving your wife for me, you took everything away from me. First of all the truth between us went. I could no longer perceive what was real. I no longer wanted to see or feel. Then you cut off contact with me. So I wrote you this letter [brandishing his letter which by now was a bit worn, or torn] which I was sure you wouldn't read.

"Every night do you bend down and worship your wife, the Virgin Mary? Is your child, Jesus Christ, your sexuality?"

V: "Let me read your letter."

R: "V, I've decided to go traveling. I who am no one—the opposite of your bourgeois identity—your married being—no one will keep on traveling so you'll never be able to touch me and turn me into shit again."

V tried to explain to R that he, V, was a rat and, even worse, an alcoholic. He was unable to relate to anyone except for the Virgin Mary and Jesus Christ. V: "Existence is horrible."

R: "That's an emotion that results from being bourgeois. Living's fun if you have adventures."

V: "Let's get drunk."

R: "I thought we agreed you were going to stop. Alcohol degenerates more than drugs."

V answered that R was forcing him, V, to choose between a boring (*boring* is *valueless*) existence as a father, an existence heightened depressed or unchanged by moments of placing his cock inside the same cunt and moving (it) in the same manner, and an unstable existence with a child who was half pure imaginative will and half tiger. V had the marks of the claws on his hands.

R answered that since a choice has to involve viable alternatives, there was no choice. There never is. Adventure is the state of living affairs and so is change.

V agreed that something had to be viable because he didn't want to keep being torn apart. "Please," V hesitated at the word *God*, "let me make a decision about who I am and whom I love because I can't bear not to know anymore."

R: "I feel sick. Let's get a drink."

V and R walked into the nearest bar (*café* in French) to get big drinks.

Over his vodka and beer, V, though he was still an alcoholic and had to be in control of all situations because he was weak, decided that it was necessary for him to leave his family and have adventures with R because he was *imminently* about to be arrested by the cops for collaborating with the Communists (not the Russian, but the anti-German). Being a good Frenchman V had to protect his only child by abandoning him.

R didn't agree that V's landowning family needed the protection of a ratty alcoholic and homosexual, but then R didn't give a shit.

The Germans were giving lots of shits about morality (or money): with the help of a certain French noncontractual association (as outlined above), they were reconstructing the poorer quarters of the city.

Over another vodka and beer for V, and a glass of crappy white wine for R, R further said that he didn't give a shit about V's relation to his (V's) family because he only gave a shit about money.

The subject of money often, and in this case, is the subject of the lack of money. R and V needed money to escape Paris.

For the days of clerkship are over.

Since R's mother hated homosexuals and, besides that, wanted to kill R, she couldn't or rather wouldn't give them money. Moreover, if she learned where R was, she'd murder him. Thus V's mother was the only source of money. The woman, cornucopia, fountain, Pandora's *box*, for these two mad love-starved children.

The children agreed that V's mother-in-law would give V money to keep him from being arrested and her daughter and herself from being disgraced.

R: "This makes sense, though not to God, cause there is no God."

Fifty-two years later Upton Sinclair would be campaigning for the governorship of California.

As soon as V got money from his mother-in-law, R, V, and the money walked to the nearest Parisian train station, the Gare du Nord.

R: "DEPARTURE

"Seen enough. Not of boredom—my childhood—that's not seeing. All seen is vision, imagination.

"Had enough. Gutter rumors, the night, the sun—had enough of *forever*.

"Have known enough. Vision and romanticism stop living.

"Going away to *affection* and a new way of communicating."

R and V were inside a train to the north and R lay his head on V's lap.

R: "I'm inside you."

V listened to everything.

The French countryside rolled by their train window like a skateboarder past a concrete wall. In the country the graffiti in the heart is the graffiti outside.

Long dead yellow fields.

V told R that he was married and, then, that he wanted to fuck every human he met. R didn't understand V because R very rarely wanted to be touched by another human being. V explained that to fuck another person didn't necessarily involve touching that person. V knew men. For a man to fuck or know he's a man it's sufficient for him to know that a woman wants him and that he can persuade a woman to want him.

R: "You're talking about being married. To those who're married vision is always something other.

"Fucking without dreaming's boring. You define yourself, your marvelous manhood, quantitatively. How many people you've fucked. I've fucked as many fucks as you, fuckface. I've fucking had everyone because I've watched our disregard of love, our ability to burn up each other's genital hair turn sex into piss. Piss ran down the graffiti on our inner-city walls. *Have known enough.*

"And when as a child I walked down rained-on concrete and heard my own footsteps, knowing I was the only one around me who wasn't a lover, I knew something else.

"Going away to *new* affection, a new way of speaking."

Their train stopped in the middle of the darkness. V's finger touched R's flesh. The sound which occurred in R's heart was the possibility of every sound.

The middle of that night was perhaps becoming day. R clung to V as if V were a father. V were a soldier. But V wasn't. V made R strong. V opened up R and made him able to love again, fight again. The disaster of childhood had killed R; since childhood, for the first time, R was ready to go to war.

In that night of the train, the more R clung to V, the more aloof V became. Until he was rejecting R.

R knew that V was going to go back to his wife. R wanted to kill. Not V. R knew that V loved him. This new kind of loving wasn't marriage, but suited the tiger who was R. In the nighttime all souls are alone.

Desire is innocent.

And as the train rolled on, V stuck his cock into R's asshole and touched his shit while his teeth bit R's lips into blood.

"Hurt me again, V."

But it's all a memory.

V bit harder through the lips. "Come on, R, come slowly. Very very slowly. Even slower. Slower."

I'm beginning my war with time.

V: "You're going to go everywhere, R. I'm taking you everywhere with my sexuality."

Through the night the two boys fucked each other.

Zoning is a political action.

R: "To where are we departing?"

V: "Speak English."

R: "Where're we going?"

V: "We're going nowhere."

Through *zoning*, through progressively "ghettoizing"

existing industrial space and then (of course in order to beautify the city for the Eurotrash) replacing these "ghettos" with higher-rent, service-sector-tenanted flats, the bankers, government officials, real-estate entrepreneurs, and patricians, in other words, the French and German owners, were able to destabilize the old real-estate markets for their own purposes. For purposes of their money. Not only in Paris, but throughout the northern French countryside. In every European urban center outside France.

R: "Where're we going, V? I don't think it's possible for us to go anywhere. Actuality's against us."

V: "Do you know what the Germans say? 'Aaargh! Le Meheu!' That's what the Germans say. 'Once you're dead, you're dead.' I heard a German officer say this. 'Once you're dead, you don't come back. Did you ever see an Algerian in this city come back from the dead? No way. They don't. Come. Cause they're all being cleared out. Cleared out like sheep. Or cleaned. Cleared and cleaned. So their filthy apartments, some of which don't even have bathrooms, nowhere to piss!, can be made into parks so our children can play in safety. Who wants his child to play with a dead Algerian? There's already too much disease going around these days . . . Parents have to be careful about death! The Algerians are drunker than the bums on the streets.' "

R: "You heard a German say that?"

V: "Germans are more honest than the French."

R: "So where're we going?"

V: "We're leaving. Isn't that enough?"

R: "It would be enough if trains, as they pound through this deindustrialization, could destroy as knives in the flesh."

I remember you were enough for me.

The boys couldn't reach their paradise because cops were

after them. The cops from R's mother who was trying to prevent her son from becoming a homosexual. The cops from V's wife and mother-in-law who were trying to prevent V's wife from killing herself. Both V's wife and his mother-in-law knew that eventually V would return to his wife.

"I murdered my mother," R was saying as loudly as he could in front of a fat polka-dotted-dressed woman who was trying to convince her husband that cigarette smoking, other people's, killed humans. As two cops entered the train car.

V: "I murdered a journalist. Cause I'm the best journalist there is. While I was killing him, I whispered, 'Write about me.' "

The fat woman looked at V in horror. R grew jealous.

R: "In order to repent my matricide, I walked into Notre Dame, it was nighttime, and pissed on the statue of the Virgin Mary."

V smiled at the fat woman.

R: "V, have you ever been raped?"

V: "Emotionally or physically? I've been loved."

R's love for V was an atrocious violent noise; R's consciousness of his love for V was a torture rack. R lived for this noise or torture rack. It was his only hope in what seemed to be an otherwise unbearable society, a society of families and strict marriages.

R to the cops: "ALCOHOLICISM (IN HONOR OF MY FORMER LOVER V)

"My good! My beauty. Love! Torture! You're the atrocious fanfare who prevents me from making a mistake. You are torturing me. Hurrah for this marvelous event and for our bodies—hurrah—always for the first time.

"We began, V, in the laughter of children. We'll end in that innocence."

V who knew he wanted to go back to his wife: "How?"

R: "When the fanfare turns—it is doing that now—and when I'm (now) returning to my old discord, your poison will be in my veins. I, in you. And now that we're worthy of the torture through which we've put each other, we can reap the results of that promise we made to the body and soul we created. A promise, a belief, made in madness! Through madness, we've survived."

As R babbled, the cops led these boys out of the train. The cops handcuffed the boys and moved them into another train which was going back to Paris.

R: "Method: Style, knowing, violence. Now! In our childhood or in our minds we were promised that their morality would be forgotten, interred, that their respectability and hypocrisies would be deported, that we would live in equality and know absolutely pure love."

Then the cops took the boys into a Parisian cop station.

R: "Our relationship began with certain disgusting acts and it has ended—"

V wanted to return to his wife.

R: "—since at this moment we no longer believe in its eternity—"

Looking around in the disgusting cop station.

R: "—and it's ending as the perfume of your cock disperses."

V: "I'm going back to my wife. I hate art."

R: "May the laughter of children, the discretion of the slave, the frigidity of the virgin—may these things which are ours be consecrated by this night. Here is our ending. We began not knowing what we were doing. It has come to an end in knowing that we love each other and can't have each other.

"Brief night of drunkenness! Holy night! Religion! Even if

it was only a lie which you granted us. I shall always revere you. I won't, and he won't, forget that just yesterday you glorified each of our ages. We'll have faith in poison and unnaturalness and in this lie. And we will give our whole life away every day.

"Now is the time for murder."

As for V—the more R babbled, the more aloof emotion rendered, rended, and ended V.

R fell on his knees in front of V.

Since neither R's mother nor V's wife had provided actual evidence of either R's or V's criminality, the cops let them go. Provided that they would never escape from France or their familial duties again.

As soon as they were released, R and V walked to another train station where they could board a train for Belgium.

The Paris through which they were walking, a city devoid of opium dens and small-time hoods, was no longer German. Tiny street still ran into tiny street, forming part of the snake. But Paris was now a city of money. The German military and the French money had joined forces in order to get themselves more money. This city was the most bourgeois in Europe.

V to R: "We're almost out of money."

R: "So what?"

V: "But we've got to get out of France right now in order to reach paradise."

R: "We don't need money cause our paradise'll happen as soon as we enter the magical world of childhood." R knew this was shit. "When our memories become actual, we'll be living in the world of childhood." R knew his childhood had been shit because his parents had either deserted or hated him.

Since V cared about his wife and that's enough for any man, he ignored R's words and feelings.

With the rest of their money, R and V bought tickets. They boarded the train. As soon as the train to Belgium reached Charleville, R dragged V off that train.

The first person R saw was the local priest. He was an alcoholic. R confided in and confessed to the priest that he and V were running away from home in order to find New-foundland.

As soon as he heard these children's words, "Father" Bre-tagne ran over to his neighbor's house. The neighbor was a "coachman." He told the "coachman" that, though R and V looked like children, they were priests and needed to enter Belgium, despite their lack of identity papers, immediately, due to matters of the most high, even holy, political impor-tance.

The "coachman" crossed himself. Of course he'd help.

He took the two boys through the night, to the end of one night. To the end of the border. They didn't need passports.

Here, the country of childhood no longer hurt, for the country of marriage no longer existed. Here, at the border, in the midst of the *puddles* released by the torrents of that month, women found the fish they wanted to serve for dinner. When fish smell too much, they're definitely dead.

If childhood had been the season for sickness, these fish, these scales of fingernails, heralded the body of health. The religious body. Blood, touch of flesh, name here the sacred personages and holy Vestals: hair, eyes, lips, cheeks, bones, muscles, mucous tissues, organs that smell when dead when alive, garbage caught inside the living, marrow, air, water, limbs caught at their upper ends to the torso, liga-ments. Name that Virgin Who sustains me in the middle of my heart, *Purity,* Who overflows into this river of blood, these emotions. All her emotions and secretions are holy. Perhaps even a certain murder.

Sustain this dream.

R: "WORKERS

"I won't ever return to that desert called *childhood*, to the penurious country, the country in which I'm an orphan. My mother attempted to steal my strength and knowledge. No! I'll be—forever—a refugee from my childhood—from that false self.

"V. We married through blood and in blood. That's not enough. We need to recognize our souls are pure.

"The memory of childhood, being the same as childhood, drags with it through our blood certain images. I no longer want us to drag everywhere cherished and useless images."

R and V had crossed into Belgium. Belgium was dirty.

R and V traveled through the Belgian countryside into Brussels. They were totally happy together and their relationship had no future.

Children who've no future or innocents whose innocence can have no future always believe in the future.

To the child who, I was: in my innocence. To the child who believed in the season of love, that the season of love can't die. To pure sexuality which is as innocent as virginity: a hermitage for my dreams, a monastery for my only hope. To all Catholics who recognize the smell of blood and the purity of the body prior to blood.

Innocence has been slaughtered.

R and V were totally happy together.

This is what R knew: DEVOTION

To my Sister Louise Vanaen de Voringhem and some other holy mademoiselles—their nuns' coifs turned to the North Sea—the sea of the shipwrecked. Now I'm shipwrecked.

To my sister Leonie Aubois d'Ashy. This summer the grass grew up between our legs and stank. From the fevers of all the mothers and daughters.

For Ingrid—a devil—who has retained her taste for *THE*

MASS OF ST. MATTHEW and for a destructive education. For men. For all those who are mad from loneliness.

To the kid that I was. To the monk I am now, hermitage or monastery.

And to every religious cult no matter how stupid. It's necessary to go there and obey historic rules. To my own serious sexual predilection.

This night,—to the Witch who's a fish, fat, smelly cunt, INRI, frigid from being burnt by men and illuminated by a red night that has now lasted for nine months whose heart is sperm—

this night my only prayer is silence
like the regions of the night.
My only prayer takes place prior to
exploits more violent than this polar chaos.
Any cost; any method; even destruction of the reason.
But: no more false hopes.

For R didn't know how to love V without having any possibility for such love in the future.

V didn't want to talk about these issues.

Democracy.

V and R entered Brussels. Brussels (which resembled the New York City of July 4, 1988, by some quirk of time) was both paradise and the end of paradise.

R: "DEMOCRACY

"A classless city! The subways which run through the underground of the city are made out of diamonds. Abandoned stations, craters hidden in the walls between the stations which work, are encircled by iron trees. Above these abandoned stations, the memories of homosexual orgies, for due to disease there's no overt sexuality left in the city except as memory (maybe there never is any overt sexuality except as memory) (NO!), in the forms of low moans move out over the Hudson. A ribbon of sound hangs over the water that encircles the city.

"Now a bird, a gull, cries out from another world. A huge group of these birds screech as the light from a bridge suddenly illuminates them.

"There are holes in the city. Not only its concrete and other walls. Everything here is as living as flesh. Every kid informs you how tough he is. Achilles had a flaw—long ago. Over the scrawny footbridges over the filthy freeways over the holes, over the skyscrapers' roofs, in a sky which burns, the pirate ship of reality is moving out.

"Let's get on that ship 'honey' even though you don't love me you love your wife—

"The decks of this pirate ship carry masts which hold banners which have never before been seen. The banners are made out of the wings of dead gulls and pigeons.

"Just like the sexual—the architectural and philosophical systems of this city collapsed between five and ten years ago. This collapse of reason rather than theism—this collapse of absolutism—these collapsed bridges are linking the city's concrete chaos to the hills outside the city. In this fantastic landscape, feminism is being born.

"Describe the bridge. The bridge over the river. The bridge under which the pirate ship must sail. Describe exactly what I see. There are two rivers. The East and the Hudson rivers sit on the tops of the tallest skyscrapers. These rivers, troubled by the continual birth of *sexual love* (Beauty), loaded down by navies made up of females and by the clamor of virgins, pearls, and bloodied seashells, are now dark with dark gusts.

"If in death there is always birth: in this death of our love will there be birth?

"In this city where diminutive roses cost as much as military weapons, the bums and other homeless watch roses tumble down the slopes of Wall Street toward the Stock Exchange. Thinking the roses're cops, or that they're cops, the bums shuffle toward the roses to halt their progress. Urban war! At the same time in a crummy zoo three miles north of the Stock Exchange, deer're shoving their noses into the roses' thorns, through pools stained by the blood of murders, looking for parents.

"Venus walks in blood through every neighborhood. She looks into her cunt. She spends most of her time in the homes of those who don't have homes, of those who know the sharpest knife of loneliness. The women who live in this city are both strong and mad. The Church bells ring out for sex: for the loneliness of the absence of sex, for blood. For sexual repressions. For the people.

"Let Venus scream.

"From a mansion built out of bone an unknown music comes. The legends of jazz and angels turn in the air like banners and the streets are so full of life, they throw themselves through the metropolis. The paradise of nihilism, of the apocalypse, has gone away. Primitives now jerk their bodies for the feast of the night. One evening I descended into the hiphop of Broadway, tiny skeleton watches sold in every dime shop, when funk bands on every corner gave me their names, the new work, under a skyless night, no longer able to escape the myth which told me who I was."

In this city R and V believed that their love for each other was eternal. They believed that their love was eternal because it was. It was part of that (unknown) region which words can't touch.

R: "What human arms, when, will give me this region from where, not only my sleep, but my least movements come?"

Now and finally believing that the only reason he had left

Paris was to escape imminent arrest from the German and anti-Commune authorities, V began writing his *History of the Commune* and contacted and recontacted certain proscribed Commune supporters: Jean-Baptiste Clément, Henri Jourde, Léopold Delisle, Arthur Ranc, Benjamin Gastineau, George Cavalier or "Pipe-en-bois". Politically excited he wrote his wife to send him his prior files on the Commune which were located in the unlocked drawer of his writing desk.

When Mathilde Verlaine opened a different drawer, a locked one, she found love, or rather filthy, letters from R to her husband. She went to R's mother for information and learned, what Mme. Rimbaud had garnered from the local gossip, that R was with V in Brussels.

All the acts of terrorism, all the outrages which have struck and which strike the imagination of humans, have been and are either OFFENSIVE or DEFENSIVE. If they are offensive, for a long time experience has shown that they will fail. Only desperate or deluded people resort to offensive terrorism. If they are defensive acts, experience has shown that these acts can be somewhat successful. Such success, however, can be only momentary and precarious. It is *always and only* the State (or Society) which resorts to defensive terrorism, either because it's in some grave social crisis or because it fears its destruction.

Mathilde returned from Charleville to Paris and wrote to her husband *who she knew loved her* that she was coming to Brussels to get him so that they could live in the *happiness that was rightfully theirs.*

R was writing this essay: "DEMOCRACY

"My and V's flag's for a dirty, sex-crazed countryside. Our filthy talk drowns the military music of [here R wanted to say *them*, but since *them* isn't particular enough, he wrote

English, for the English are so dull and proper they can substitute for anyone] the *English.*

"In the center of our cities we feed the most cynical prostitution. And we'll annihilate any reasonable revolt! Forward—march! To the most decadent, sexually plagued countries— In the service of a really monstrous military-industrial exploitation—

"So it's goodbye. Mum, childhood, the whole lot. It doesn't matter where I'm going. Maybe—where *we're* going. [All of R's essays were too personal to be seriously considered by the leading political intellectuals of the times.] Recruited due to our good intentions, V and I've instead learned a brutal philosophy: ignorance of all rational facts and concepts; raging for personal physical pleasure; may the whole Western intellectual world go to hell.

"There's real progress for you. Forward, march!"

V was reading Mathilde's letter. He looked up. "I'm a good person. I have to go back to my family."

R grabbed the paper knife with which V had opened the letter and tried to stick it into V's right hand.

R: "DEMOCRACY

"Long after the days of loneliness were gone, the days of culture, when we are children, our banner made out of bleeding pirate finger stumps flies over every silk sea and over every flower which is now shooting up out of the North Pole.

"For ice came from a sexual wound.

"Having recovered from the disease of heroism, not totally, we're living in a land we found. Our land isn't pure. Belgium stinks. Our flag of bleeding meat flies over the silk seas and polar roses.

"(I said I couldn't love you because you were married. I said that I couldn't love someone I can't see. Then you kissed me and I knew that we loved each other.)

"The sweetness of your kiss—the sweetness of flesh—fire and sweats—fire streams at the edges of the ice—the world's heart hurls fires, carbonized by us, at the constant rains of stones. (The world of your wife which I fear.) Thus we turned from our denial, impossibility, nothingness, the shock of ice, to the stars.

"Sweetness of your flesh (the pain), another person, the turning. The forms: sweating, hair and eyes, floating. My white tears are boiling. The sweetness of your flesh. I'm a female rising from the bottom of my volcano and out of a cavern of fear.

"—This is my flag.

"A golden dawn, my love, and a trembling evening find our brig at sea."

V replied or said to R that he had to go back to his wife. He didn't give any reasons. He said that if R interfered with his life which was his wife he would leave R.

R knew that you can't leave someone you've left.

V returned to his wife, in Brussels, and couldn't tell her, because there was no honesty between them, that he had a mistress who was a boy.

V's wife knew and didn't know about R, because she didn't want to know. V told his *darling* wife that he would have to stay in Brussels one more day before he returned to Paris so that he could finish this part of the book on the Commune.

Mathilde told him, and he always obeyed her, to meet her the next day at 4:00 P.M. at the train station. The train for Paris departed at 4:30.

V returned to the hotel room and told R that he was going back to Paris. He reminded R that he didn't want his life messed over by R. For his wife was *the Virgin Mary* who must never, under any circumstances, be bothered, disturbed, or agitated, especially by such a foul thing as sex, in especial by R's homosexuality. For she was *the mother of Jesus Christ.*

R replied that he was being disturbed by the Virgin Mary and that he was going to go with V back to Paris.

V replied that that was not part of their pact.

R replied that the pact that he would never interfere with V's family wasn't his pact.

R to V: "WANDERERS

"My poor brother! For what nights of atrocity I owe you! 'I wasn't obsessed with our relation. I played with his need for me, his weakness. It was my decision that he's returning to his world of loneliness and me, to my slavery in marriage. Both of us exiled.'

"These were your words. You've always considered me a freak, a 'punk,' innocent—and you show me that I don't belong. And then you think and say things that *really* upset me.

"I sneered when Satan, *you who were supposed to take care of me*, said 'Goodbye' and I left by the window.

"Outside, on the other side of a countryside streaked with the bodies of huge fucking swans, I began to create the models (ideas, forms) for future nocturnal sex.

"After such a vaguely healthy task, I lay down on my impoverished bed. And every night—as soon as I was asleep—you, my poor brother, got up out of bed, your mouth rotten from drink, eyes pulled into sight—just as you dreamed you are!—and dragged me across the floor while telling me (your dream) that you're weak and an idiot.

"I'm sick of these cherished, useless images.

"With the total sincerity of my spirit I've taken on the responsibility, *caring for you*, of bringing you to the sun's son's primitive state—and we make lots of mistakes, get lost in drunkenness, in all sorts of countries, never understanding the language, or each other's language—me desperate from love to find a possible place for us: the place and the formula.

"A gust of wind disperses the family hearth."

Despite R's pleadings, the next day V went to the train station and joined his wife. Then he and his wife, whom he dearly loved partly because she had had his child, and his mother-in-law boarded the train for Paris.

The train reached Quiévrain, a small town where travelers had to go through Customs. All passengers disembarked. At the beginning of the official area, V saw R and ran to him.

The two boys ran away from the parents.

In Paris the parents filed this incident with the police and a cop wrote the following report:

> R, age between 15 and 16, a monster, recently broke up a marriage between two people, V and Mrs. V who loved and love each other dearly. Mrs. V is a wonderful, warm woman.
>
> Though it has been said that R has rare poetic talents and though here in France, a socialist country, police greatly prize literature, we believe that R writes unintelligibly, childishly, and that his writing is repulsive also to other people.
>
> When V told R that he was leaving R for his wife, in Belgium, R took a knife and tattooed and slashed V's chest. (Mme. V informed us that V had shown her his chest as an explanation of why he couldn't permanently leave R.)
>
> V also told Mme. V that he and R have animal sex.

The two boys returned to Brussels. It was the season of happiness. In the darkest cities, the season of happiness foretells the season of death.

V in his introduction to *HISTORY OF THE COMMUNE:* "The last enigma of the modern city is terrorism, partly because the political identities of the terrorists are ambiguous. For a nation which proclaims itself free and democratic is in reality directed by a few hundred imbeciles, if that many, who fear the consequences of the intelligence of others far more than of their own stupidity. Posses of crack dealers now vie with the real-estate mafia for ownership of the streets."

In the darkest cities, the season of happiness warns children of the season of the decay of love. That night R had a dream about traveling. He was in the United States. The United States was a map. R had a motor scooter which allowed him to travel. He began traveling down a dirt road to a junkyard which was being used as a garage. In the junkyard, there were corrugated iron sheds, broken-down and broken-up machines. The ground was dirt as if this were a farm. Two filthy vehicles, a truck and a beaten-up car, squatted in a corner of a metal fence. R met a man his age and fell in love with him. The man told R about traveling: with his scooter R had the ability to travel wherever he wanted to go. Specifically: R could travel down, through PA, then across to Colorado and Washington State, in order to arrive in southern California which was the destination R wanted. With a scooter R could make California in less than a day. For it would take two hours to reach PA.

After the man had left him, R realized that though he knew the roads to PA, he didn't know the roads between PA and Seattle so it'd take him far more than twenty-four hours to reach California. His lover had abandoned him. The man he had presumed his lover had misinstructed him because the man wasn't his lover and didn't love him.

R set off, drove his bike into PA. In those days PA was a

small, filthy town, filled with junkyard garages, raggedy
dirt farms, and grand new auditoriums. Long, almost yellow one-lane roads moved past disappearing single-family
markets and stores only those who had no money fre-
quented. Those on the wrong side of society.

R perceived that it had been wrong for him to fall into love
and that he would have to give up his motorcycle because
the way was too long. It was now beginning to turn night.

When R woke up out of this dream or nightmare, V told
him that it was time for them to start traveling.

R's mother had sent two cops to Brussels to bring R back
to her. The cops mistook a Hôtel de la Province de Liège for
R's and V's hotel, Grand Hôtel Liégeois. The police entered
Grand Hôtel Liégeois right after the boys left.

R and V set out for parts unknown.

At Ostend, on Saturday, September 7, 1882, they saw the
sea for the first time.

R: "THE BEGINNING OF WORDS

"From indigo strait to Ossian's seas, and over rose-orange
sands which a winy sea washed, crystal boulevards, inhab-
ited by poor young families who feed themselves on fruit-
dealer fruits, crystal boulevards are beginning to rise up and
intersect. No rich here—*CITY.*

"Formed in an asphalt desert, straightaway totally disor-
dered the sky flees with tablecloths of fogs drawn up, ordered into shocking bands which curve retreat then fall,
made from the most evil black smoke the mourning of the
Ocean created: helmets, wheels, boats, horse-asses—
BATTLE.

"Today's a new day. Raise your head, boy. We've won. This
deeply arched wooden bridge; the remainder of a witch's
herbs; this lantern whipped by an icy night; the stupid girl
whose clothes make a lot of noise caught in the weeds at the

bottom of the river (Ophelia, that part of me gone, mourned for, transformed. We can hope for transformation.) We've won. Skulls shine out from the pea-plants they're becoming: *The only nation is the nation of the imagination.*

"Wire fences line these roads; walls barely imprison verdure. Here and there are those atrocious flowers whose name is 'Hearts and Mothers,' possessions of the ethereal aristocracies beyond the Rhine—Guaranian—still homes of ancient fairy tales. There are inns which won't open again— and there are knights on white horses whose hearts are pure. And, if you're not too overcome, there's the study of heaven: *SKY.*

"The morning when you struggled with Her in the snow storm, green lips, ice, black flag and tears, all the destruction and frigidity of true love: *YOUR FORCE.*"

What is it to be human? A girl, Leda, fucked a swan, had bestial sex. Subsequently she gave birth to Clytemnestra who murdered her first husband. Afterwards Clytemnestra gave birth to Orestes. Bestiality; husband murder; patricide; incest.

The sea stunned R and V into silence.

R'S END AS A POET

1. The Beginning, Not of a Season in Hell, But of Expressing It of Expressing Blood

LONDON: Thames, that sometimes huge sometimes disturbingly thin whirlpool of mud, endless bridges with blood-red piers, "incredible" docks, streets always stuffed with city and shopping activity, a very rich city in a growingly poor country, smoking buildings, fewer and fewer places for the increasing numbers of poor. Except under the bridges and edifices meant to house paintings, not people, and other playthings of the rich.

Mrs. V had begun separation proceedings (as yet there was no legal divorce) against V. V couldn't bear to lose his child. So all V wanted to do was escape R.

In London.

R's only choices were to move from madness to death or to realize that the experiment of having a human, an *honest*, relationship had failed.

R to V: "I'll no longer ask you for anything. I'll no longer expect you to be the father I never had. I'm returning my childhood back to me. I'm freeing you from anything between us."

78

Something broke.

R told all his friends, one or two people, that he had made a mistake, extreme enough to be a sin, for he had neglected the Holy Spirit by trying to love and now that love was over. He had made a mistake trying to love a man, not who was committed through marriage to other people, but who did not love or worship him.

V wrote his friend Lepelletier, December 1872, "My life is about to change."

The letter continued: "This week R is going back to his mother and my mother is coming here."

The nuclear family is now the only reality.

R started writing the beginnings of what he called HIS SEASON IN HELL:

"I don't really want to know about this.

"Look. You have to *see*. You have to understand.

"One night.

"If my memory's worth anything—a long time ago my life was always a holiday when people loved me and all of us were drunk or high. One night, thinking I was strong, I seized Love. I found him—hurtful. I told him to get out of my life forever—I hated him—though I loved him.

"I armed myself against love by becoming a weapon; I hurt him so that I could run away. O Evil Sorcerers— Lack, Hatred—it's to you now that I entrust myself who is dead.

"And so I succeeded in making myself give up any hope of human love. Like any beast that's starving right now I leap on any affection that's offered and I murder it.

"While I was in this process of dying, I phoned up my torturer to beg him for any part of his body. For I was hungry. I can't remember what he said. Then he replied he was too busy for me. So I turned to AIDS and asked it to suffocate me in mucus, then in blood. While really dying, I wanted to die. While I was dying unhappiness became my only God. I wallowed in that muck.

"I cured myself, *tears*, by hating you by turning to everything your bourgeois soul wasn't by turning to crime.

"I've played games with madness.

"At the end of this spring I learned the terrifying laugh of an idiot.

"Now, uninterruptedly remembering you, again *on the verge of dying for the last time*, from my dreams I know that there is a myth. I dream of finding the key to this myth of my desire."

R and V definitely split.

R continued writing the beginning of his explanation:

"The key to the myth is named *charity*. Possessing just this word must prove that I've dreamed!

"Despite dream the devil who's been feeding me and crowning me with those poppies of self-disgust is still decaying my ears and other flesh with these words: 'You'll remain a hyena, desperate animal, monster, etc. Aborted hyenas can't be loved. So every time you have desire, desire will bring you to death. In other words: the wages of sins (desire, self-pity, etc. etc.—add to every sin another sin named *ignorance*) are death.'

"Dear Satan. Just don't be so irritated with me. It's only that I've taken on too much.

"*You*. Though I know I'm a coward in several little ways, for *you* who love the absence of moralism or social-realist tendencies in a writer, I'll tear out certain hideous, overwritten pages from my notebook on being damned."

Pagan blood will rise again.

2. *Interlude*

R returned, again interminably, to Charleville and his childhood. But his childhood no longer existed, for rejection in
love creates a real and permanent (until death) wound in and
below the flesh. As a human is able to deal with death, so he
or she with the rejection of love.

V was happy to be a family man again even if he could no
longer stand sexually touching his wife.

There are only models of defeat. The Prussians didn't
abandon Charleville until July 24, 1873.

R felt that the world was his mother, V's family, the Parnassian poets, and that V and the whole world were an army
fighting his one-man army. R knew that he would survive,
but he didn't know how. He didn't know where happiness
was, geographically, in these deserts of pierced childhood.

R to R's only friend, Delahaye, who now worked in an
office: "I'm writing childhood songs."

R wrote:

"IF YOU'VE GOT BAD BLOOD, YOU'VE GOT BAD
CHILDHOOD

"The white fuckers have come to America. With guns!
Now we'll have to submit to religion, put clothes on our
bodies, work for their money.

"I received a wafer which was a bullet called 'grace.' It
wasn't my fault, mommy. I didn't know V was going to
happen.

"I've never done anything bad. Seriously bad. I've never
hurt anyone's heart. But this clock will not strike any hour
but one of pure pain!

"I'm going to be lifted up and taken like a little child to the
paradise of love where I won't be rejected.

"Goodbye to all phantasms, ideals, misconceptions. The real graceful song of the angels is rising up from the rescuing ship; the ship of reality is leaving; their song is divine love. I have two loves. One is earthly; one, divine. I want to die by my earthly love and I want to die from divine or poetic love. My two loves are trying to kill each other.

"Lord. Save those who have been shipwrecked.

"Here's a little play about some of the shipwrecked:

"MEDEA

"There was a king, in Greece, and he was tired of his wife. He married another younger wife. This wife didn't like the first wife so she decided to murder the child of the first wife and the king.

"This was her plan to murder the child: She ruined all the seed corn so the people began to starve. When the king asked the gods why his people were starving, the gods, bribed by the younger wife, replied that the people would stop starving if he killed his own child.

"The king took his child to a place in order to kill him. Just as he was about to murder his child, a gold male sheep flew by, snatched the child up, and took him away to Colchis. Far away.

"When the child grew up, he killed this ram and gave him to the king of Colchis, Aeetes.

"King Aeetes's daughter was Medea, the witch who will never tell us what she knows and we can never know.

"Now when Jason came to Colchis in order to steal the fleece of the dead golden ram, he first stole Medea's heart, made her forget her family, her homeland, her duty. She lived only for Jason and his adventure: she defeated her own father, killed her own brother and scattered his cut-up limbs in the sea, and had Jason's father sliced up and boiled alive—

all for the sake of what Jason wanted. Adventure. She gave Jason two children. Then he told Medea he was going to marry someone else. Medea complained. Jason the king told Medea that because she was protesting his actions, she was exiled. Medea was a brat like me. She wasn't going to be exiled and become nothing and suffer any longer because of her loving a man who was incapable of love, because of her loving a man more than he loved her.

"Here is a confession by a friend of mine, Medea, who's also in Hell:

" 'Oh husband, Divine husband, My Lord, please listen to the saddest of your maidservants. I no longer know what to do. I want to suicide and I don't want to suicide. I'm out of my mind. My mind is mad. I'm drunk.

" 'My life has stunk and stinks like your dead fish.

" 'Oh, please, forgive me, I didn't mean to say that, Jesus Christ, of course, everything is good. What are these stupid tears? And there'll be tears and tears—tears'll build up into reality—this is what I hope!

" 'I was born submissive to You, Lord, and I've let another man beat me up and reject me all over the place. Now I need friends to take me away from this pain, but I have no friends. I fought Fate—You—by loving a human man, so now I have only pain and torture as lovers.

" 'I don't have to cry all the time I can do whatever I want because Jason's exiled me set me free he doesn't care about me—

" 'I am the slave of a husband out of Hell. This husband likes to make women about whom he doesn't give a damn fall in love with him. He's just that kind of guy. Because he thinks he's powerful, he thinks he's a man. A real king. But I

who've lost my reason my sense cause of this man, I who'm now dead to the world: I'm not going to let myself be murdered. I'm not going to let him kill me.

" *'How can I describe him to you? I no longer know how to say things out loud: I just cry. I need a (real) husband.*

" *'I used to be uninterested in men . . . I was always a kid . . . his romanticism seduced me . . . I left everything to follow him . . .*

" *'This is the sort of thing my husband said cause he was a romantic: "Love has to be continually reinvented. But all women want is security. As soon as a woman's secure, that is, married, she becomes celibate. There are women who don't care about security and like sex—I see these women being happily devoured by brutes who are as sensitive as logs in burning funeral pyres—" "My race," said my husband, "came from far away . . . Vikings . . . the first heroes . . . who slashed into their own bodies then drank down their own blood. I've inherited this love of blood, of tattooing, I'll be as ugly as one of them, for I know who I am. Don't show me your treasures, for I'd vomit over your antique Persian rug: My jewels're stained in blood. I don't have to work . . ." he said as he took me, we rolled over each other on the kitchen floor, I fought my demon.*

" *'Nights, always drunk, both of us, he dragged me out onto the public street. There, or inside, he tried to frighten me into dying with his violence. "This time he's going to thrust the knife into my heart—But that's not right!" In those days, in those nights, he wanted to be thought a criminal.*

" *'He used to talk a lot about death—when he was being tender. He wasn't able to realize that he loved until that love had died; he wasn't able to realize that he had loved until he felt guilt and repentance.*

" 'In a dirty hole in the city, we would drink ourselves deeper and he would begin to pity, himself. Back on the public street he kicked me down then against a tree dog piss had stained, then lifting up my body, hugged me. It was raining lightly. Then he strangled me until I passed out and when I came to became angry at me for letting him strangle me: every gesture of his muscles revealed the gentleness of a girl at her catechism.

" 'That night I followed him whenever he let me. I had to.

" 'Followed him into strange, complicated actions, very far, bad and good actions. But I was never allowed into his world. What was I to him? A fantasy. I gave him another identity. Whenever I lay next to him in a bed and it was night, I was too excited to fall asleep, too unwilling to lose a chance that I might be allowed to enter his life. Since he wanted fantasy, what I wanted didn't matter.

" 'I asked myself if there was any chance he would change. Would he want to transmute this fantasy into reality? No. Change, for him, was fantastical. Yet I was, and still am, a victim of his charity.

" 'I was in him as if he were the palace. A desolate palace. The palace had been shut down so that no one could see that a person as desolate as me was in it. I depended on him, but who could love the dependency of someone as lonely and sad as me?

" 'So sadness is always renewed while perception dulls: I no longer saw the world. The world forgot me. Only his charity existed. When he kissed and hugged me as if he liked me, I entered a somber room named 'Heaven.' In this room I was deaf, dumb, and blind and I never wanted to leave. Here, I took the habit. We were two children freely wandering in and massacring the Paradise of Sorrow. We were together. But after he had penetrated me, Verlaine said,

"All this is going to amuse you after I'm gone. When your arms'll no longer hang around my neck, when you'll no longer rest inside me, when your lips'll no longer touch my pupils. Because I'm going to have to go and not come back. There are other people I care for: I have duty. Although that isn't exactly what I want . . . darling." I saw myself—he had just gone—suicide. I looked up at Verlaine. I begged him to never leave me. He said he wouldn't. I made him promise this twenty times. I knew it meant as much as when I had said I didn't want him to leave his wife.

" 'Sometimes I forget this insoluble mess and dream: he'll save me, we'll travel; we'll hunt in the deserts, we'll sleep on the pavements of strange cities, carelessly, without his guilt, without my pain. Or else I'm going to wake up and all the human laws and customs of this world will have changed— thanks to some magical power—or this world, without changing, will let me feel desire and be happy and carefree.

" 'What did I want from him who hurt me more than I thought it possible for two people to hurt each other? I wanted the adventures found in kids' books. He couldn't give me these because he wasn't able to. Whatever did he want from me? I never understood. He told me he was just average: average regrets, average hopes. What do I care about all that average shit that has nothing to do with adventure?

" 'Did he talk to God? No. I should talk to God and tell God that I'm living in the bottom of an abyss and, here, there's no prayer.

" 'As for talking to him—he mocks me, avoids me, denigrates me. "Once upon a time," I would say to him, "you were as wild as me. You thought that all straight men were the playthings of Nature in a grotesque delirium. You laughed at straight men, hideously, for a long time. Hiding,

*you became so perverted, you had to become straighter
than a straight man. If you had acted less perversely, you
wouldn't have had to become so straight—get married—
and we could have stayed together longer. Your tenderness
to me was mortal. But I'm a slave to you. I'm mad."*

*" 'One day perhaps—miraculously—you'll disappear,
you'll die, but then, since I don't believe in murder, I'm going
to go with you: when you go to heaven, I'll be there to witness
your Assumption. Ours is a strange kind of marriage.'*

"These ended Medea's words.

*"Medea killed the woman Jason was about to marry and
then she killed the children Jason had given her. She couldn't
kill Jason. As she sat on the palace roof amid flames as fierce
as her love, a chariot of snakes carried her away from Jason
and into safety. Jason wandered homeless from city to city
and everyone hated him. Medea didn't die, but became
immortal and reigned in the fields of Heaven.*

"But I, Rimbaud, I love Verlaine.

"You see: I'm not a child anymore.

"I'm eighteen years old: I know I'm getting older and
going to die.

"Quick rages, doing anything to reach oblivion total delusion or madness—I've been through it all.

"I'm sick of hating myself. No more. Now I'm innocent.
An innocent can't hate himself. Innocents are free, not pris-
oners even of reason or charity.

"I don't regret he's been my life. Each has its own
season—yesterday he rejected me, the day before he desired
me—I depended on him for a while, not now.

"As for planned happiness, domestic etc. . . . not for me.
I've got work. Actually, I don't have a life: I live in fantasies,
sleep in dreams. Now I'm going to try to live my dreams."

Another piece written in a town growing gloomier and gloomier:

"SOME NOTES OF A PERSON WHO'S IN HELL (continuation of IF YOU'VE GOT BAD BLOOD, YOU'VE GOT BAD CHILDHOOD)

"According to the priest here, saints are people who can cope with anything. They're always happy even when they're living in countries of burning bombs and they never fuck though their genitals are burning up.

"All the people who work for money think saints are lower than bums. No one in this society wants saints anymore or artists; all they want is money.

"The world's a continual farce. My saintliness doesn't belong here. Rather I should learn to conduct a dinner party that farce called *life*.

"Who am I kidding with my innocent act? I'm in torment. My eyes are burning up again. Where's torment's always! Forward march! Fight!

"He doesn't want me. Again and again, rejection. Rejection never stops: the blindness rolls around inside the eyes while the body opens like a rose into wound. Where can I go to? Around me everyone seems to be managing to have a decent life. What can I use to make my life better? What do I do with time?

"If you killed me, at least you'd love me. I gave myself to you. I have tried to kill myself—I'll do it again! I'll throw myself in front of horses!

"I can get used to rejection.

"To God's rejection."

In the meantime, V was happy that R was out of his life because now no one could accuse V of being homosexual.

R felt that he was living in prison because Charleville was the land of childhood and childhood had died. Dead dogs can't eat shit. There was nothing left to do with the burnt logs and the weather stunk like cunt. Even though it was summer.

The Germans are always around.

After Christmas had come and gone, boredom made V forget his fear of homosexuality. In those who are sensitive, boredom leads to physical debilitation and even degeneration. V wrote to R that he, V, was dying, and so the prison gates opened a little for R.

3. The End of Poetry

R:

"This is about me. The story of one of my mistakes.

"For a long time I boasted that I had any characteristic— was anyone. And I derided Great Culture, those who are now considered to be great writers.

"I loved naive painters, primitive painters, schizophrenic painters, fashion designers, comic strip artists, popular art, any literature which is low and brutal, Church Latin, badly offset porn, the first novels ever composed, fairy tales, kids' adventure books, dumb children's songs, rock-n-roll. Anything but culture.

"And I dreamed of the Crusades, voyages of discovery unknown to our history books, dreamed of nations who exist outside documentation, of suppressed religious wars, revolutions of this society, major shifts of race and actual masses even continents—topological revolutions: I have believed in every desire and myth.

"This was my childhood.

"Language is alive in the land of childhood. Since language and the flesh are not separate here, language being real, every vowel has a color. *A* is black; *E*, white; *I*, red; *O*, blue; *U*, green. The form and direction of each vowel is instinctive rhythm. Language is truly myth. All my senses touch words. Words touch the senses. Language isn't only translation, for the word is blood.

"At first, this is all just theoretical.

"But I wrote silences, nights, my despair at not seeing you and being in a crummy hotel next to you. I saw wrote down the inexpressible. I fixed vertigo, nothingness. My childhood.

"You want to return to your wife. So you have to make a decision whether you're going to stay with me or return to them. The pain of hell into which you've put me is worsening.

ODE TO A DRUNK FLY
(IN THE TRADITION OF LANDSCAPE POETRY)

Far from the maddening crowd,
What can I write cause I'm still crawling on my knees
(this is the only way I want sex)
surrounded by the tender wood of bar chairs
in a lukewarm mist?

"I know that nature poetry's shit. But I need something, a belief. But a belief, rather, holding on to a belief, can go too far. For instance, the belief that V and I loved each other. Belief then becomes hallucination.

"In order to keep on having this belief, I considered hallucination sacred. No one and no thing can penetrate obsession. The nonnegotiable distance between my desire for V and V's torturing me led me back to virginity.

"Because I was living in this shit of lies and couldn't forget V, I hated everyone and the world.

POEM IN THE TRADITION OF THE
POET MAUDIT

Come come come
What I've been wanting
In every bit of my flesh
To happen.

I've been so fucking patient
That I've forgotten
Reality:
How badly he treated me.

Here's a way, monks,
To put an end to pain:
I longed for him so much,
Disease touched my veins.

Come come come
What all of me
Wants to happen!

All nature is mad, oblivious;
The fucking flies drink down blood;
Nature must be good.

"I love fire! I love every part of fire: burnt-up fields, shops
which are so dusty you can see their air, drinks that burn
down my mucous membranes. I love! I have dragged myself
through stinking alleys, eyes closed, offering myself to whoever turns me on, to the God of Fire.

"My myth.

"My German general. If there's one fucking cannon left in
these ruins of ramparts, bombard us with shit. Our own
shit. Bombard the windows of the most expensive depart-

ment stores! Bloomingdale's! Harrods! My general IRA. Get into our living rooms! Make our greatest and densest cities, New York and London, eat their own trash! Fill every bedroom full of the rubies of blood! Mein Herr General—myth.

"Uh oh. The fly drunk on the piss in this crummy hotel's toilet's now in love with a diuretic—and the sun has just burnt him to death!—

"This is the story of V and me.

"Look. Each person has the possibilities of being simultaneously several beings, having several lives. The good family man doesn't have a sense of responsibility. Simultaneously, he's my angel. Simultaneously, his family's a pack of incontinent dogs. In front of men such as him who believe they're respectable, I love to talk about who they really are, the people they don't want to know and socially and politically chastise. Look. I have loved and worshiped a pig.

"This society hates and locks up its madness because they hate and lock up themselves. I know the system of schizophrenia. Nevertheless I loved a pig and couldn't stop.

"My health was threatened by me. I became scared. For many days I hid in sleep. Awakening, I continued dreaming the most anguished and hurtful of my reveries. I was ripe for death. My vulnerability for him led me through a road of dangers to the limits of reality, to Cimmeria, a country of shadow and abysses.

"Now I've begun to travel in order to divert all the obsessions that have become my brain. On the ocean—which I adore as if it's washing away stain—I saw the Cross of Comfort rise. I know lust has damned me. Sexual ecstasy, the translucent worm just like my father when he tried to rape me, has always been fatal to me. But I've never had a father. My life is too immense to devote to happiness's strength and beauty.

"Lust's tooth, sweet point of death, warned me as the cock crowed—ad matutinum when Christ comes—in the dirt of the dirtiest of cities—

> Oh heights oh depths
> Whose being isn't a wreck?
>
> I've studied happiness
> Which no one wants to shun
>
> I love it
> Each time your German cock hums.
>
> I had no more needs
> You took charge of me.
>
> You owned my thoughts and feelings
> I no longer had to do anything.
>
> Oh heights oh depths
> Whose being isn't a wreck?
>
> This moment you stop owning me
> Now my life flees.
>
> Oh heights oh depths.

"All that is over with now. Today I welcome beauty."

V's mother sent R fifty francs for fare to London. R met V in London, January 10, 1873. On April 3 V boarded the *Comtesse de Flandre* for Antwerp so that he could return to his wife. Who didn't want him back.

Finding himself alone once more and with no economic resources, R left London and went back to his childhood where he wrote, "This life of childhood, this endless highway I'm on no matter what happens to me, mythically impossible to change, Tigger-tiger (R's stuffed animal) I'm always a child, I'm now more unchangeable and tougher than any bum, hey look at me I don't belong anywhere I've got no friends: so I fucked up my whole life. Now I see that I have. Fuck Verlaine.

"I wasn't wrong to despise wimps, nice men, who'll do anything for a kiss, who think they should be sweet in sex and so cater to women, when today, actually, there is only violent separation between men and women."

R soon guessed what kind of life awaited him in Charleville the land of total insignificance: that of a peasant, without a penny, without a friend, without the slightest distraction. What a hole!

"The contemplation of nature fills my ass, here. I'm yours, O Nature, O Mother!" R wrote Delahaye.

R and V again met, traveled to London, again split. This time because they were accused by close friends of being homosexual. They reunited in Brussels where V shot R in the wrist.

R: "A boy had an affair with a married man. The affair ended. That's a usual story. *But V and I were both virgins when we met.* Together we banished virginity. Can you banish virginity without banishing it forever?"

The judges of the Sixth Court of Summary Jurisdiction sentenced V to jail for two years. R, setting out for Roche, then for unknown realities, wrote: "I can live without Verlaine, but can I live without sexuality? Is it necessary for me to throw sexuality away?

"TODAY I THINK MY RELATIONSHIP WITH HELL IS OVER. It was hell, the ancient hell. Hell: I believed that if I loved V enough, we would love each other.

"All I know is that I've been returned to earth violently;

I've a duty to myself to survive and to see what is. I have to deal with the truth, with nothing else.

"Did V's charity to me almost cause my death?

"I, starving, fed on the dream that V loved me and I lived a lie. So forgive me, You who knows that only truth matters.

"I have no friends. Where is there any help for me?

"Yes—this dawn is at best difficult.

"I've won life: my eyes're no longer swollen and diseased; my thoughts, no longer dreams. I've forgotten that I can't live without him. My love of criminals, mad people, obsessed tortured souls—these genital or social rejects can go to hell for all I, who've been to hell, now care.

"In a Thatcherite society it's necessary to be absolutely modern.

"Hard night!

"The blood he let out of my skin, now dried and stiff, hurts me and there's nothing else in my life but memories of him. Mental war is constant.

"Nonetheless this is the eve before the morning.

"May I accept the influxes of vigor and whatever real tenderness floats by in these barren waters. And when dawn comes, armed with my patience which burns, I shall see the cities of humans which are splendid.

"Was I saying that I needed a friend? Fuck that. It's better to laugh at old false loves—to destroy heterosexual bonding—I know the hell most women live through. *Fuck everything. I can now possess truth, not only in my mind, but also in my body.*

"*The imagination is nothing unless it is made actual.*"

AIRPLANE

LOSS OF VIRGINITY

"QUESTION: Why do women become whores?

"My answer: It's not *women;* it's *girls.* Girls also freely fuck men and murder. It's our American way.

"Question: Why do girls become whores?

"Answer: A lot of girls do for a while. The ones who don't just for a while, die.

"When I was a girl, the strongest feeling in me was to go out. That's how I put it. As far out as I could go, in any way, concerning anything. Then beyond. I didn't know what *out* meant, or it was this feeling I had in me. Like banging my head against a brick wall. Doing anything really stupid or really repetitive or sex was an easy way (at that time) to get out of jail.

"Once out, then everything mad and all shining, wet. I actually saw angels rise out of the bottom of the sky of night where I was at university in Connecticut. Since then, to me only angels, and never God, have mattered.

"At university, my arms were thin, but my ass was full and high, like a black person's. In high school, I used to tell people I had Negroid blood in me. My lips were too full to mean anything but sex; my hair is still cherry red. My best friend and I would walk around the green square in front of our dorms, looking for boys, but we weren't whores back then.

"Until that night when I inadvertently left college, the main thing about me was my hatred of my parents. This hatred was nausea to me because I knew I wasn't supposed to hate them but only passively allow their hatred of me. My father was a judge and my mother had disappeared on account of suicide. The judge. For me in those days, despite what all those left-wing students thought who went further down south to help their black brothers, freedom meant not being nauseous. For there was always a buzzing, related to nausea, in my head and I never wore underpants.

"I wondered if I ever thought about sex, or only about parents. That must be what they mean by *innocence*. I still lick the menstrual blood of my heart.

"I knew two kinds of men. Or boys. I didn't know any men except for the professors and they were monsters. Sometimes a girl fell in love with one of them. Falling in love with a monster. The boys were either college boys or 'townies.' My girlfriends and I had imbibed class before we had had education.

"The 'townies,' rough boys, all had cars. Driving when the sun had descended into its half-light, serene gold lying over the tennis court like a blanket, or without an auto, snooping around the grounds, he or a professor (who was covertly searching for one of his young female students) would see this girl, snatched jacket under her right arm, long unshaven unstockinged legs wet from running, in speeding silhouette against 'The Castle' (an actual castle brought over from England, brick by brick, the college legend had it, to be a dorm). Only girls lived in this place, but some of them sneaked males, if they were steady boyfriends, into their rooms. Then, vanishing into the shadows in the back of the library, where Harriet had seduced a creep into taking off his dirty underpants, not in order to make love with him, but so all of her girlfriends hiding in the bushes could laugh at him; then

emerging, only to spring, with a sudden show, not of underpants . . . but of nothing . . . into the particular car that was
waiting on that particular night.

"It was a college boy's car. As fast as he could, he drank
down the liquor he had. The next part of the night was spent
searching for more booze. Rather: for a joint that would
accept our lack of ID. It was sort of fun. After another bottle
of vodka and a number of beers, he ran the car into a tree. So
we had to get out.

"I didn't know where we were. I was half pissed (angry),
half curious, and maybe even in love with the danger. Since
the tree and the car were caught up doing something to each
other in the night, we stumbled with our arms around each
other down this geek path until we saw this geek house and
he kept asking where there would be more liquor.

"The house, even in darkness, looked, well in the darkness it smelled like there had been whore murders and pimp
deals and other unspeakable acts going on inside its walls.
Crawling. The windows were crawling around in themselves and touching broken wood panes like a girl wants to
touch her first john. That's what I think now. Windows
should be openings into heaven, for the soul should be in its
own home and see out of its own eyes. But in this house,
there were no sober inhabitants.

"I learned that there were people of this house. Something
older; a whore; something who had, when a man, crippled
himself; something less than a man.

"The whore did the housework.

"We walked into this crumbling house. I didn't have any
way of going anywhere else. People always have to go somewhere and somewhere is always nowhere. My boyfriend
because he was looking for liquor.

"Just in the door of the house, I either remembered a
dream or saw a dream:

"I was standing on tiptoe, listening. I was flat against a wall and, on its other side, were my parents, the judge and my mother who was now living. Were they talking about me? Words I can almost understand. I know they are saying there's something wrong with me. The way I really am. I can't control this wrongness because by birth I'm wrong. They whisper: everyone says this about me. I grew scared because I realized I was how someone had made me. Suddenly I couldn't hear enough of what they were saying to understand what they were saying. I thought: this is even more frightening.

"Then, in the dream, my boyfriend didn't want me anymore and I wanted him almost more than I existed. All he wanted was booze.

"When I looked down at the floor corner, I saw a gun.

"I wanted to scream but I didn't.

"Something, someone, was moving on the other side. Of a wall. It sounded like a shuffle, a cough, someone old. I ran through the hallway, through which a bit of morning light was now beginning to trickle, light which relieved nothing of all the nightmares of the world but just stank, grey, into another grey kitchen and hid behind its stove. Like an animal.

"I could smell the stuff in my cunt.

"I crouched there for a long time. When a hand picked me up by both the blouse and the back of my neck and said, 'What're you doing here?' I felt safe.

"But I didn't say anything. I didn't know where I was. I didn't know if I liked this strangeness cause I wasn't with the judge or if I was so scared, I had stopped feeling.

"A woman walked into the kitchen. She was wearing some sort of dress and nothing else, but she wasn't sexy. For she was over the hill the way whores get over the hill, perhaps because they've learned too much about men. The old man told her to cook something. She threw some brown and yellow hair wax–like stuff into a dirty frying pan and then red meat.

"I thought the woman would help me cause she was a woman not a man. Men torture women and women help women except when they hate them—that's what I had learned in college though not from the college.

"The woman told me she hated girls like me. I had everything because I had rich parents. I didn't know what a man was. I was just a little thing, an object or a have-it-all, who fucked.

"But I didn't fuck.

" 'Women are subservient,' she said. 'You're stupid. You don't know you're a slut. Cause of sex. Not cause of food or clothes. Cause of sex.' Her eyes looked down at my legs.

" 'For you, sex is cars, going fast, liquor down your boyfriend's gullet—and you get in trouble.'

" 'I'm in trouble,' I said.

" 'You don't know what trouble is. For you trouble is having to tell your daddy something he doesn't want to hear.'

I was remembering.

" 'My daddy's the judge of this county.' I was remembering.

" 'You read in a book that you meet some man who tells you that he cares so much for you that all he wants to do in his life is make you happy for the rest of his life. If you'll only let him. And you say, "Yes. Yes." You'll let him, OK. He says he's never been so happy. And for the rest of your life, you live in happiness.

" 'Real trouble is sex;' the whore said, 'you don't know what sex is.'

"The bacon fat leaped onto the table. I didn't want her to hate me cause I still wanted everyone to like me.

" 'Look. I just want to go home.' She looked at me, but she

wasn't seeing me, maybe she wasn't seeing all of us, all of us who didn't yet know what sex was. Now all I wanted to do was get out of this strangeness and back to the environment which I understood even if I didn't like.

" 'When you finally want a man,' I remember the whore saying in all that I didn't understand, 'you find out that you're worth nothing. From that day on all you're going to do is get older and stink between your legs. When you finally want a man—what was it you were talking about? Love?'

"I was watching the grease jump like a bloody rat out of the black pan. If I could fry that hard, maybe I could get away.

" 'I'll tell you about love. Now that you're here. Love and luck. Love and luck. If you're lucky enough,' she stabbed the slab of meat and turned it over, 'to want a man who wants you, he'll call you *whore* and step on you and disregard all that you, if you're proud, call your rights. And you'll beg him for more, for something; you'll crawl in between his legs and up cause he loves you. You need him to keep paying attention to you.'

" 'I don't want to hear that. That's disgusting. That's not true.' The only thing that was true was that I had nowhere to run.

" 'How do you know what's true 'bout men? That's a boy with you and he drinks himself dead.'

" 'My father.'

" 'A father isn't a man. A man like the man who owns this house. When he was in prison, I waited for him. I didn't know whether or not he'd want to see me when he got out. I waited for him and I didn't see no other men. I was working as a bar-girl to make my way and even save up money for us. Carried huge mugs of beer to them for forty minutes, then danced for the same guys twenty minutes. Those men didn't tip much cause I lost my glamour down on the floor. One of the girls was always vomiting in our toilet, but she wouldn't say why. I knew. When a Vice Squad—a woman—tried to bust our boss for not giving us our legal rest periods, she got offed. Better to vomit than get killed. Better always to survive,' said the whore. 'But I wasn't surviving—I was doing everything for him even though I didn't know if he wanted me.

" 'When he found out what I had been doing—I hadn't actually let a man touch me—not where it matters—he had been out of jail about three months: he almost left me. Instead of leaving me, he hit me. I'd never before been beaten by a man. And now you don't know anything and you come where you're not wanted.'

" 'I don't want to be here. I don't know where I want to be. I need a home. Not the judge. The judge.'

" 'You don't know anything, do you?' The woman who knew probably too much spat. 'Not even fear.'

"I shook her housedress. 'I want to go.'

" 'Do you?' The woman looked at me. 'You make your own decisions.' She went back to her stove. Something white had dripped over the second pan's side.

"It's no good yelling you're desperate. Cause you can do what you want and I was too scared to leave even though I didn't know where I was. Since all I had was her, I followed her. Down the hall. At the end of the hall, she told me, like my mother, to go away.

"I went looking for my boyfriend's voice. It or he was in this room, drunk, around a table. Two other men. They were sitting up at the table, unlike my boyfriend.

"One man held his arms in that funny way, jangled almost mangled, so you know the brains inside his head look like his limbs or worms. His eyes don't look right either. Or mine didn't, cause it's hard to tell who's seeing whom, so his jangledness made me feel nausea. Guess my boyfriend felt nauseous too so he wasn't my boyfriend anymore.

"As I entered the room, one of the feeb's arms reached out for me, or did something like that, but an arm of the other man stopped him. This one or man was older, a tall big-boned man, gaunt, the thin skin hanging off the bones, skin grey from gristle like an old piece of meat brown with rot. At least the half of him that was above the table. 'No,' he or the arm said. 'Not now.'

"I turned around and ran away, out a door into early-morning light. What would have been early-morning light in a world that I knew. I didn't know these men. Since I didn't know them, I didn't have any reason to be scared and I was scared. Maybe I was scared of something in or part of me. I didn't know.

"I am scared of the unknown and I love it. This is my sexuality.

"I saw a smaller building behind the big house and ran into it. I climbed up the barn's stairs to a loft. One corner had been walled off into a room. I sat on the bed. I was safe from fear because I was on a bed and there were walls all around me.

"Since I was safe and I still loved my body, I took off my blouse and skirt and threw them on the floor.

"Through a crack in the door, I could see an eye. Either I could put my clothes back on, acknowledging both the eye and my fear, or I could ignore both. I felt it was safer and more dangerous to ignore both. That kind of danger made me feel good. I sensed something. Down there. I couldn't smell myself yet.

"When I was a kid in their house, way before I knew about boys and I knew about boys before I knew about sex, just before I was about to go to sleep, I would put the middle finger of my right hand, cause I was right-handed, into the wet softness between my legs, then lick my finger. The liquid tasted like the vanilla between the two chocolate sides of a Hydrox biscuit. Afterwards I told the judge I wanted to eat only Hydrox cookies.

"I had a small compact in a pocket in my skirt. I pulled it out, then looked at my face in its mirror.

"The big man, the feeb, and a skinny guy who looked slimy as a ghost walked into my room. The big man ripped the bedsheet I had wrapped around part of my body off. The men looked at me.

"I wanted my body to be mine. Deep in me I didn't want it to be theirs. Something in me was revolting. Something in me was screaming, 'No. No. No.'

"So just as I was learning about my own body, I learned this kind of revolt.

"No one was going to touch me but me. That's how all of me felt with a scream. But it didn't matter how strong I felt it cause the slimy man lifted up my right breast and looked at it. The older man grasped him, pushed down to the raw floor, held him there.

" 'Keep away from her.'

"I held what I could get of the sheet around my breasts as if my body were a baby. I didn't want a baby cause I didn't think about having a baby.

"Now I was fear. Not quite all fear cause fear stinks. All of me was screaming, 'Get out!' I watched the three men walk out of that small room. I knew they hadn't gotten out.

"The feeb turned around and told me he'd care for me. I sensed I didn't have to fear him. My intuition's always right.

"I was learning about my body: Everything's also positive.

"As soon as the three men had left the small room, I

smelled my skin and it stunk. Fear makes you wet, but it's
no orgasm, and I didn't yet know what an orgasm was. I
crawled my body into a corner behind a bed and was rigid.
I don't know how many hours in the stink and stillness. I
thought, 'No human is like this.'

"Fear is what makes humans inhuman. Another time, I
saw a young cow being branded in front of a lot of men. The
dripping heifer smelled like ammonia. I guess it's the nitro-
gen that smells. I also thought, during those lost hours, that
bodies that become rigid become diseased. Or maybe it's the
other way around. I didn't actually have the time to think
even though there was endless time.

"I don't want to be like this ever again: Men coming to get
me. My body is mine. There was this hard thing that came
out, was me and said, 'No. No.' "

During this time, morning, Airplane's boyfriend woke up,
sort of, the way you wake up when alcohol's become so much
part of your blood that it's too thick to flow out through any
of your body openings, though it keeps trying, sort of woke
up in a headache, whatever had he done last night, remembered Airplane. Didn't want to, know Airplane. Didn't want
the responsibility of her young dependency. Wanted his
survival so the hell with her. If you walk away from things,
and people can be things, it doesn't matter if the thing lives
or dies.

Finally the girl decided she had to escape. There was
sunlight on the bed. She looked out the jagged window over
the bed. She didn't see anyone. She walked out of the barn
as if she were free and then, cause she was hungry, into the
kitchen where she had seen the whore through the half-
a-wire screen which served as a window. Knew that a
woman, no matter how much she hated her, wouldn't
kill her.

There was all this food lying around on the tables that

served as counters in the kitchen, half eaten, food discolored and mixed with all sorts of other objects, cigarette butts, old semidried yellow blobs that must have once been human spit; blood, some brown hairs, mainly lying on dirty white and grey broken china plates, a cut loaf of bread, a half-dead mouse. The smell was bad, but the girl was still hungry. Hunger doesn't go away when it can't be satisfied, and even gets worse.

"The white sink was three-quarters full of oily water. I could stick my mouth in the top part of the faucet's cold stream and then the top half of my head. Afterwards I felt I had washed some of the fright away. Long before, when I was a child, I had known that the judge despised me and I had dreamed about sex. Having sex would make what was outside me like me.

"The whore turned round. I told her I was hungry.

"Everything that happens to you, even things that happen to other people that you read about, becomes memories; these memories lie, somewhere in the body, maybe not even in the mind, wherever that is, and shape all you do, the body. Your desires. I was still a girl, and there were no memories in me but those of childhood. The judge who hovered over me. A woman who left and perhaps rejected me before I was old enough to know her. In my memories, I had no control. Being touched or sex was only a dream. My flirtations with bad boys had been this dream's actual edges.

"I knew the whore envied me because I was a child.

"Now I saw that the big man limped. He moved into the kitchen. He was watching me as the woman talked to him.

"I ran out of the house. The feeb was standing by the barn and told me he'd protect me. I knew he was harmless and I needed a guard, Virgil to Dante, so that I could start the journey out of childhood that I was being forced to take.

"Later on, I worked as a stripper and was sick of it, sick of fighting the men who became indignant when I refused to let them shove dollar bills—the least valuable paper their numbed fingers could pluck—up my cunt. I met a guy who looked like a jockey, though I had never seen a jockey, a pimp. I knew he'd protect me from being a stripper just like now I intuited the feeb'd watch over me.

"I've always been stubborn and believed in myself, intuition.

"The feeb climbed up to the room in which I had slept and was now standing.

"The feeb had hair like a horse's mane.

"Feeb: 'It won't hurt you none. Just lay down.'

"I did what he told me when there was still sunlight either cause I wanted to be protected or cause I wanted sex. Though I didn't yet know what sex was. Or maybe these two reasons were the same reason cause I didn't yet know what sex was.

"I needed someone to lead me away from the land of childhood.

" 'Don't let him in here.'

"The feeb shut the room's door in obedience to my hopes or fears. He was still in the room.

Feeb: 'I ain't gonna hurt you none. All you got to do is lay down.'

"In my mind I saw the big man limp away from the barn. I had forgotten about the one who oozed.

"Someone told me that for the Chinese there's no difference between inside and outside the mind.

"No one can ever harm me. Humans don't do that. There's a child who's sleeping in a bed. The child wants to play, to tease. The feeb said, 'I won't let anyone in.' "

At another time, in another place.

She looked up and saw someone whom she couldn't see.

He was tall, thin, and his skin was translucent like that of the men who go to sex shows. He was going to marry her or do whatever men did to women when they intended to care for them. She closed her eyes.

The door opened.

"I know human beings can't hurt each other because to hurt another human is not necessary."

The sex maniac about whom the girl had just dreamt walked into the room.

As the feeb said, simply, "I didn't know you were here," the thin man took the feeb's face in his hand and turned it around on his neck.

"Hurt me. Hurt me."

The sex maniac said, "Look somewhere else."

The two men could do whatever they wanted to each other, gang violence, and because they were men, it didn't concern or disturb the girl. She lay in her dreams.

Then the sex maniac pulled a gun out of his pocket.

"None of this concerned me cause human beings don't really hurt each other. If humans actually hurt each other, any belief or faith I would have, the world, would collapse."

There was a sound, pop, and the world collapsed, but she didn't know that had happened. You never recognize an end when it's happening. You only know it afterwards, like an illness from which you're supposed to have recovered and can't.

(There's something here about the death of love: Love doesn't die if it hasn't been born.)

The pistol smoked against the sex maniac's flank as he stared at the girl. Since she had never seen a gun before (her father the judge didn't allow them in the house because he thought them evil), she was curious.

As the girl reached her hand out, the thin man put his gun

back in his pocket. She hadn't been thinking anything or else she was between two worlds. The world of justice and kindness in which men killed each other only for reasons and maybe not then, and the world of insanity. A cat who's been given two opposite commands can't act because she's trying to grow a second head.

Perhaps being an adult means being a mutant.

Now she was listening. Sound and silence had become inverted.

"I could hear the silence. 'No, I'm not dead,' I said. Inside. Inside my head. I'm curious."

"This tall man is my death," she said to herself.

"He's got hands and a coat. There's reality. I need reality. Things. 'Hi!' I said this to him in my mind, but the words weren't coming out. There was a dislocation somewhere.

" 'Hi, mister, you don't want to be so tall and frightening.' My mind swerved. Or something in my mind swerved. 'All of me doesn't want this thing to happen. This bigness.' All of me was screaming, but nothing was coming out of the mouth like an asshole that doesn't work. The body of the world is dislocated.

" 'Don't you see what you do when you touch flesh?' I said. 'Don't you see? You change the world.

" 'That's what we're doing; that's what we're doing. Touching flesh.

" 'But this world is decaying because nothing, like the words *I love you*, means anything and anything means nothing, everything's always about money.' They said.

"I know bigness. So big you can see its material. It's so big that when the feeling happens down there, you can't tell what's going on in there, what's going on in there. Everything becomes lost. It can be anything, it and what goes on in there, and as long as you don't die, you survive.

"This is what sex was. Death, then sex. I didn't recognize it at first. This is when I learned that I can close my eyes, fight however I have to, and survive.

"I learned something else about this thing, sex. You don't understand your own wants but at the same time you can't deny your own wants without going so crazy that you can no longer bear your own craziness."

JOURNEY

LATER on the rapist thought this: *"Who are the men who rape? They're always asking me this. Who's 'they'? Everyone. Why are you the way you are? They ask. As if I'm a fuckin' freak. As if I'm not human. All of them want to stick things into me, find out how every little part of me works, basically they want me to be dead.*

"It all has something to do with sex. I tell them: Look, I'm always scared. That's true, but everyone in this world's scared and most of everyone are zombies. I learned that this world is insane. There aren't any rules in an insane world. A world of power. It all has something to do with sex. And men have the power, within all the fear; those men who deny this, lie."

After he had raped her, the tall thin man carried the girl out of the barn, into some sort of car, that moved by an engine, and she didn't fight him. She even seemed to cling to him.

She was clinging to him because she had decided to survive. Somewhere in sexuality was her strength. Later on, everyone would hate her for this. Somewhere in absence, between an act only feeling remembered and a flight, the activity that was her mind decided that males have the power.

That for a female to get her power or to survive, she had, at least at first, to get it from a man. Love is free. She didn't know what love was. She would survive. This male, the one who had taken her virginity or raped her, it didn't matter which, was as good as any other man. She'd use him. If things worked out, she wouldn't be a dumb cunt all her life.

Perhaps it's men who dream of love and women who dream of survival.

She was holding to her rapist, sometimes falling into his lap, while he drove past filling stations on top of living earth, horizons of yellow grass. Huge advertisements on endless white dot the skies of the eyes. The landscape is full of holes, something to do with what should be the heart of a country.

Radios competing with phonographs in the doorways of drug- and music stores filled all this sun. Hot, hot days don't burn up the mind. No need to do anything to the flesh, to remember the flesh: the flesh will take care of itself. Businessmen went to whores and peep shows. Identities are holes no need to pay attention to the sun. The rapist drove the car swiftly, but without any quality of haste or of flight, down a clay road and into the sand.

" 'I'm alive,' I kept thinking to myself, 'I'm alive! I'm alive! Even the dirt in this landscape grows.'

"The kids in the state weren't allowed to drink.

"Usually growth is so gradual, humans can't perceive it. This slow kind of growth is mathematically calculable. So human science works. But, a few times, growth is so rapid that humans can perceive it only as separation and disintegration. Such growth or disintegration also happens mentally.

"The next thing I thought to myself is that I could no longer live without the rapist. I talked out loud for the first time since we got in that hot car.

" 'Promise me you're not going to leave me.'

"He promised he would never leave me and I didn't know what that meant.

"I didn't understand why I was saying what I was saying, but my consciousness had gone somewhere.

"All I could think about was what he was like. Should I say that? Would he be offended? Should I say that? I noticed there was some blood between my legs. If I told the rapist I hurt where the blood was coming from, would he be annoyed or would he love me out of pity? Later, I learned that his mother had been a drug addict. Lots of mothers are drug addicts.

"(Sex show:

"(Husband: Where are the rubbers?

"(His newlywed, very young wife, turning over in bed: What do you need rubbers for, darling? It's not raining.

"(Husband to himself: Dumb.

"(Husband: All right. Turn over and I'll teach you something.

"(Wife: Are you going to teach me something nice . . . or are you going to hurt me? I don't like it when you're mean to me. My mother always made us wear rubbers when it was raining.

"(Husband: Your mother's been dead for ten years.)

"It might be that people have no psychology. People'd be better off if they were dead.

"(Husband: Turn over. ([The wife turns onto her stomach, more curiously than obediently.]) Now raise that up. ([His hand lightly punches the side of her stomach.])

"(Wife: Ow! I'm not a fucking man! ([She does as she's been told. She's now in the doggy position.]) This is stupid. ([She doesn't move.])

"(Husband, as he pats her rump: I'm teaching you that you're dumb. ([Pontificating.]) This is the 'dog' position and it's the way that you get the most pleasure when you're fucked cause that's how your genitals're made.

"(Wife, looking at the sex show audience, lifts her right leg in a triangle, like a dog, and pees ([the audience loves this]): Woof! Woof!)"

The car stopped in sand, not of the desert, but the kind of sand or rubble right outside urban centers.

" 'Look at yourself. Look at yourself.' I didn't want to look. He held the back of my neck in his fingers and turned it to the car mirror. My mouth was open. You only look when you care what you see.

"I only wanted to look pretty.

"Exhaling cigarette smoke, 'Ain't you ashamed of yourself?' he said.

"No, I wasn't ashamed of myself. Shame isn't the same as not wanting to look.

"And there was something else. There is something else. I was waiting to look for myself. Something to do with blood. Even then, I sensed that blood is who I am.

"(Sex show. The point is that the smell of sex is everywhere. Whether or not you do it. It lies on the skin and it's the air in the mouth. Here, the women don't need feminism to allow them to curl around each other like cats, or to put their heads on each other's shoulders for consolation, or to hold hands. The women support each other, not because they are sisters, for we're all brothers and sisters and yet we torture each other in perhaps uncountable ways, but because suffering, each one's particular problems, runs through all of their flesh like air can run through a window screen in the full heat of the drowsing summer. They smell each other's cunts and love and hate men. Who, in turn, adore and mistreat them. Cops often follow them when they leave the club, for being *bad* women, women protected or defined neither by men nor by respectable jobs. The cops think they indulge in every form of evil: junk, theft, disease. They are women whose legs are automatically spread open and to whom men can do anything. Anything can go into any hole. But these women smell particularly, of sex.)

" 'I like what's happening between my legs,' I told the rapist. This statement scared him.

"There's innocence in the world and there's what is other than, perhaps comes after, innocence. I had been innocent. In the house with my father, the judge, and then university, making out with all those boys. It's a kind of innocence, letting boys touch you and feeling nothing. The flesh must be the mind. What did some philosopher I read at university ask? Wittgenstein. I never understood questions except deep down, where understanding can't be verbal. And then there's something else in the world. Wildness.

"Innocence; being without virginity; wildness.

"Even when I was innocent, I was wild. I knew something about what was between my legs and whatever else was me. Wildness doesn't have to go away when you lose your innocence.

"I wasn't going to look at myself. Yet.

"I told the rapist I was hungry. He started the car. Identity must be a house into which you can enter, lock the door, shut the windows forever against all storms. And so we entered a city, its outskirts.

"It's as if my eyes and ears, in this journey, were beginning to close so I would have no more pleasure (something I as yet had only a hint of and the blood was still coming out between my legs), so all I could want to do was survive. Use my rapist for survival and then, as soon as I could, drop him. Locked-up eyes ears made the body into a prison, a fortress so I could survive. I will survive, I will I will.

"We drove up to a filling station. Buildings were just beginning to appear. I started to get out of the car for the candy machine. My body was halfway out of the car door. The rapist said, 'Who told you to get out?' He kept the car moving so fast through the filling station, then around the corner of the next street, that I had to cling to the car seat, then to him, to stay alive.

"He reached over me and closed the door without stopping his car. 'Don't move.'

"Past one-story office buildings erected against nothing. Advertisements against the sky could have been pictures of those cocks in sex videos that look as if they're pink plastic. As if the city had been built in protest against the existence of nothing and at the same time was nothing.

"The traffic noises were one level; the moving air, another. These two levels never met.

"Just beyond the office building complexes, brown and brown, wood town houses were dead dogs. In the rubble of so-called civilization you can find anything.

> "This is the end of Democracy. If in the world of truths it is *proof* that decides all, in that of facts it is *success*. Success means that one being triumphs over the others. Life has won through, and the dreams of the world-improvers have turned out to be but the tools of *master*-natures. In the Late Democracy, *race* burst forth and either makes ideals its slaves or throws them scornfully into the pit.

"Some of the wood houses, town houses missed windows. The grass was the color of gasoline. Gasoline neither dies nor suicides.

"Between two wood houses, the sky was getting dark, grey and grey, a neon sign (BAR) lit up in front of an ordinary black building.

"Identity is a house. Then what is safety?"

"She flung her legs upwards as if they were sticks and

then they weren't sticks because they locked around his waist and she could hear her own noises coming out and lying like animals in her nostrils and mouth, mule noises, and then her body was a drilling machine, she was not animal she was thing, against him against him, I'm a machine I'm a machine I'm out of control, and boom the orgasm just came it was large it made her into it. Come. Like death. The screams didn't come from anyone. She didn't go where this pleasure or perfection led her because she was each sensation totally. The cock began to pump liquid up and down its length into her vagina. Deep in there where there is more sensation than surface feeling, she felt this enter in waves and she, the mucous membranes exactly there, pulsed in complementary time, come come, it's called coming, she said to herself afterwards, you can't stop it when it happens; you can't do anything about it."

The stairs turn back on themselves as if their ascensions are almost unsuccessful. One of the hands of the rapist pushed the girl up these stairs. As if she were a machine, slightly disinclined to work.

At the top of the stairs the room was long and narrow. A bar was one of the long sides.

The girl felt alone because she saw no one in front of her and there was almost no artificial light. She walked forward because every human has to go somewhere.

". . . as if you're describing a myth. But you're only at the edge of myth, you don't yet know what the myth is."

Real light, falling through a window at the far end of the bar, had a weary quality. Perhaps the light that also exists when the world is far away. The girl wanted everything to be far away because she had been hurt too much.

"No one," she thought, "ever talks to me.

"In the back there was some talking, but I couldn't see

nothing. It all sounded like whispers. The men. Dream. What I like to do is dream. When you dream, society's far away and you're safe. I could be in this safe place if I could keep dreaming. I still didn't know what the men wanted of me.

" 'They get exactly what they pay for. They know this an honest place.'

" 'Hmm-mm.' The tall skinny man was squinching his lips around a toothpick.

" 'Yeah. Honest.' The other man looked like a woman. He was short, powerful, and fat, so powerful and fat that he no longer needed to move. Everyone came to him as poisonous insects come to a spider. 'How much do you want?'

"The sex maniac replied, 'Don't want nuthing. Just keep her for me.'

" 'Keep her?' The fat man asked with as much curiosity as he could find. 'You've never wanted anyone more than you've wanted to kill some mosquito.'

"As answer the sex maniac motioned somewhere, anywhere, cause there was no outside, only what was, the dust and whatever light it took to make sure that dust appeared, played.

"In my dreams, beyond society.

"The tall, skinny man said, 'You're going to take care of her.' A finger was pointing somewhere.

" 'I'm not afraid to die,' I said to myself, but I was, I was. Then I realized there's no time for terror.

"The rapist turned to me. 'I'm going to take care of you.'

"You know when you're a kid and you believe that Santa Claus is going to give you everything you want? I didn't know what the rapist was talking about. Knowing has something to do with feeling."

"I'm going to take care of you."

LOSS OF SOMETHING
LIKE MEMORY

"THE changing room was smaller than a bathroom. A single light bulb hung from its ceiling. I draped what was left of my coat on a nail sticking out of the wall and put on the bikini which the fat man had given me.

> The night spermed.
> What have I
> done, oh Lord?
> I made this night pregnant, as if
> A night could breed nights after nights
>
> More revolutionary than this one.

"The bikini was yellow as if it were slightly damp. I thought to myself, 'It's supposed to be glamorous.'

"I then thought I was silly to be wearing a bathingsuit in a dark, dusty room whose only water lay hidden in a rusty thin hose, like a snake, over the sink.

"My mind was as blank as Eve's when she met the snake. I walked in my heels, from the days of innocence, back into the bar.

"At the same end of the bar, opposite the doorway out of which I had just walked, there was a circle of wood about five feet in diameter raised twelve inches above the floor. Someone had put music on the juke. The fat man motioned me. He said he wanted to see what I could do. For no reason at all.

"At that time I didn't know what I could do."

Later Airplane thought, "It's hard for me to write down what happened to me."

The club to which the fat man had sent her, his brand-new club, had two floors. *FUN CITY.* Fun for somebody, the man, or men, who earned the money. Earn. Airplane only realized that later on. Its ground level wasn't exactly the club. This level's first third, next to the street, held porn books and magazines. The magazines were arranged in categories of kinds of sexual activity. It's possible to name everything and to destroy the world. A Pakistani man, who probably had a gun, stood behind a high wood counter to the right of the street door.

The store, like every other store of its kind, held a certain unmistakable smell. Once a human smelled that smell, something akin to stale human piss, he or she never forgot it. Just like an acid trip doesn't remind you of, but rather brings you back into, all the other trips you've taken.

Journeying.

A plastic black-curtained doorway was the entrance to the next part of *FUN CITY.* After the curtain, a long narrow, almost lightless hall. Something like a red carpet. Curtained cubicles on each side of the hall held men or shadows or men who had become only eyes. Airplane and her fellow thespians called "ghosts" those men whose skin was translucent white and who left razor blades in the cubicles' machine slots.

The machines showed anything, any choice in a democracy, from lez sex to pig fucking (humans). To Airplane, the pigs had the most disgusting, that is, slimiest, cocks of all animals. Here, the smell like some kind of piss was more definite.

Just after the black-curtained doorway, a foot to the left, before the rows of cubicles had started, another Pakistani (the fat man always hired, when he had to hire, illegal immigrants because he could pay them under minimum wage) sat behind an aluminum table and a probably unstealable cashbox into which he put the men's torn tickets for the theatre which sat, inhuman and Mecca, above the somewhat red-carpeted stairs behind him.

FUN CITY's top floor, crown, was a theatre for humans. The smell of ammonia conquered almost every other smell, even of poppers. Broken glass often lay in the red tufts of the carpet around the huge bed on stage and more often and more thickly on the red bedspread itself, plastic like the bedcovers in airport whore hotels. The plastic's satin sheen, an added expense to the boss, was a homage to sexuality or life which was no longer real.

Or so Airplane thought when she worked, day after day, in service to sexuality.

The fat man had actually asked her if she'd like to work in a venue he was about to open, "a better place," where she could make some money which, of course, she handed over to the rapist. She first saw the theatre as that semilight which acts as gloom in the beginning of nightmares. He was telling her that she didn't have to do too much. "Just fake sex, honey. Otherwise the cops'll bust us. We have a legitimate venture here. All you have to do," he would have placed his paw on her shoulder, but he never touched anyone, "is to get up there, dance a little just like you've been doing for me, then do some sort of number, you know, husband and wife, girl on her first date, they like that sort of thing, innocence, and get your clothes off. Then, fake it, loudly. That's all."

"No sex?"

"We're keeping this place legal. If the cops bust you, *I'll* get you out. You only take your clothes off; you don't do anything else."

"Can I work with my boyfriend?" She meant the rapist.

The fat man laughed because he knew how stupid she was. "If he wants to work with you." There was silence somewhere in her mind. "You can work with anyone you want, but no junkies. I don't want to give the cops any legal reason to bust this place. No drugs and no booze. Even a hint of smoke and you're all fired. I'm taking care of you."

"I understand."

At that time in the city's short history, two men or mobs owned the downtown sex business. About five years later, these two businessmen, who represented the Jewish Mafia and the regular Mafia, would fight to death via a series of shootouts and undercover girl murders in their new massage parlor ventures.

The slob believed in family. His nephew, a skinny pimply intelligent petty crook, used to heist cars across the New Jersey state line until his uncle brought him into the legal family business. The kid was now cleaning the piss and other items out of the cubicles and hoping to be discovered by Andy Warhol. One of Warhol's stars used to help him pick up cars.

> No one will make me again,
> No one from this earth.
> No one will cover over my ashes.
> No one.

Nothing
I was, am, will be.
I'm blooming,
This nothing—
No-one's -rose.

With my pistil or soul
With my stamen which fate destroyed
My center's red
By means of the red word, I sang
Over and over
This thorn.

Airplane understood, as everyone grows to or grows up to
understand, that she needed a job. For since she knew blood
could drip down her legs, she knew that she didn't want to
live on the street where there was no medical care. The
minute you know you have to have a boss, you feel fear. Vice
versa. She didn't know yet she now feared. The job was easy,
the boss said.

"Three shows—each a half hour long."

Time was mental, maybe only in the sex business (and in
disease) and she thought she could handle that. "I won't
have to fuck anyone I don't want to fuck; I won't have to
pretend I want to fuck some stupid boss like secretaries have
to." This was what she thought to herself, but what she felt
was nothing. She had made her decision to survive. To go
along with a men's world and then kill it. She was sick
between her legs where identity partly lies, blood.

Another part of herself which wasn't buried knew that it
. . . she . . . loved danger and flesh. She was finding this out.

The rapist spent every night with her and moaned about
how his life was decaying. Once he asked her to wait in the
kitchen while he made love to one of her girlfriends.

"I don't take chances," he said.

Through her work, Airplane gradually got to know the dregs of American society.

The guy who projected the short hard-core flicks which showed, like dainty hairs, between the half-hour theatrical plays, was a Haitian refugee who had been studying to be a doctor before he had left or, more probably, had been forced out of his island, and was now trying to earn enough money to continue his education.

> Near are we, God,
> Near and available.

> Already grasped, God,
> Digging claws into each other, as if
> Our bodies
> Are your body, God.

> Pray, God,
> Pray to us.
> We're near.

> Distorted by emotion we went out there;
> We were out there just to bend
> Our asses over abyss and ditch.

> It was blood, it was what
> You dropped in the gutter, God.

> It shone.

> It flashed your picture in our eyes, God;
> Eyes and mouth fall empty and vulnerable, God.

> We've gotten drunk, God,
> On the blood and on your picture
> Which lay in the blood as if the blood was piss.

Get drunk, God.
We're coming.

The Pakistani ticket-taker was basically interested in sav-
ing his own ass every time *FUN CITY* got busted. (Which
wasn't very often considering that every time a Connecticut
police officer vied for promotion he did so by promising the
media "HE'D CLEAN UP CONN" and, even better, got a
picture of himself arresting some immigrant in a sex shop in
Conn's *DAILY NEWS*.) The Indian ticket-taker would
scream, "I didn't do it," and then, pointing at Airplane or the
other girl and her sex-show partner, "They're the ones!" The
actual boss, after that initial meeting with Airplane, was
never in *FUN CITY*, either because he might get arrested or
because he was busy having dinner, coke snorted through a
hundred-dollar bill, with the head police honchos.

Lots of pimps and streetwalkers, especially the transves-
tite ones, hung around outside the club on the sidewalk. For
real females weren't physically strong enough to handle
either the trade or their pimp's junk for more than a year or
two. Airplane didn't notice any of them since there were the
same numbers of pimps and prostitutes on almost every
other street corner of the urban mass.

Her closest friend was a girl who worked around the corner
from the theatre. The whole area was a community. This girl
was also young and pretty, light brown very curly hair and a
slim, though not thin, body. Airplane had always wanted
curly hair because she wanted cunt hair all over her head.

Cunt juice is a perfume.

Airplane's girlfriend hated men. In her own favorite sex
show, she acted as an artist's model. As this model slowly,
very slowly disrobed for the painter, she began to, slowly,
very slowly, pose in ways that made the parts of her body

the male audience wanted to see harder, then especially hard, to see. Revelation became sacred. Until the men in the audience were standing on their heads in order to see. The girl hated men.

Half of night.

The other girl who acted in FUN CITY's theatre had a model's body and the kind of hair every girl is taught as a child to want and kill for. The beautiful girl was a model whom the photographer who had done her portfolio had persuaded to whore for him. Somewhere between whore and mistress, a large space, for the clientele were six of his friends.

"One day," the beautiful girl told Airplane in the dressing room or bathroom of FUN CITY, "I took a taxi to a very posh hotel. As soon as I entered the room whose number I had been given, the door was open,"

With the knives of dreams

"—the door locked behind me. I saw a coffin. I ran over to the hotel telephone which didn't work. Finally I had to walk over to the coffin and I don't remember what I saw cause I fainted.

"When I came to, there was no one in the coffin and the room door was open. Through it I ran away."

Another time there was an actor who had played the role of Mafia gangster and whose behavior and dress had been subsequently aped by Mafia gangsters. The beautiful model blew his young boyfriend while his aging eyes watched.

"All of the people with whom I worked were very innocent.

"Of dreams stitched into the effervescent eyes."

AMERICAN EYES

"My rapist wasn't innocent, but he was never in the sex show, he was back home. I was still bleeding between my legs.

"One night something inside me popped. No blood showed this time. The popped thing, shreds of flesh in there, let loose a burning which grew, in waves, until I had to ask the rapist to take me to a hospital.

"Three streets away there was one which was the most well-endowed hospital in the city and so provided almost no care for all those who couldn't afford medical insurance.

"The entrance said EMERGENCY. I could see just as I could walk.

"Inside its door, many poor people were sitting on, sprawling over, or stumbling past folding chairs. One man was bleeding on the floor. By a counter, two nurses sharing a plastic cup of coffee were watching him. Another man who had an ulcer or said he had an ulcer between vomits was vomiting. I still can't look at vomit because it makes me want to vomit. But I was burning too much to want to. Two pimps were watching their teenage girls who were either falling asleep or OD'ing. Between each semideath, a pimp abused his woman.

"In front of the folding chairs there was a line of cubicles from one side of the room to the other. A dirty white cotton curtain, in some cases pulled aside, acted as a door for each cubicle. Here were the medical examining rooms. An old almost-boneless-and-fleshless man managed to move from the inside of one cubicle to a folding chair. Past the pimps and their girls. A nurse strolled up to him.

" 'Mr. Alberti, you have to wait until the doctor gives you your medicine. You shouldn't go near another person, honey, because you're dying of TB.'

"Now and then, a nurse happened to summon someone to a cubicle. A nurse voice called out, 'Mr. Lorca.' Another old man shuffled in a folding chair. 'Mr. Lorca.' Nurses must always remain calm just like cops. Same old duffer tries to get out of chair, can't make it. 'Mr. Lorca.' Old man manages to move left hand. Ten minutes later, a cop pulls old man out of folding chair over to hospital door. 'No bums allowed in this joint.'

"In Connecticut nobody thought politically.

"A 'nurse' ordered me to lie down on a hospital stretcher inside a cubicle. She put her hand up me and hurt me. She got angry cause I called her a 'him.' I hurt, down there, in the ocean, in waves and I was angry at myself for being sexist, for thinking doctors were male. Doctors hurt you. She told me to wait for a doctor.

" 'I don't want to wait anymore,' I said.

"But I wanted to be well.

"When the second doctor came, not in me, anyone can piss in an ocean, and I was still hurting in waves and these waves were bigger, I said, 'Look under the surface of the ocean.' The doctor or the second doctor also put his hand into me and there was a wave that shipwrecked. But I wasn't shipwrecked. Sex, you bring out my emotions. So I couldn't help but scream even though I was in public, in an American emergency ward.

" 'Shut up,' the doc said with his hand up me.

"I wondered if his hand was having fun. Somebody has to have fun. Sometime.

" 'It's just like having a baby.' He said.

"I had always known there's something wrong with the American family.

"When the doctor told me to shut up, I shut up as if I were a younger girl.

"But my shutting up didn't make the pain go away. The pain was getting worse, then worse, as if the sea were raising itself toward something mythic. 'It's alright,' I said to no one, even though there were men in the room. Cubicle. I was clinging to something. I didn't know what that something was and I have to find out if I'm going to live.

"They all left me.

"I waited in the cubicle for medicine. I could hear screams outside me. The screams came from all directions as if I were in a loony bin or as if I were mad, though I've never been in a loony bin. I've been lots of places.

"Afterwards a third doctor told me that my infection was nonspecific or undiagnosable. He gave me synthetic morphine and sleeping pills to stop the pain.

"Taking my medicine and holding my clothes about me, my arm linked through the rapist's arm, as if we were the figures in a tarot card, I walked into light which was either twilight or the beginning of dawn. A mirror, a quick movement of the metal bars of a stretcher on the outside: I saw myself as a ghost who wasn't going to die, not a ghost but only semiopaque flesh. Pale shadows move only in the uttermost profundity of shadows.

"The rapist and I were linked and I hadn't died.

"Since I hadn't died, I no longer felt pain or knew any of the problems I had had about my life.

"Not dying can make things easy.

"And so we, or I, moved through the next two weeks. With the help of drugs. I forgot I was still sick between my legs and I almost forgot everything else.

"Something realized, two weeks later, I was very sick. I wasn't innocent anymore. They say suffering changes a person. What I hope is that that's not the only thing that changes a person. I knew that, in Connecticut, only the rich get well, or get medical care, and that everyone dies. The poor get junk, one way or another, and they die too. It's the American way—to forget even before it's happened. Even in my junked-up state I could recognize history.

"I started working the sex show again to have the money to go to a good private doctor and the rapist, I called him Mr. Sam, liked I was working the sex show. 'Everyone has to get off.'

The new doctor looked like a European gentleman. Fat chance. When he touched her, it was with an impersonality which wasn't cold but rather was distinguished.

The tall man was kind and hurt her as gently as he could. The girl wanted her mommy and knew that she had almost never had a mommy, only a judge. She felt hot on and inside some parts of her skin,

"I thought that if I could just call things by their proper names, I could get rid of evil and hurt. I knew that in order to do this, I had to be naïf.

"How can anyone be naïf, for no one in this world can remain innocent? I had to let reason purify my inner life.

"What the fuck is *reason* in this life, a life of disease and sex show? Perhaps I had become too polluted, not down there, but socially, as everyone becomes, to be pure *even down there in the blood.*"

and she felt cold on other parts of the skin. She kept her eyes closed.

She must have been crying inside her eyes because as soon

as the doctor or her public left (the boyfriend didn't count because he now only partly existed), she began to cry actively, hopelessly and passively, as a child can cry.

After her visit to the rich doctor, for weeks she lay in the improvised cot in her boyfriend's and her apartment except when she was working in the sex show to pay for the expensive antibiotics she now had to take.

Afterwards she never could remember what had happened during this time. Except for the sex show so the sex show could have been the only reality.

"Sex-show girl to sex-show guy: Doctor, I think I need a doctor.

"Sex-show guy: I am a doctor.

" 'But I *need* a doctor.'

" 'You're acting crazy, Miss . . . uh?'

" 'I think I'm crazy, that's why I need a doctor.'

"In this show, I played a *very* young, innocent girl who, because of her innocence or stupidity, could do and did whatever she wanted. Such was the strength of the innocence I had lost. So, perversely, I liked the role.

" 'I think I need help,' I said.

"I sat down on a chair opposite the doctor who was also sitting on a chair. He looked like Santa Claus. Actually, I was getting the two mixed up.

" 'What kind of help do you need, miss?' The man felt that he was getting somewhere. A first step, somewhere. It's important for humans to go somewhere, given reality.

" 'Well, if I knew what kind of help I needed, who I needed, I wouldn't need your help, would I, doctor?' I was getting kind of angry.

" 'You're not crazy,' my doctor-to-be or not-doctor-to-be decided. Something had been decided in reality.

" 'Oh yes I am. Mad. I see men all the time.'

" 'Oh dear,' the doctor answered. 'That is mad.' He thought deeply for a moment. 'Where do you see men?'

" 'Everywhere.'

" 'That's serious.' His thumb rubbed his chin as if it were a cat.

" 'I see men,' the girl said quickly so that he would understand everything, 'when I go out on the street and reach up to wave at someone and I've forgotten to wear underpants because I hate underpants, doctor. I see men, cause I'm so scared, when I'm going back. . . . when I'm back in my own house, cause I'm scared all the time and I'm alone.'

" 'If you're alone in your little itty-bitty apartment, how can there be men, there?'

" 'What I like to do, doctor, is to sink my naked endlessly,' the girl was looking at her own skin. . . . 'soft body into lilac- and rose-colored water, bubbles bursting against the hard ceiling, for hours, oh, and hours, oh, and hours. Oh. I like.' Her fingers played with her own skin. 'What do I like? For hours I bite my fingers then slowly slip these very fingers into the waters of the ocean, where there are big fish, down . . . I know there's buried treasure. Cause there are pirates. Doctor. And these pirates are . . .' Suddenly she sees the audience. '. . . men!'

" 'This is impossible, Miss . . . uh . . . If there were men watching you commit private acts in the privacy of your own home, men would be rapists.'

" 'Doctor, there are many men watching me right now.' Turning to the sex-show audience, her right leg dangling over the stage.

" 'You're totally mad. Whatever your name is.'

" 'Do you know what I'm doing right now? You can't see my right hand, can you? That's cause it's hidden where it's the warmest, no, the second warmest, in just a mass of

oozing squishing flesh. . . . stroking. Stroking. You can't
know what I'm feeling, can you? I'm flesh. Tremors here; no;
tremors here, little bitty tremors like the dashes typewriters
can make. Straight line of shivers . . . oh—oh, where's this
hand going?

" 'Up a calf, no, oh do it to me, it's an animal that has to
get to its home, you're all animals that have to get to your
home, sniffing . . . sniffing . . .

" 'I love it in here. I can be here and you can't.' She takes
her fingers out and licks them. 'Doctor, they're watching me.'
She turns to a man in the audience. 'You're watching me,
aren't you?'

"(When he was off work pimping and he could relax, my
boyfriend took acid. I knew the acid had hit the moment he
said this city is decaying 'RIGHT NOW.' He was standing in
the midst of buildings that were melting. I would try to
persuade him, for a half hour, that he thought he was about
to die because he was perceiving incorrectly. Then I didn't
care anymore.)

"The girl talked to her new friend in the audience. 'You
know, my hand's very warm when it's in here.' She put her
hand back into the warmth so that the man could compre-
hend her teaching. 'All of me, my flesh is warm cause it's lots
of furry animals running around scatterbrained cause
they're not being taken care of and looked after and fed. You
could feed me.'

"Another audience member, a guy too old or too bored to
get it up puritanical style, who knew all the lies, answered,
'I can.'

" 'Doctor, there's at least one man out there!' "
. . . Dreams . . . of what? Something she saw last night?
" 'Miss . . . uh . . .'
" 'Just call me Halo. Halo's short for Halitosis. My mother

named me Halitosis, but she didn't think that was a real name.'

" 'Miss Halo: you are a very sick woman and need immediate attention.' "

An audience member, watching the girl's hand play with her tit, suddenly slumped into his chair.

So with a sigh, the first part of the sex play ended. Though the audience wasn't versed enough in fine theatrical technique or interested enough in anything but their own immediate sexual gratification to appreciate the artistry of the text and acting, except for a few black couples who had perhaps also come here to laugh at whites, the girl and her acting partner were able to make the men laugh almost against themselves.

" 'I need lots of attention, doctor,' Halo said seriously. 'More than any man can give me. That's my problem. Do you want to see something?' she said even more seriously as her hand padded back to where it fell, felt safe; then, as a child looks at a wound, slowly enough to be imperceptible and innocent, began uncovering one breast. Since she knew she was a child looking for something, perhaps herself, she no longer saw anyone else.

" 'I want to know things, Miss Halitosis. First of all, when did your serious condition start?'

"There were now two children. One child was uncovering her breast in order to see what it looked like. Licking and smelling wonder. The other child was answering the teacher's questions thoroughly as she knew she should do. The second child asked, 'What condition are you talking about, doctor?' while the first child flicked the tip of a nipple. Fingers like tongues.

"The doctor's breath had begun to be audible.

" 'When did you first see men?'

"The child thought for a moment. Or remembered. 'The day I was born. Now the whole world seems to be made up of men.'

" 'I see.' Half of the doctor was listening to the patient's replies and half of the doctor was staring at something. 'Genetic or genital disturbance. Proof that puns and other forms of word play are early modes of perception. Mumble, mumble. And this mad delusion—that of seeing men—when did it turn, dive like a smelly fish, down, into paranoia?'

" 'I don't know what you mean by "paranoia." ' Some child is staring at her nipple. That child looks at a man in the audience and asks him whether he knows what 'paranoia' is. Like young girls ask old men the meaning of 'penis' on the streets of the city.

"Man: Uh.

" 'Doctor, I'm not paranoid. I'm a girl.'

"The doctor felt that half his head, since he didn't have a body, was going somewhere else and desperately grabbed it. 'Let's abandon that line of thinking. One can't trust primary theory anymore.'

" 'Do you want to check whether I'm a girl?'

"The old geezer in the audience who knew all the lines or could make them up faster than the actors stood up and said, 'Yes!'

" 'It's not time to get up yet. Wait your turn.'

"The doctor was being neglected. 'I want to know, miss, what it is that you want. What is your deepest desire?' He mumbled.

"Girl to herself, inaudibly: In those moments right before I wake up, I keep thinking up my lovers. Thinking up lovers is thinking about lovers you don't have or miss. R doesn't want me. [R stands for *rapist*.] Actually R doesn't know whether or not he desires me. His confusion forces me to decide he doesn't want me. Then, I fantasize I'm with a man who's not R. Since *this* man wants to marry me, *he* wants to be with me. The moral of this fantasy is that I'm holding on to R until I have another lover. This statement or theory, in turn, explains why I'm so stupidly hanging on to R who doesn't care about me. Actually the truth is that R would love me if he could.

"Having located her desires, the girl said, 'Doctor. I want Santa Claus.'

" 'What do you want Santa Claus to do?'

"The girl has by now entered into the other world where there's neither shame nor guilt. She realized that her boyfriend was feeling more and more guilt now that he was drinking between the days. She put her finger in her mouth and bit it. It is very simple: the sensation of touch feels good.

"Taking the finger out of her mouth, she showed it to the audience, half aware the audience was there, no longer aware of the evil doctor who clearly didn't want her naiveté. The long finger was wet. So she spread her legs. And her mouth fell open. Maybe.

" 'Oh. Darling.' Maybe the audience was one huge lover. 'Oh oh. Darling.'

" 'What do you want, darling?' the doctor asked the girl.

" 'What is it that you want? What is it that you want?' The girl, murmuring over and over as if words no longer had meaning, fell backwards over the stage, her legs open to the audience in the manner of a temple. The rapist, before he had started drinking heavily, had more than once said to her, 'Let me see you masturbate.'

"And she would lick her hand, tasting it while wetting it, vice versa, then tentatively insert one finger in the flesh she couldn't see. They said it was a hole, but it was impossible for her to think of any part of herself as a hole. Only as squishy and vulnerable flesh, for flesh is thicker than skin. She was wet up there. When she thrust three of her fingers in there, she felt taken.

"No one said, 'Let me see you masturbate.'

" 'Come here, little girl, and tell me what you want for Christmas.' The doctor's paw patted his lap.

"The girl trotted over to Santa, placed herself in his lap, and placed her arms around his neck. This cat had been weaned too early. 'I can't say what I want.'

" 'You have to say what you want.'

" 'I can't! I can't!' the child cried. 'I'll whisper it.' She whispered something into the man's ear.

" 'You have to say that if you're going to get it.'

" 'I can't. I can't.'

" 'It's up to you—'

" 'I want a man to fuck me.'

" 'Tell me how you want a man to fuck you, child.'

" 'I can't say,' said the girl, shaking her head backwards and forwards and reaching for his cock.

"Santa's pants sprang off at the slightest touch. The girl grabbed at his cock as a child dreaming he's drowning yells out of sleep and awakes. 'I don't know what I want,' the girl said.

"They fucked and they didn't fuck. Neither of them actually took their pants off cause they had seen a cop in the audience. In reality, the girl was desperate to fuck and scared to fuck because fucking was how she earned money and got power.

"The girl said, 'Oh, Santa. Oh oh.'

"Obviously the fake fucking was getting good. At least for her. You can never tell what the other feels. She added spontaneously, 'I'll do anything for you. I'd even . . . oh . . .

oh yes. Ah . . . Oh [short sharp scream]. I'm going to go crazy. ooooooooooooooooooooohoh. Oh [low short sharp scream].

" 'I don't have to pay you cause Santa Claus does things for free.' Afterwards Halo said to her psychiatrist.

" 'Santa Claus doesn't exist.' Now that the man had fucked her, he could show her what he really thought of her. The audience loved this one. 'If you think a man could love the likes of you for free, you're sick.'

" 'If the world in which you live is sick, you have to live in the imaginary.'

" 'Do you think it's possible to destroy poverty or any other social ill or rejection by an act of the imagination?'

" 'No.' The girl bowed her head.

"The doctor was beginning to control her. As control always works, through the imagination. 'Isn't it necessary to perceive the truth? Can you perceive the truth by lying to yourself? Are there really men out there who want you and, if so, how do they want you?'

"As he said this, the doctor's right hand reached under the girl's skirt. Holding her there like a vase, he turned her over so that her legs were in the air. The audience could see that his hands were beginning to give her pleasure.

" 'Is your body lying?'

"She remembered that the rapist had made her know. Perhaps *come* equals *know*.

" 'Show me how you come.'

"She comes.

" 'Is your body sick now?'

"The doctor was beginning to control. So the girl turned around and kissed him.

"Time wasn't dead yet so I wasn't free. Yet. There's no such thing as fake time as there is fake sex. As soon as I got home, I got into bed. I just happened to look up, one time, time going so slowly, drop by drop, the blood leaking out of my heart, and saw him standing there, looking down at me. I didn't want to see him, or I didn't want to see anything, cause there was nothing to see.

"I pulled myself back down under the blanket, into the warmth. He must have come over to me. I knew that. I could feel him look and catch me like I was a soaring ball.

"Somewhere in me I felt, actually physically, a part of me wanting him.

"When he drew the blanket off me and put his hand over my mouth, I began to whimper. Even through all the drugs that had become the stuff under my flesh, I knew what he wanted to do. *Wanted* is the same thing as *must* in a man. He told me that it's sick for a person, man or woman, to have less than two orgasms a day.

"That couldn't have been the alcohol talking.

" 'No,' I found the guts which told him. 'The doctor said. I'm not allowed to.'

"Either it didn't matter what I said or my words sounded halfhearted, for he immediately slipped his hand down to my cunt, as if he could persuade me by pleasure to let him do it with me. But I lay there motionless, refusing to feel the pleasure I felt, as my act of rebellion. Usually physical pleasure rose in me at any touch.

"When he felt me, I thought there was a violence in that touch and that he was unsure of himself. He had often said that he didn't really exist. Maybe that had been the alcohol talking.

"Then he gripped the top of the undershirt I wore as a nightgown.

" 'I hurt. I don't want to.'

" 'I won't hurt you.' "

There are different kinds of marriages. He took her wrists, placed them above her head while she thrashed, then put a finger between her legs which she didn't like. The finger went up.

"Around that time I decided I wanted to be a boy. I found a cheap barber, there were lots of cheap barbers in Connecticut. This one was unusual because he was willing to cut my hair as short as a man's. He was Italian. I knew short hair was no good for my work, but I didn't care. When I'm determined, I'm determined even if I don't understand why I'm acting as I am. And the audience didn't like me at first, having a woman who had no hair to be their sexual fantasy, but I worked so hard, I persuaded them I was sexier than before.

"It's not that I wanted a penis. I've never sympathized with Freud when he said that. Freud didn't understand the relations between sex and power. Looking like a boy took away some of my fear.

"Maybe I didn't want R sexually as much as he wanted me because I was really lesbian. If I was a lesbian, I would have control over my life, my vulnerability, the thing between my legs, my need to be touched though not my need to touch (I had that anyway), all of my childhood which remained, all which should be allowed. If I had control over my vulnerability, I couldn't be hurt as profoundly as I was being. Sexuality must be closely tied to reality because by being a lesbian, I could make the reality I wanted. Not drugged up in a bed or in a sex show.

"I *had* to change something. I didn't know how else to change it except by wanting to change.

"It was like having a boyfriend. A real boyfriend, one who'd put his arms around me and hug and kiss me and even pretend he was taking care of me. When I had been in

school, both high school and university, all of the other girls
had spent all their time wanting one. I hadn't understood
why I didn't care. But now I knew, though I still didn't want
a boyfriend, that if you had a boyfriend and more than
anything else you wanted him to love you, to want you, but
he didn't: then you'd wish and wish. Cause if you wished
right, he'd love you.

"Everything was the same. I wished not to hurt. Let me
alone. Let me alone, all of you, and there'll be no more hurt.
Then reality'll be what it's like when I'm in the bottom of a
bed, the ocean, under all the covers. There all of my flesh is
warm and I can't see anyone who frightens me.

"Maybe I was praying in the right way. Cause I thought
that if I prayed in the right way, hard enough, I could be a
boy. But I didn't turn into a boy and my sexuality wasn't
lesbian."

The man she had adopted as her protector told her over
and over that she should like sex. A person who didn't like
sex was sick. She thought that maybe she was crazy without
realizing she was crazy. She could be sick because she was
letting men hurt her instead of feeling pleasure.

"I wanted to go to sleep," she told the solicitor after everything was over.

"I knew he wasn't going to stop until he had taken me so I
decided to get it over with as soon as possible. You can do
sex that way, a woman can—faking—but the problem is that
at least half of you is screaming. Another problem is that you
have to hide this screaming.

"That is. Sex. You can can't lie to yourself sexually. If you
don't want it, it's the most disgusting thing in the world.
When he touched me, I was disgusting because I didn't want
him touching me. I was sick, you see.

"My skin started trying to leave my body while another
part of me wanted to go to sleep. Until it was all over.

"So I turned over, on top of him, and started doing it to him, touching his cock and then sucking it, alternating, as if I were a boy. You see, I had to become a boy.

"I knew I could give men pleasure. It was the thing I was good at. Maybe I think I'm a boy cause I understand men physically.

"I did this as well as I could, then, as fast as I could, paying total attention to his rhythm, so he'd go to sleep like me, as soon as possible.

"I guess I was living as if I were dead. Living in fear. First, there's the fear of sickness. You keep trying to figure out how you got sick, as if you did something wrong, sinned, but you can't find any reason. Reason just comes, like death or love.

"Then there was my fear of him. I don't know why I was so scared of him and why I stayed. I could have left anytime. I didn't depend on him for anything. If I were a boy, I wouldn't be scared of another boy and I wouldn't be scared of the world outside and my sexual vulnerability wouldn't be a source of fear."

Whenever a man touched her sexually (unless it was violently), Airplane had orgasms because she liked sex.

When an animal's dying, the animal absolutely doesn't want to die, but this ferocity often means nothing. When a human's dying, the human sometimes realizes that his belief in justice and society is ungrounded and that this death, and this life, is meaningless. Airplane learned that we all die alone, and so we live alone.

"If I'm going to live and die alone," Airplane said to herself, "I might as well stop being scared." And so she began to recover physically.

She no longer had to stay in bed all the time. One morning she came home, she was wearing a nice dress and a pair of heels. She had been looking for work so she could leave the sex show. The skin of her face was white with strain. She saw her cot, her bed, and threw herself down on it. The bed hadn't been made. Since the rapist was at his job (he was now an editor in a book firm), she was free.

Airplane turned over on the cot and saw a grey man's sweater draped over a brocade-covered armchair which they had gotten off the street. They hadn't believed in paying for furniture. "Shit," Airplane said, and threw every piece of clothing she could reach without too much effort around the room.

She could do whatever she wanted until the prison gates closed again—he returned—but there was nothing she wanted to do. She couldn't find work. Having to work in the sex show for money was just blots in the dead of time. She wasn't dead, yet, though she was in prison. She had made this prison, not the rapist. He didn't even make her come.

She had to go out. Though she knew there was no hope of work. She took the elevator downstairs and looked out of the large building. The part of the street on the Puerto Rican side was filled with broken glass. Like her throat.

"I'm trying to learn a new language," she thought to herself.

She walked down the street into a stationery store. The people who moved by her were old and looked like animals, the way people look when everything's wrong. Inside the store, she didn't want a magazine or anything else she could think of.

Later that night "I won't" she told her boyfriend, "I won't do it anymore." Her face was twisted and set.

Her boyfriend was in a taxi. He told her to get in. Something was always the color of blood.

"I don't want to anymore."

"Either go back to the house or get in the taxi." He had almost white hair.

She leaned forward, as if someone had abandoned her before this and she was now trying for her second or last chance, and placed her hand on his arm. The taxi wasn't moving yet.

"I want you to take care of me," she said, "and you don't."

"I don't know what you're talking about."

She realized that's how she saw his face. Dead.

"I don't care what you do," he continued. "Get in the car and stop making a fool of yourself."

Something in her, she, felt all wrong. "I don't want to do it. I don't want to get involved in all that mess that is sex. I want to be clean because I am clean." But she didn't dare say this.

The car was in motion. There was something immense she was trying to grasp. She was on the edge of something foul. Not the sex show. That was just money. Clean. But not for him. He wanted it dirty; he got off on sleeping with those he thought the lowest manifestations of humanity; his eyes, the windows of the soul, were what were melting. He was a manifestation of some primeval lizard and that made sex foul, as absolutely frightening as the strange is.

"It's not sex for him," she thought to herself, "it's descension into slime or his real self." She shook to touch him and she had been touching him. "He wants to die.

"Death," she thought, "is a lizard who basks in the sun."

She wondered if there was another kind of man and if she cared. His hand came over her mouth, his nails going into her flesh. While they passed in the taxi beneath violet, green, red neon lights real humans must have made, she could see glimpses of him watching her as she struggled, ineffectually pulling at his hand which was whipping her head this way and that.

The cab took her to a seedy club. There were no marks left

around her mouth. They danced together. In another room, some men were playing poker.

Then she started to drink. Her boyfriend disappeared. She walked over to the other room where he was, he gave her more to drink, and he killed a man. Then he took her away.

"I'm not dead: I've got my cunt. I've got my cunt; it's not a hole; it's an animal and I love the animal."

She went to the funeral of the man her boyfriend had murdered. There were two kinds of people in this uptown funeral. The first kind were there to see who was crying. They were a kind of vulture now often found in society, a vulture who feeds on media. The second kind were waiting for the funeral to end and the funeral hall to turn back into the gambling joint it usually was.

The girl was the only one crying. She didn't remember how she had gotten into one of the funerary limousines, who had placed her there; she was sitting opposite her mother had put her there; her mother had killed herself in order to get revenge against her mother and all women who were still alive; her mother had never loved her because, above all, her mother had wanted to be the eternal child. So it was all death. In the moving car, she had nowhere to go anymore.

Maybe there had never been anywhere to go even when she had been innocent: the family was just a dream. But you need at least, one dream, to live.

She knew they were burying the body and the coffin was closed, you couldn't see the face, cause something horrible had happened to it. Or so they said.

When the girl got back to their apartment, her boyfriend was gone.

"I didn't know what to do. I wanted my mommy and daddy to come save me. But mommy was dead and daddy didn't save me, he'd never save me. Sure there are daddies who care: my daddy doesn't do anything. If I'm going to survive, I have to save myself.

"I became two people: I was (still) a child who wanted caring parents and I was a human I had made. The human I was making had a will as strong as a god's, like those gods in Norse mythology, cause the one I was making had to. The will isn't ferocious or uncontrollable; it's an adult. Whereas the child's freedom in geographical terms is sexuality. That got me mixed up for a long time: being two people or rather, being the same person as a child and as an adult. And I knew I was hurting and I clung to my hurt.

"I always knew I was beautiful. My beauty was that of loving sex and most people wanted to fuck me. I love fucking even when I don't like the person I'm fucking.

"I don't know how I got in that funereal car; I don't know how I managed to leave my boyfriend a few months later. The money I was making helped. I guess sex shows are good for something or someone, besides for the businessmen who always make money.

"A few years down the line, I heard he had married his half sister, only a year after he had left the apartment. Who had some degenerative disease. A child who's born to such a woman has a fifty percent chance of being infected. Within a year of the marriage, R and the woman had a kid. I never knew anything about his childhood. That's American."

CAPITOL

GIRLS WHO LIKE TO FUCK

1.

DADDY was a drunk, and mom had decided to be a crip, but I didn't mind them too much. Quentin came back from Harvard with all these ridiculous *theories*. He told me Freud had said that all women are naturally masochists, though he didn't say that that simply.

I understood what Quentin meant and I got angry at him. "They teach you stupid things in universities and universities are no good for anybody." I was angry, though I didn't know why.

I had never known Quentin. Or anyone. It's impossible to know a person who's always fantasizing about you and about whom you're obsessing.

I saw Quentin as someone who desperately wanted to touch me but never could because he was mean.

All these men wanted me; well, maybe they did and maybe they didn't. They say "I love you" that means nothing to me it doesn't touch me that means they want something from me.

Quentin wants something from me.

Daddy and mommy are dead and they should stay that way.

Who am I? That's not quite the question which I keep asking myself over and over. *What's my story?* That's it. Not the stories they've been and keep handing me. My story.

I fuck every man in sight. Men open me up or sex with them opens me up, so I learn something about myself. My story has something to do with opened-out flesh.

When Quentin came back from Harvard, he was more mixed up than before he couldn't get anything straight.

Quentin was still sharing my bedroom (when he wasn't in college), though we were too old for that. There was nowhere else to go. I disappeared into my bedroom and, after I heard mommy and daddy close their bedroom door, curled up into my bed. Through all the walls, I could hear Father telling Mother in this high whining voice he used when he was trying to assert himself that he was supporting her so she should be properly grateful. Then I heard Mother really cry.

I didn't give a shit. I decided that sleeping with a lot of men doesn't go far enough, far enough into me. Because the guys who sleep with me and Quentin say, "You've got whore blood in you. You sleep with every man because you want to be hurt because you've got whore blood in you." Their saying this reveals that they sleep with me but they don't perceive me so their sleeping with me doesn't open me up far enough.

I've decided I'm not going to sleep with every male.

Then, from his bed, Quentin started to tell me about Harvard. "It's a Jewish university," he said, "but most of the universities around there are Jewish, everyone knows Jews have the most brains. Though that might not be true now that Jews are fundamentalists too."

"Weren't they always?" I said. Cause I wasn't listening. "What is it about Jews?"

"Because their god is simply horror, they're outside the

range of God. Not only of our fucking familial respectability, of love, but of God too."

I remembered I was unable to be loved because I was sick or because my mother had taught me I was unable to be loved so I fucked every guy I could lay my hands on. Women have always been taught to hate themselves. That's history. And they have to deny that by not allowing themselves to fuck around. Maybe: to be whores. I wanted to tell my brother about history. "Outside the law," I said. "People either do what they're told or they go outside the law, find . something else, maybe themselves."

"There were two kinds of Jews at university. The first kind had made themselves out of the past. Nazis. I learned nothing in university. I wanted to escape the compulsion of having a past, like the Jews, but I couldn't find any past, I couldn't find any past to escape. I can't find a past and a future. Father says that nothing human matters. That must be part of my past too. The past I can't find. Meaninglessness. I wanted to leave . . ."

"I fuck," I said.

". . . but of course I wasn't ready to leave school yet. I stopped going to classes. All the students around me, Capitol, anyway, were insane. Though Harvard has the largest psychiatric staff of any college in the country, the students who are really mad don't go anywhere near the psychiatrists cause the psychiatrists might see the razor blade marks on their bodies and have them locked up. A friend of mine who popped pills every day, he didn't care what pills, and took pot to come down, worked in one of those houses. Stately homes for rich American youth. He said, there you can't distinguish between the inmates and nurses and doctors because all of them piss on the walls and fuck around."

"Fuck you-know-who, fuckface."

"It was awful, Capitol. There. There was a buzzing in my brain. Being in a dentist's chair and the dentist is drilling. The doctors, actual doctors, tried to find out what was physically wrong with me, but they couldn't find anything.

"The worst pain is when consciousness hurts because you can't get away from consciousness."

I didn't want to hear about other people's problems.

"You're a slut, aren't you, Capitol? You do it with every boy and you don't care. Father said women are diseased and have no respect for anything living *their own flesh and blood curses them* and Father said nothing matters."

He was sick but so, then, are most men. Because women hold the repositories of life and death or of time in them, women know that both the material and the measure of living is time. Time to humans is painful. I could spit on men because they're weak.

I got out of bed into the cold, walked over to Quentin's. I put my arms around him and told him to get to sleep. "We're not nothing. We're our stories."

"Mother never wanted to have me. She had me only cause she had an unknown disease and the doctor told her getting pregnant would cure this disease. You're the same way, Capitol. Don't you think it's sick to fuck, to fuck only out of fear, loneliness, and other evil emotions?"

I looked down at him. I had decided I would never fuck a man whom I loved.

It was nighttime.

"Orpheus looked back," Quentin said, "I stopped going to classes, failed three out of four courses, and now I've left university forever. The nearer I got to this house, when I was traveling home, the louder the buzzing in my brain grew."

Father ate only hamburgers, steaks, and lamb chops; he said that all other kinds of meat and most vegetables were niggerfood. Father was searching for his bottle. Mother had hidden it, locked it somewhere in their closet. Father told her to get it out for him. Mother accused him of being alcoholic. Father replied that all businessmen have one or two drinks when they come home. Mother said that any drink made a man into an alcoholic. "Shut up," said Father. "I've given you everything you own." He was crying.

Quentin named the buzzing for me:

"The quarter of an hour before I was back here was when the buzzing was the worst, worse than when I had been in school and when I was finally with you. As I entered this section of town, I couldn't hear what anyone was saying to me and I couldn't see the buildings in front of me."

It was dark in our bedroom.

"Though I didn't think I saw anything, I remember seeing: Wood boards on the empty houses. Pieces of black dog shit. A young boy cried out. Our town was brighter, in colors, than it had been in my mind in university. Light, but not neon, colors: the yellow women wore wasn't the yellow of the sun. The pinks of young girls' cheeks weren't . . ."

Now I knew some of it. I could begin to touch the buzzing.

"Some of the women have prams. You said that women have babies in their blood. Sometimes two prams. One of the babies squalls; a young woman walks over to it . . . her, him, whams the cheek, 'Shut the fuck up.' The buildings aren't tall until you come into the center of town. The businesses here, at the edges, are crummy, like people who know that their lives'll always resemble prisons. Sure everybody has a story, Capitol. Eventually, if they make it to anything besides death. Isn't that what Harvard's supposed to be about? Meaning? The town has always shifted away from descriptions: not that it doesn't want to exist, it just wants to be safe. There've been no major radical political movements in America since the thirties."

"Huh?"

The bedroom was dark.

"Harvard was another world. They knew what terrorists were there and maybe who. Maybe they even make them up, those snotty Harvard tenants, maybe they make everything, the outside world, that's how they own. In Harvard I was taught to know, Capitol, know because known, *known* as in *own*; I was taught to remember what I didn't and can't know."

I was only half listening to this. Maybe, like, cause of the buzzing in his head he couldn't see, so I couldn't hear. Only I didn't hear or hadn't heard cause of what was going on inside or as me. Feeling. Nothing made sense but feeling. I don't mean sentimentality; I mean sensations. Either some portion of the inside surface of my skin moved, or else there was nothing. For this reason, I've never and don't need to say anything to anyone and I let them say whatever they want to me. I'm happy whenever I rub up against someone like a dog.

My brother said. "I remembered and finally I saw some low-cut houses running along the green like rats. I was now about half a mile from here. I wondered whether, if I stepped on their tails and gouged out their eyes, like a poor kid who lives with rats, I could eat them for dinner. My daddy'd drink whiskey and my mommy'd be a low whore."

"Blood," I said, "drink your own blood. I want to go to sleep." I put my hand on a cheek which I couldn't see. "You're the whore because you've got the maturity of a three-year-old and I'm not going to stick with you because no one sticks with whores."

"*Schwartzertown.* That's what mother used to call it . . ."

"You're as disgusting as they are."

". . . I was being forced to go back home by instructions in my head. A hand in my head was clenching and unclenching itself. The instructions decided I actually had an hour or so till D day.

"I walked up and down, then down that long hilly road mother used to walk every morning to get us fresh eggs, and I came to a short stretch of white sand and then the ocean.

"A boat was effortlessly moving, as if propelled by nothing and no one, across a sheet of water. Since there were many kinds of time here, the hand could no longer control me.

"For instance, I looked away from the water and saw areas of suburban life that wanted to be progressing as fast as possible and, at the same time, wanted no time, invulnerability, wholesomeness. Isn't wholesomeness untouchability?"

I knew who I was. Now.

"The ocean was another kind of time. Time like blood."

"Is blood untouchable?" Maybe, finally, it is, as are all things. I thought that women are sane because they're ruled, not so much ruled as pulled, by their menses. Little did I know.

"I knew it was time to go back to the terror (don't say it, *doom*) that was ticking in my blood."

"You don't want to fuck me, do you?" Every man or boy in this town wants to fuck me and they know who I am. You can't ever leave me, don't. "Terror (doom)," I said, "like everything else, has to do with babies."

A few weeks later, Mother disappeared. I shouldn't have been scared when it, that, happened because being crazy, she could do whatever she wanted. She had lied all the time. But despite all my reason, my blood knew doom. I learned about blood. The cops who didn't give a shit said that she hadn't suicided but been murdered but no one could know. And then, she who was in my blood wanted me to be dead.

I asked him, why don't you do it normally? "Why don't you do it normally, Quentin?"

"What do you mean *normally?*"

"With another person?"

I knew Quentin knew what I was talking about, but he had already fallen asleep. I snuck outside. The moon was going somewhere and from somewhere, but nobody saw where. I had no intention of going to sleep ever again or doing what they told me to do.

2.

Will you be my daddy? I wanted to say. No one can tell me what to do. Sometimes I'm in ecstasy and I want to fuck every man in town and I don't care what the face is on the body I'm fucking. That's not evil it's ecstasy.

During the day, Quentin and I walked down to where the swans were. Here I felt peaceful. I hadn't seen them because, for a long time, it had been winter. I had been scared they died in the cold and I couldn't bear when living things die. It's the helplessness, but I don't know whose helplessness.

It was winter and the swans were OK. They came glided ran over to me as if they were in the right proportion to the water and air and so controlled their own existences. "Snake-necks" I called them.

There is a myth.

Quentin stood at the side of the bank on some concrete while I put the bottoms of my legs into the water even though I knew I wasn't supposed to because the water was polluted. Hair and weeds. Rimbaud had told me, he's always instructing, that the people who tried to suicide cause of love or money or just out of stupidity in the adjoining river and were too stupid or unlucky to succeed had to have their stomachs pumped. Swans never have to have their stomachs pumped.

Quentin told me I'd better get out. I was up to my waist in mud and reeds and weeds and water and a swan was waiting about a half a foot from me.

Against my wishes and better judgment I did what he said. I sat down on the bit of the concrete that sloped into the water and mud in my clothes so stiff from the wet and cold they stood out from my body and made a noise as they scraped the stone.

"Why don't you wring your dress out do you want to catch cold?"

The water was rippling or waving, against itself, here and there, as if it were remembering to whom it belonged. Maybe everything's alive. There were some baby mallards, grey ugly, and they were running through the water without any shyness to investigate our human doings. Quentin wanted to ask me, again, why I fucked with every boy in town, but he managed only to ask me if I loved every boy with whom I had sex.

I knew the real question and I placed one of his hands over my breasts. I knew what he was asking and what I could never ask. "I don't love anyone," I said that wasn't the correct answer. "Look at the fucking water, Quentin."

"Do they have some hold over you?"

"Of course."

"Do they have some hold over you," my brother continued as the sky grew darker, "that you spread your legs for them? You're barely anything else but a child. Maybe you want to be hurt by them or, maybe, cause you're a woman, you want to be pregnant."

I thought he didn't understand anything about women. No man did. I had learned to pay no attention to what all men thought, but just to take what I wanted from them.

That wasn't exactly it. Something to do with hatred. That this was my brother confused me.

"I'll kill them, Capitol. I will Father won't find out Father doesn't care about anything I know who, what he is . . ."

I know what sex is and I'm a young girl.

"Afterwards he can find out afterwards nothing'll matter cause there'll be some freedom."

"We'll run away," I said gleefully.

"I'll take the money Father gave me for tuition. School just teaches you how to fuck like those men fuck you. You hate those men (you fuck), don't you, Cap?"

My fucking and fucking mattered to him: he was a man. A boy-man, my brother, and a man. There's no man who isn't sexually jealous.

"You hate those men you fuck."

I didn't hate anybody I did I did. I had to be open to him cause he was my brother. Open to what was inside him so now I put my hand there.

"You hate those men, don't you?"

"Promiscuity is basically a compulsive, illusory attempt to create object relationships, doomed to failure, for the promiscuous girl is flying from a frustrated experience with a mother who she feels didn't nurture her properly. I hate Father." My hand was still there and there plus my hand had something to do with the ocean. It wasn't the ocean. It was a thick pole in the middle of the ocean. I could come around it he was inside

I couldn't stop this although it was against me cause I had to be open to him vulnerable skin gets bruised don't hurt me again I got hurt before I was born. "I hurt."

Concrete.

With Quentin I didn't know who was taking care of whom and I don't think he knew, but knowing isn't the same as or necessary to doing: Openness and the flesh do.

I looked up at him and I could see him thinking and not

thinking because he wasn't able to think. Then I could just see the skin of his face. I think we had the same breath, the flesh meeting. I saw his eyes looking down at me. I couldn't bear to see him looking down at me. I couldn't bear anything but exactly what was happening because it was all of me and I didn't know what he thought. His left hand was under me I must have been crushing the blood out of it. Blood is somewhere. "Quentin, I hate them, that's why I do it with them. That's not why I do it with them. (Fuck.) I don't hate you I do it with you."

(Afterwards I started to want and I'm not sure if I wanted to want.)

Then I saw it coming out. I've never again wanted to see anything else.

I've heard you can use it as skin lotion and it's good for your skin.

I don't know if Quentin knew (saw) (wanting) even though he had done it.

That's what it is: not *it*, but *wanting*.

Quentin was in love with suicide. I got up and draped the wet cloth around me. "Quentin's dead," I said. "Oh, I didn't mean that. You know the first time I ever saw a penis?"

Quentin was looking away from the bank, toward the river. It all looked stagnant, but not as dead as a dead man's face. Or even more, someone who's about to die. Father. "The first time I saw a penis was Father's. I was in Mother and Father's bedroom. I walked into the bathroom where Father was standing over the toilet, I hadn't known he was in there, and I saw it for the first time. It was standing away from him and looked weird. I had never seen anything like it, some part of the body and yet not part of the body, opposite to it. I immediately knew I was seeing what I wasn't supposed to see and I felt disgusted or frightened or both and I got out as fast as I could. Out of the bathroom. Freud said, you told me, girls always want their fathers, sexually. You think that's why women are sluts, don't you? That's just why I fuck everyone. I only thought that penis was weird."

Quentin was crying.

"The first time I was ever loved was when I was fucked. Loving has to be fucking. If it isn't: there's nothing. I fucking know it isn't. Mother and Father hate us."

Quentin said, "You and I."

The river looked as it always did, faintly disgusting, only faintly. The warehouses on the other side of the liquid were or looked empty and the shopping carts that always lay like dead horses in the river held the water stagnant in their manes. We walked to and reached the riverbank.

The sky was dark but not so black that you couldn't see. I had never cared about Quentin because I knew all he cared about was death. You can't care about a person who's more dead than a rat or enclosed than a living flea. Father had taught Quentin to want to die. Mother had taught me I should. That's what parents do.

Maybe cause we had done it, though both of us weren't sure if it meant anything, or maybe cause of no reason at all (no reason humans can know), Quentin started revealing facts about himself.

That he had fucked lots of girls. He said. In college. He was horrible to them, physically and, worse, mentally, cause he was so passive or uninterested that they fell in love with him and then fantasized he loved them. Quentin couldn't love anyone. Not even enough to say "No." "No, I will never love you." "I held a knife to her throat," he said.

The riverbank was more desolate than the pond's and the cold. I sat down on the cold. I could see little figures, across the water, standing on part of a white building, white like flesh. "Who?"

"I've been in love with every girl. I've never cared for a girl. I was horrible."

"Don't cry."

"I'm not crying, Cap."

I say every dirty word out loud cause that's who I am. *I compulsively and indiscriminately look in men for what I miss in contact with my crip mother.* (a book) I say every dirty word loudly, but I can't say aloud what he does to me sexually when he's doing it. He was touching his own cock. "Are you going to . . . ?"

"Do you want me to touch myself, Capitol?"

"Yes."

Then, "Don't cry," I said as I touched, a rubber, and then his hand took away my hand while, still crying, he watched his cock and my face which was watching upwards to the sky, under him, and I almost asked "What?" while liquid came out onto my face. I put my hand into it and gasped and I don't remember if he was crying.

"I hated him. I don't hate him. He's too weak to hate."

"Who?"

"Father."

"Quentin." I was still rubbing in the stuff. And smelling. I fuck everybody I can, Quentin. I didn't say that out loud because something else had happened. Somewhere I was open. I gathered my muscles and stood up.

We went back home.

3.

"Let's go," Quentin had said. He had turned back to his cold part. He was warm only when he was wanting to fuck me.

Fucking me (for a man fucking any woman) was destroying what I should be, a perfect enclosure, by hurting penetrating opening me up, all that he shouldn't do especially to his own sister. Virgins have to want to be virgins so only men know and can know virgins whereas we were made to carry life, be unclean. Now Quentin was a cold fuck and we were going back home . . .

. . . down a path where since the sky was now almost black, the branches sticking out could poke away one of our eyes. "You'll know it when it happens."

This was one of my favorite times being by the river. Cause time is material. I liked the shapes of the leafless branches of winter that only appeared when you were right next to them and meanwhile the tree trunks, trees blown over and cut down by the storm last year, took on other shapes, always metamorphosing depending on the changing distances between them and you. Dreams emerged as we walked. The river began to appear the mirror it would be when there was no more light in time.

Time too can totally go away. I know we are really nothing; that's why I like this night.

I wanted to go back to the riverbank to see whether the swans were sleeping or were hurt by all the darkness. They couldn't be dead cause when you or a swan dies, time dies. I told my brother I was going to leave him.

"It's late," Quentin replied. "Capitol. It's time to go home."

I kicked a stone that being material must be time. My foot hurt. Time must be antihuman or time was human and humans were antihuman. Fuck Quentin fuck him fuck him. Cold fuck. All he cares about is himself. He doesn't know dog shit. He doesn't know what it is to fuck. He doesn't have any responsibility because he has no relations to the world so he should die.

"Capitol. We're going back home now."

"Fuck yourself."

"Now."

I stood as strong as I could I looked at the water cause I belonged somewhere. I was confused. I didn't know where the part of me who fucked every boy in town had gone to. The other me, new, didn't hate him and hated him because he didn't love me. (I want to kill you.)

His hand was raised somewhere. "Are you going like I told you?"

Half of me hated him and half of me didn't. "I didn't hear you say anything."

"Capitol." His arm swung and met. I looked out, I couldn't see anything, and said, "I'll do what you want. OK. I'll do what you want." I looked at him though I couldn't see him, and didn't move.

"We're going back, Capitol, now."

(I had forgotten about the high school boys. But what I hadn't learned yet was that it wasn't only my decision. The more Quentin wanted to touch me, the more he was unable to touch me, not because of guilt, but because he wanted to remain in love with death, frigid. Nothing in him, and sexual desire wasn't the strongest of these impulses, was going to make him grow up. I didn't want to be in this world where people had no protection against being hurt and I was.)

"You shut up you shut up," Quentin quickly said to me he quickly came over to me and shook me.

I looked out of my eyes, but I couldn't see anything but my blood. "Tell me everything," I said again, "tell me what you're thinking about tell me everything."

My brother slapped me.

"You tell me everything you're not one of the bimbos I

fuck, *fuck screw,* you've got to tell me everything, you are, Quentin."

"Shut up. Shut up."

I opened my eyes and *my* hand on *his* cheek was burning hot

In the dark

we walked past the brick wall of a deserted factory. Along the river. I remembered there had been graffiti. Quentin said, "You're going to do whatever I say?"

I said, "Yes." But I didn't want to go home.

"Go up against that wall and masturbate."

While I started to do what he said, which was easy, he stepped away from me and then stood still. While I was doing what he told me, I said that from now on he and I would fuck our brains out with each other and we wouldn't care about anything but physical pleasure and I murmured "Quentin Quentin" and then I explained I wanted a home Mother and Father weren't a home cause she had decided to be a crip, him a drunk, sex (with Quentin) must be a home.

When I finished masturbating, Quentin took me back home.

4.

I want to be dead, I thought when I got back home. Mother and Father were in their bedroom per usual. Since I knew Mother's every movement and emotion during a day, due to her love of pills, I knew she wouldn't be asleep yet. Mother's rigid schedule, as if she were an athlete, was this: in the mornings, as soon as her beautiful green eyes opened, she was in a lousy mood, a bitch. That must be from where I got my sweetness. In the early morning no one was near Mother. Fifteen minutes to an hour after she had imbibed her first meal of dex, she was in a glorious mood, friendly, everything an American mother should be. Now gaily, now timidly, depending on their natures, her children would venture into her room and asked her for favors and for love. Gradually my mother became more frenzied until by late afternoon she was physically shaking, but she never drank. One drink would turn a man into an alcoholic. Mom was only a crip.

(In the late afternoon sometimes she would disappear. We knew she was out gambling.)

When my father returned home and began his (home) drinking, Mother, at the peak of her irritability, took her first Librium. She had scored this Librium from Father who had been prescribed it for heart attacks, though actually, being rich, she could score anything. An hour later, she was sensual and would walk around or sit in her bedroom, naked. She and Father never did anything. That's what Father had said.

This was how, though I wasn't yet grown up, my life was run by drugs.

When I had said I wanted to be dead, Quentin said to me he wanted to go back to Harvard because everything was dead there. Good and dead I said, but he couldn't get a joke up anymore.

Back in my parents' house.

Mother kept on taking drugs, but we didn't think of them as drugs cause Mother was a child, then a crip, because her Librium was legal, and because Mother had always instructed us that drugs are evil. "One puff of pot leads to worse things." That's what both Father and Mother told Quentin right before he went to Harvard for the first time, but they neglected to tell him what *worse things* might be. Quentin must do everything in his power to reject the evil pot-seducers who hung around those college campuses like fleas.

Father was too alcoholed up and sweet (naive) to notice Mother was a drug user. He worshiped the ground she rarely walked on. Mother and her friends were too rich for her rich friends to notice that she was increasingly unable to perceive whatever it is we call reality.

She had always been abusive to Father. I will never be like my mother because I hated her guts or, rather, she hated mine. Just after Father had had another heart attack and was now out of the isolation ward, in a private hospital room, recovering or not recovering (nobody really cared), I saw Mother standing outside his hospital door. *Mother was as popular as a young girl.* All the old people told me. One of her girlfriends was saying that Father *had been* a good husband to her.

("Choose a good husband, Capitol. Nobody's going to take care of you but you.")

Mother, in a voice as loud as the other woman's, answered, "Oh." She looked at her red fingernails.

"Though you've never loved him."

"Oh."

But whatever Father heard as he lay dying (he didn't die that time) (we all die), Mother must have loved Father, whatever *love* is, because the next time Father had a heart attack and this time came so close to death that the doctors told Mother he was, Mother's perception of reality started to decrease. Rapidly. Mother needed a man.

Quentin was going cold on me cause he was too scared to feel to trust. The only safety he knew was to fuck women in his head, in actuality to throw them over to hurt them. "Keep your hands off me," he said to me, "don't you know any English besides the word *us*? Get that cigar off the mantel."

We didn't know that Mother was crazy only that a great

deal of money was disappearing. Every day new clothes, five differently colored versions of the same designer dress or coat, would appear in one of the many closets. Mother owned them all. Mother was spending more and more time in bed.

"I used to hold you like this," Quentin said to me, "I wasn't strong enough was I you are the one with the strength."

"I don't want to be. I want to be loved."

"I thought you were going to be strong enough for me because I'm not strong enough."

I could cry because humans are so stupid.

Winter is the most hateful season. Winter is death.

Whenever it had been Christmas or my birthday, Mother had given me a minimal sum of money because she had felt she had to. Now, as ice was living in the blood of the earth, she called us into her bedroom, asked all of us what we wanted as presents. We had never before been asked what we wanted: when the blood had first come down between my legs, I had been told it was carrot juice. None of us said anything. I wondered whether Mother had decided to like me because I looked exactly like her only she was beautiful. I fucked every boy in town.

Quentin disappeared totally from me. For he didn't want to die anymore and something had to die.

Quentin.

A week before Easter, Mother disappeared. She had never disappeared for more than three hours before this. I was scared for another reason. Because I knew.

For a week no one knew where Mother was.

I fucked every boy in town. One of the men I was fucking was a French professor at our local university. Because he was older and dictatorial, I turned to him when Mother disappeared.

I had told Quentin I was going to marry him in order to get back at Quentin, in order to get Quentin back again.

After Rimbaud had informed me over the pay phone that Mother had disappeared and Father was too drunk to know, I followed the French professor out of the artists' bar in which he hung out, desperate to prove his purity, in the filthiest part of the downtown area, three whores too worn out to make it to New York and a dirty mag store complete with flashing neon green . . . followed partway down the street just like the dog I want to be until he turned to me and told me to go home.

"Do you want," the French professor inquired, "me to be your mommy?"

"Keep your nasty old hands off of me it's all your fault." I don't think I've ever had anyone to talk to.

Since a woman has to be perfect intact to be worshiped from afar (that's what Quentin wanted of me), a woman who needs isn't whole.

A week after she had gone, when the cops came to our apartment, Father was still so drunk he was almost dead. "I didn't do it!" was all he managed to say. The cops told my brothers and me we would have to accompany them to the cop station to identify the body of a woman they believed to be my mother.

I asked them where had they found the body.

"Did you love them, Cap, did you love them?"

"When they touched me, I died."

Only Quentin and I went with the cops. Though I had never seen a dead body before, I recognized Mother. I don't know what Quentin said when he saw because I was screaming. I don't remember anymore about being downstairs in the morgue. Upstairs, when I asked the cop who seemed to be in charge of her case how she had died, he looked at the case file and said, "Pills." A bottle of empty pills had been found on her body. Since both madness and despair are motivations for suicide, I asked him whether she had suicided. "No." "Why?" "The evidence pointed the other way." Then she had been murdered. But to prove that, it would take three months until the cops could do an autopsy because morgues are as overbooked as jails. By that time it wouldn't matter how she had died. It's cops' job not to give a shit.

Quentin and I walked out of the cop station through some streets, hand in hand, but Quentin still didn't want to fuck me.

As soon as we got home, I cried out loud. I didn't cry, I cried out loud. I shoved his hand against my throat. Where the heart is. "You fucking, stinking bitch. If you don't love me—I don't care. I will have ecstasy. Whatever else happens: the whole bloodied world gone to hell. My emotions *will* be free. I don't care what the pain is. I don't care what the rules are. I can't bottle up and maintain all the death you've given me. Death—to not admit my needs. Death—to not fuck. Death—to not feel every feeling there is. I will be free. I will live—you fucker, you you," I shook Quentin. "You Fuck.

"I'll live in all my disastrous insane emotions and I won't hide anything like the sailors whom I love live in ships, ships slipping through, hiding under the waves' dragon wings . . ."

Quentin looked at me as if he no longer saw me.

I told Quentin I fuck every boy I can get hold of because I want to fuck my brother.

"I have an illimitable courage for rhetoric and know or care for little else," Quentin said.

"I won't be dead."

Quentin didn't suicide because he became an artist. In order to become an artist, he made friends with those whom our general society considered evil, low-life sex industry, gamblers and beauticians. He himself became a gambler. He wasn't yet actually making any art, for he was drinking and learning to be silent.

Writing is one method of dealing with being human or wanting to suicide cause in order to write you kill yourself at the same time while remaining alive.

For the rest of his life, Quentin would drink cause drinking was a way of moving among people without having to touch or be touched. Not having to belong. Ever again past death. Who gives a shit how your mother died or if you have a real father. Only stupid Oedipal-obsessive theorists care about that sort of thing. "Cap," Quentin said, "Cap." He took a wife, but he wasn't sure who she was; any kind of sex except the kind of sex you're supposed to have in marriage drove him into fleshly hardness. I need anything, anything, that will stop me from living in the kind of death the bourgeois eat, the death called comfort. Quentin said. The ways we're supposed to touch each other and present ourselves. May all that go into silence. I have to be American. My need to be American is to get what I want, viciously, viciousness is sex, to just keep going out. There. Drunks don't need to be touched.

I self-destructed, motherfucker, years ago. Died in every way a person dies except physically, everyone around me died, that was childhood. Fuck it. Throw it away, keep on drinking, keep from sinking into that sentimentality called contact.

Quentin started drifting. It's as if he swam down the Mississippi, huge waves carried him safely to all the places he wanted to see but not live in. Touch, but never hold on.

He needed to turn away from everyone and, finally, that takes unhuman stability.

Do you care now do you do you? No man has ever cared for me. I loved my brother and my brother went away. I want to be an artist, he said. Men worship work.

Me. I am my mother.

Quentin was Orpheus. He knew if he looked back, he was going to die. Looked back at whom? He didn't remember. Maybe a woman. So a writer has to be fucking alone, he said, not to a novelist, he avoided novelists for the ambitious poseurs they are and hated their literary talk. A writer has to be alone because if he really touches anyone, which must involve looking back, he dies. But to be a great writer, you have to perceive. So: you are playing with death.

I can see Quentin in all his faglike clothes, which he couldn't afford, laughing, masses of envy bitterness greed insecurity stubbornness agree to any vice but the truth. I don't give a goddamn what you do, I say, I've learned to be in pain. I am my mother and I fuck whenever a man will have me no man tells me when to fuck and when not to fuck.

THE LAST DAYS
OF RIMBAUD

MEN always understand each other.

". . . solitude is a bad thing in this world. Personally, *personally*, I regret only two things. Not being married and not having children. I am living out the worst punishment: being without other people, being an outsider. What is the point of this atonement if I cannot, one day, before I'm too old (and old age is coming up, sitting on this shoulder), settle down in a nice, middle-class neighborhood and have a family of my own, mainly a son to whom I'll devote the rest of my life by raising him in accordance with my etc.

"You see," said Rimbaud.

"See what?" said Father. Speaking because he wasn't totally inebriated yet. Men always understand each other. Or: males.

"That I shouldn't be here with a drunk and a whore too young to be a virgin, that I'd be with my son if there was any justice in this world."

"There isn't," Paw himself explained. And took another drink. "Haven't I explained this to you over and over again? Man is always fooling himself; maybe he's on earth to do just that."

"Yeah," Rimbaud said, "God."

"Not God, but man. Man fools himself that he or God exists."

"Well, since she doesn't exist," pointing to an imaginary woman, "maybe she should at least learn to act decent." Rimbaud's voice rose. "Do you know what your daughter does?"

"She's not mine," said Paw. "She's not no man's."

I know that.

"She's now doing what bitches do and she's going to end up the way bitches end up if one of us doesn't do something about it."

"Her mother ended up," Father replied.

"That's what I mean. And they leave younger bitches."

Father started crying. "I'm just a trouble and a burden to you."

"I ought to know that. And you're a man. Or you were before you started on that stuff you use as a substitute for your mother's nipple. But your daughter's worse. There's no telling what she's likely to drag in here. She's a whore, but her mother the bitch couldn't even get it up to teach her that whores are supposed to earn money.

"So I'm supporting all of you.

"She takes anything in and when it leaves, bawls a little like a dog who's been kicked. You know why you kick dogs who stink. Where she takes anything in," Rimbaud stated, "is this house, plus she's wearing her cunt out which should be virginal. No man will ever want to take her away from us and impregnate her. Work saves."

"Given the welter of female emotion, the female is unable to know or to value work." Father.

"She's your own flesh and blood."

Childhood was an education in how adults treated flesh and blood.

So the only thing for a man to do is to settle down with a wife and have children, the most rigid setup possible, to counter his natural tendencies toward disorder even suicide. "Sure," Rimbaud said aloud, "that's what I'm thinking about. Flesh. It's her goddamn flesh. There's something the matter with it. It's hot. Like nuclear energy run wild. I think either we do something with her immediately and that something can't have anything to do with schooling cause she'll just fuck everything male there, or else throw her out on the street and let her survive like the wild cats do."

"It's not right, Rimbaud, for our own flesh and blood or for someone's flesh and blood to be out on the streets." Father sobbed a second time.

"I should have been a poet, but I've the burden of this decadent family. I am forced to concern myself with money, with no help from either of you. I who hate the musk like garbage that rises off of female flesh."

Those were the days in which there was the smell of something other than human desperation.

"Either lock her up in this house yourself," my older brother continued, "or hand her over to me and I'll get the shit out of her."

Father protested, though he didn't care what he said, that I was still a child. As if anything could matter.

Rimbaud knew a slut who'd never be loved. We'd be better off rid of her, thrown out onto the streets, but then he should have been a poet.

"Nothing *can* matter," Father said, "because no man can do that which matters and he knows matters."

Jason or Rimbaud went out and got me. Out of the outside. I had been drinking coffee because I couldn't get booze because it was too early in the morning though I didn't like the taste of booze.

Inside, the sun was shining through two kitchen windows as yellow as piss. "That's what they should have named you." Rimbaud's fingers were on my arm.

I looked up from them as much as I could, through the hair over my eyes as if all the world and I were a mess. But my eyes were so big, I could see through all that hair, eyes too big to be scared.

Quentin when he had loved me had said I looked like a victim.

"OK. I'm late I've got to be going."

I could feel his eyes.

"I'm going to school."

"We're gonna fix that right now."

"I'm vulnerable and I survive."

"Come here." The fingers didn't move, but tugged.

"I'm not going to go anymore near you. I'm going to school."

"You've been handling men even since you were ten and blood traveled down your legs, but you're not handling me." His fingers were as white as the skin under them.

"Mother's dead," I said.

"You sluts always want to get your way. You act like babies, thinking we're stupid. You've made a mistake this time, haven't you?"

"Mother made the mistake;" I said, "mistakes are human. Not finally irremediable."

"You're going to school," he replied, "and afterwards it's time to learn something from me and it's about being hurt." Rimbaud had been hurt when he had been a kid. "Either you'll do what I tell you or you'll get hurt."

"Hit me," I said, just like Verlaine had pleaded to Rimbaud in my literary book.

"You don't think I'm going to hit you."

"Father became drunk so he could manage Mother, and he didn't manage her. No one manages death."

"But I'm your brother," Rimbaud answered, while he let me go so quickly I stumbled, in their house, against the wall near the stairs, trying to keep my kimono shut. "I'm going to teach you to not be a slut."

I've always wondered how some people teach other people. Death and blood transfusions teach. Quentin, at least, had gone to Harvard to learn and had learned about Freud whereas Rimbaud was part of America who know that book education has nothing to do with experience. When I looked up from the stairs, I saw Father watching his children. The first time I had dreamt about Father, I had dreamed that a huge, translucent worm with opaque teeth and no other features was chasing me. Never again I kissed Father. "Do something." I always wanted my lovers to be my father. "Do something."

Father smelt. "I'm watching," he answered. "Nobody's going to hurt you. Not in this family. Capitol."

I threw Rimbaud's arm against the wall behind it with a strength whose source was unknowable and then I ran up those stairs. To where the bedrooms were.

"Capitol."

"Capitol."

I could hear both of them from the beginning of the black iron fire escape in my bedroom. I finished climbing out the window; the window slammed down; got out.

Father, a kind, gentle man, and a wimp, because he couldn't stand up for himself, believed in the American values someone or some people had taught him. Honesty and hard work. If a man's honest and works his butt off, his life will be valuable, but my father's life wasn't valuable. "The present is always grim, and the future is supposed to be worse." —Father.

I don't know whether or not Rimbaud and Dad noticed that I wasn't there anymore though they say that men run the world. The feminists. The feminists say, too, that women, unlike men, are good because women don't have aggression in them. My problem is, that given my circumstances, that is my family, I don't have enough aggression in me.

"I guess love must be based on absence." —Rimbaud.

Though Father was saying about me, "Rimbaud, she wants something."

"She's going to get something. 'Bout time." Rimbaud had a faraway look in his eye just like a visionary.

"You don't understand her. You've never understood anything about women. She's not bad: she's sick. Women're always sick with wanting to eat up your soul. It's all in *JANE EYRE.*" Father read books. I inherited his love of reading which proves that inheritance is important for human beings. A huge inheritance can make a miserable person's life happy. "A man has to keep himself away from women, cold and hard."

"Speak for yourself, drunk," —Rimbaud. "Mother ate you up, but there was nothing to eat. Women's lower mouths have bad taste or taste bad."

"Never had to taste one," replied Father. "I've never abided perversion. If a man's going to have anything to do with a woman, he has to destroy her."

"Why that's what I aim to do with . . ."

"I don't actually mean make her into a whore or a physical corpse. By *her,* I mean *wanting.* Without their wanting, women are nothing like everything else."

"Well, what's your fucking problem? Rhetoric and booze?" asked Rimbaud. "I know how to take Capitol in hand and I'm willing to do it and save you all the effort so you won't have to look at the blood on your hands and you're crying again."

Father couldn't stop crying, so Rimbaud left the flat to find me. He knew that the most likely place for me to be, if I was alone, was in the motorcycle garage to the left of the apartment building. Crouching in one of the back corners like an animal who's frightened. Knows it's about to die. Fear smells like cunts do. All over. I was scared all the time; when the fear came up, grew, it took me and made me absolutely passive. I always do whatever anyone tells me to do even if I hate the person's guts. All of their guts. At the very same time there's a spot between my legs since it's almost burning up is almost my consciousness. Since it involves another person, sexual need looks like fear. I don't see any reason not to play my fear out, not to swing it in their faces like a live cunt.

Rimbaud thought, our whole fucking family.

Sure I was where he thought I'd be. Into a corner, on the ground, all the time as low as she can get. Jason or Rimbaud was thinking. And that's where she wants to be that's why she's there that's what she wants to be cause she's a whore. Our whole fucking family. They might as well have committed a lot of murders their genes are so bad.

Despite all I got myself off the ground. I was once as low as you can get and I changed myself into a successful businessman. Now they all depend on me as if all I am is strength. Since the act of poetry's weakness, it's disease. I am proof, Americans, that a man who is low and filthy even perverted in his very mind can become the acme or acumen of American cleanliness.

[Looking at Capitol.] Look at what the fuck I'm responsible for. A cunt who spreads the legs attached to her for anyone cause she's too stupid even to know what a sexual disease is.

I had crouched down lower so my legs were spread out

and my ass was in the center of a used tire. "Didn't your mother teach you how to be a whore like the whore she was before she died?" Now there was a question. The garage had fleas for light. "You aren't naked enough to be a whore, but you've got more gook on your face than clothes."

"I do what I want. Just like Mother. But unlike Mother, nobody really touches me because nobody means anything to me nobody will ever have anything to do with me again now that I've been perverted into a monster by Mother's suicide, so I do exactly as I want." As I spoke, I pointed my right middle finger at my chest and thumped into there as if it were a weapon. I don't know why. I was angry. And I had no intention of suiciding or even of hating myself now that Mother had suicided. "And do you know what I can do, if I feel like it, with these things which you don't even call *clothes?*" With my hands, I tore at my green dress though it wasn't my green dress that I was tearing.

"You don't even know how to do that." He kicked me. "Maybe you need a man to help you." Father would have said that people are only the repositories of their inheritance if Father had been sober enough to put mind to lips. By rending my dress, Rimbaud was carefully informing me that I depended on him because he had paid for my clothes. Family education is a sound, unforgettable education. I've been educated to know that truth, that I have been brought up as a whore to be a whore. If poetry is the salt of this earth, females by education or economic training are more poets than males. I told Rimbaud this while he was ripping up my clothes.

But. Only poetry is rebellion and Rimbaud had gone, rebelled against his inheritance in order to make himself into a businessman. He was still a poet. A dead poet. Dead poets don't have ears.

I put one of my fingers up my cunt, withdrew it all white wet, and said "See" while I showed it to Rimbaud.

"See."

"I've seen what you are, slimy slut, and I'm going to whip it out of you."

"Whip? Like you're a slave trader? Go on. Big boy."

"Like my own flesh and blood."

I knew a poem by the original Rimbaud:

> In olden times animals came as they ran
> Glands larded with shit and blood, not the curse.
> My father himself proudly displayed his member,
> His sheath's wrinkles and the grain of his purse.

. . . Not having loved women—although his cock was full of blood—he had trained his soul, his heart, all his force, to strange and sad errors or wanderings. Following dreams—his loves—which came to him by chance, both their beginnings and endings. Since this bizarre suffering possesses its own unquestionable authority, all of you must hope that this soul, wandering and lost in the world, and who, it seems, wants to die, will right now find value and real consolation in suffering.

Jason or Rimbaud hates when I say things out loud, especially the things he wants to repress. He says I'm scared all the time cause he's scared. So, out of the garage, I stood on the street and said in as loud a voice as I could, "These are the boys and men in this town who I fuck," and started naming names. Quentin's name wasn't among these names. Since most of my clothes were still in the garage, people were staring at me.

"You do a thing like that again, I'll make you sorry you ever drew breath." Rimbaud hit me.

"I'm sorry now," I said. I was beginning to be sorry I was me and I didn't know where to go with or in me. When a man loves you, you wake up like plants out of the earth, and I was dead and perverted. Both my soil and my blood are sick.

Rimbaud's poem continues, somewhere, "Truth: this time I wept more than all the children in the world." Keeping hold of my hand, my brother dragged me into his Ford which was parked on one of the corners. The left side of my face was still smarting. I didn't care about anything anymore. Except I didn't want to be Shirley Temple. I didn't want to be myself. Sure I got into the Ford with him. "I'm going to hell, Jason. Do what you want with me. Rape me. Lobotomize me into a good little doll. I'm going to hell. I'm bad and I don't give a goddamn. You'll never touch my brains and my heart. I'd rather be in hell and be hell than wherever and what you are. Brother."

He turned to me, and, even though he was driving, smacked me. "You'll be in hell even more," he muttered, "when I've finished with you."

He could have run someone over while he was hitting me. Men don't have any sense of responsibility.

When he had driven some way and turned, came back to the apartment building, rich, ugly as his bearded face, he opened his car door.

About three months before she had offed herself, Mother had told Quentin and me that she had a boyfriend. The boyfriend worked in Father's shoe company, the company into which Father had married.

The day after I saw Mother's dead body, I phoned the company. I asked to speak to the boyfriend. I told the boyfriend Mom had just died.

Boyfriend didn't know about whom I was speaking. But

don't you know Father? I asked. Of course he knew Father cause he worked for Father.

The boyfriend asked me to convey his condolences to Father.

I decided that I had to learn why and how Mother had died so that I could know what it is to be a woman. To be me.

If memory is a tool by which I'm making myself, why do I make painful, even deadly parts of myself? I'm not sure who's in control. I spent most of my childhood fighting against parents and men in order to control what I call my life.

Perhaps it'd be better if I do nothing. I miss the swans and plants grow. Do memories spring up like plants?

Thinking about what he had to do with me though he didn't want to be thinking about me, Rimbaud drove on to his office. A man named Earl was already there. They left the building together.

Earl was a Jew; Rimbaud said that didn't bother him. Preverts were worse. Jews and Italians were into the pornography business in this part of Connecticut and Italians didn't let anyone into their part. History always repeats itself.

"I don't have a Jewish accent," said Earl.

"I don't hold a man's religion against him or a man against religion. I asked you to have lunch with me cause I need the advice of an expert." R never had any expression on his face and he was thin. "What do you do with a slut?"

"You don't know?" asked Earl. He reached over for a ketchup bottle.

"When she's your sister and she advertises her sluttishness all over town."

"It shouldn't matter to a man what a woman's doing. They don't have any brains to make their doing noticeable. If she's a slut, make your money that way."

"Money," R replied.

"Americans got out of England so they could make money any way they pleased." Since Jews have brains, they know history. "You going to be told what to do by a woman . . ."

"Girl . . ."

". . . or are you free to do with her as you need whatever the hell she does?"

Father had said, "History always repeats itself, at least in blood." We knew.

R opened a pack of cigs. "I'm not paying for your goddamn lunch for philosophy. How do I sell this bitch?"

"They've got a lot of religion in this country now?"

"So? Religion doesn't have anything to do with me."

Earl looked at R funny. "This government loves religion. They're not going to let the only way poor people can now make money alter their new shiny religious surface, the screen behind which they can now hide their criminal doings. All they're doing is trimming a sucker like everyone else, but they are and they can be better at it."

"They believe in Christianity." Rimbaud had never known if he was Christian or not.

"Why shouldn't they? The Haitians believed in the white missionaries who showed up with black books; the Haitians knew power when they met it."

"So what am I supposed to do? Lobotomize the slut's clit into a Bible so she can go around begging righteously for more of my money?"

"She wouldn't stand a chance against the TV preachers."

"Listen," R said. "Sex is a sucker game unless a man keeps a continuing, expanding profit. I don't want to be in a high-risk business."

"I don't mean to put you off," Earl answered. "If you can learn to keep your head down (your name out of the papers), sex is the surest business there is."

They were sitting in a drugstore, at one of the Formica-topped tables next to a large glass-paned window. Through a fence across the street, Rimbaud could see grimy kids. That, somewhere in his memories, returned him to himself as a boy, doing something in the haze of pollution like mauling and being mauled. He was now no longer part of their world, misfits losers vulnerable fucked-over; he was never going to be fucked again.

He'd do something about Capitol.

Earl swallowed a bit of the lukewarm coffee. "I can put you in the way of a little business. The kind of business you're looking for. Sure."

"It's not that I give her anything." R explained. "It's that she won't believe she's nothing. And she's costing me."

"You're a businessman," Earl. "Money has no value. If you want to go into this little business I'm talking about, family business, you know that it's going to cost you. You have to spend money to start a good business. Like a car. You wouldn't run your car without gas and oil, would you?"

"She's been running me."

"Well, you have to set her up properly. A woman will do what she's told if she's been told clearly. It's when they get confused, they act up. Women aren't your problem, Rim. Sex is good for business otherwise it doesn't matter anything."

Rim agreed. "So how much money do you think it's going to take to set her up?"

"The thing you've got to learn," Earl, "is that to set up business, you've got to spend money like a whore. Funny, how things go. You see, every dollar a whore spends, she spends double in her own flesh. Pockmarked, junked. And that's your profit."

"That'll teach her."

"She don't exist. I'll tell you about moralism and religion. All the jazz the politicians're now saying. Every whore gets junked then the holey cunt finds religion—you might say she's supporting our government—and when she dies, she'll find out religion's nothing."

"Money in my pocket," Rim. Not my brother's mind, but rather his flesh held a memory of love. The second a human begins loving, he or she is better off dying, the memory whispered. Flesh is always whispering and it hurts, itself and others, when restrained. Mass murdering. "For those who love." Rim was looking through the fence at the kids who believed that this parking lot full of rubbish and half-dead dogs was their playground.

Once upon a time he too had hated his mother whoever she was but now he had forgotten for a long time.

As he walked over to the real parking lot where his Ford was, he congratulated himself for growing into responsibility. Finally. Taking care of his family. Providing for the goddamn sons of bitches. Son of a bitch and bitch. They were his family so their beauty was foul. He was keeping this circus, bitch and son of a bitch, together. When he got some money stashed, he'd get him a decent wife, a nonbitch or a nothing, and then they'd have a son whom he could teach properly, to have his values.

You can't teach a bitch nothing because bitches live in blood. He had always known that. He hadn't changed.

There was poetry somewhere.

Pieces of a dream unreeled down the back of time.

"Our Fathers," Father had said, "had their children to support them in times like these."

These are the times when we no longer have the myth of escape. Go to the multinationals, think tanks for your myths of information, but never look to the home.

What is it? Shards.

"What time?" asked the man who had once been a poet.

The poet had sung for a bit until what seemed to be the causes of his singing frightened him into failure. Reaganite failure. Shelley sang though, now the scholars say, he had been a shit. To women.

Shelley isn't a shit to me and if men aren't shits to me, they don't exist. Is that true? Shards of memory. Father was trying to not exist; Rimbaud, unlike Quentin who had disappeared from me, would disappear for me.

Either Mother had never had a boyfriend and had been mad (loneliness, sexual deprivation, thwarted ambition) or her boyfriend had lied when I had informed him of Mother's suicide and, perhaps, had killed her.

I didn't see any other possibilities.

Was the latter true? Why would he have killed her? Because she gave him money? At her funeral, the family lawyer had informed me about a million was missing. The only people I knew who carelessly murdered were the rich people I read about in newspaper stories.

I want to know who I am and I don't know what's real.

Yesterday over the phone a friend told me that when she was living in a seaside resort, she noticed that a whore was working out of the flat next door to her accommodation.

Shards of memory. A sailor whore port town. One night, my friend (an actress) was walking home through the early hours of the morning. Leaves fell into an ocean which didn't exist. Noticed one shadow among all the other shadows. As if noticing a memory. Rushed to get her door open, inside, where she'd be safe from.

As her door finally was opening, the shadow emerged into a woman. "I haven't talked to anyone in three weeks."

I could have said that.

The actress went with the whore.

Entered into the whore's flat, her world. This world was one room which was empty except for a mattress on a floor and a lamp with a red light. Sailors get serviced easily. I don't remember.

The whore took one of the actress's hands into her own. "I've seen that ring before." Rings are for marriage, belonging to the world. Shards of memory.

I will remember so that I can dream.

There were empty bottles pyramid-packed into one corner. My father was a drinker. "I remember," the whore said. "I hated the person who wore that ring. It doesn't have anything to do with you. Have something to drink, dear."

The actress had two tumblers of whiskey. Into the waters of the nonexistent sea.

This is between women.

"What's your name?"

"I knew a woman with that name. Hated her hated her." The whore said.

Since my family are dead people, I know that dead people never win and live in the bottom of the sea.

Wanting to abandon the mad whore, the actress looked ahead of her, then saw the shoes the whore had on. Men's oxfords.

"I'm dressed as I used to dress in England."

The slut had a man's voice, but wasn't a man. My friend said that women are strong, that when they act as men, they become fragile.

The whore screamed for help.

When Rimbaud entered the apartment, he walked past Father, ignoring him, up the stairs to his workroom.

I opened that door he was looking at his watch as if the goddamn watch which every businessman wears was going to tell him something about life. "So you've come back," he said, but his eyes didn't move from the watch. He knew damn well and I didn't have to tell him nothin' that I had nowhere to go so there was no coming back because (I thought—they had taught me) no human wanted to have me. At the dinner table, Rimbaud had said no man would have me no matter how much I spread my cunt lips—

("How I spread my cunt lips," I inserted.)

(If I could, I would have fucked over every man.)

("Childhood. The whole of poetry is there. I have only to open my senses and then to fix, with words, what they've received.")

He asked why I had been knocking on his door. I asked him if he had gotten a letter from Mother.

"Were you expecting one?" He wasn't interested. "Were you expecting the dead to tell you what it's like there so you can have a new place to spread your cunt lips?"

"Just tell me, Rim."

"Tell you? Tell you what? That Mother's dead because she suicided? That she suicided because she was female or mad? What could I possibly tell you? That all that you have, that all that anyone in this family has, in possibility, is what I give you. What are you looking for now?"

"Money."

"Eat it."

"Just give me some money. Some of it's mine. I'll do anything you want if you give me a bit of money. Please. After that you can think and say what you want about me."

Rimbaud, after his experiences, knew a whore, a girl desperate for money without a chance of getting it, when he heard one. But he hadn't made me low enough yet. To suit his weakness, his insecurity, his inability to do anything but attempt to control. *He was the first sane member of our family.* He thought that poetry is dead in this modern world.

"I need some money now," I begged, "because. I owe it. To a friend and I can't hurt a friend."

"What the friend's name?" He knew that everyone who knew me in my school (but I didn't care) hated me.

"It's a girl. In school." I couldn't tell him that I was pregnant cause then he'd do something horrible to me. All of them knew I didn't have any friends my own age.

"You know that our mother's dead and every penny I make goes on supporting you?"

When you don't eat your dead meat, a child in China starves. "Yes." But even then I knew I was going to be like Mother. No matter what men did.

Let the children in China starve. "Now, get out of here." He didn't hand me any money.

I knew that he was planning some new business in his mind and that business had to do with me. I knew as if we were born to get married to each other cause I can hear blood, power. I knew that this brother had never taken care of me and that now he was going to take care of me. All I had to do now was find out the details of caring or maybe I didn't care, maybe I should get the hell out of there.

Rimbaud came down behind me on the stairs, placed his hand on my shoulder so that I had to turn around into his face, and gave me a fifty. Said, "I'm taking care of you."

Since he had a beard and skin that was all wrinkled like a sailor's, he looked old. Something to do with memory.

"Childhood. Innocence. Innocence is the plague. O Nature, O Mother."

Father was resigned to Rimbaud's haphazard, violent aggression, but Father was financially dependent on Rimbaud. He didn't seem to like his son, but he didn't seem to like anyone.

"I'm dying," Rimbaud said, "rolling in platitudes, nastiness, and greyness. What do you expect, I persist stubbornly in worshiping full freedom."

ODE TO ANONYMITY

Four young girls lean against the wood bars horizontally crossing a gym wall. All of them wear black cotton sleeveless blouses and black cotton full skirts. One girl leaves the group by herself and half walks, half struts, very slowly, across the floor. Her strut, as her head falls toward the floor, turns into a swirl. Falling without falling. All the girls are moving, alternately lifting skirts and showing their white underpants, or stepping high, as they've been taught is proper. They can be good and they can be bad. They forget their roles and just move. They rest in the center of the gym, out of breath. I am not one of them. Me: Capitol.

All my brother cared about was money. Business. His money. He didn't care whether I was a slut. He had stopped drinking, though he didn't believe in Jesus Christ yet. "I want to," Rimbaud said, "slowly, carefully, climb up the ladder of common sense. I don't depend on anyone but myself." He depended on one body. My body. I was so fond of my body, and dumb about what men do, I let him think this. I let what happened, happen. You might say that *dumb* means *fond of the body;* I will never let this go.

Rimbaud intended to reach and cling to the topmost rung of success on the ladder of my body. I remember that what existence was for me was that there was nowhere to escape.

Rimbaud walked past. Then I heard his and Earl's voices together in the living room below.

"Been much busy?"

"Not much. Not since I talked to you."

They were talking about me. I walked down into the living room. Rimbaud told me to get out. I got out and I didn't think I had anywhere to go.

I went up the stairs. I could still hear them talking.

Mother had hated me despite her slight and unexpected change of heart a few months before her death. She had made Rimbaud the sole trustee of the scrap of money she had left for my education.

"She's just a girl." Rimbaud.

"You need capital before you can use her or anyone else."

"That's what I'm saying. She's a girl."

"Since women don't think, women don't know how to think," Earl added.

"I haven't beat that out of her."

Since I'm not dumb, I knew what they were talking about. I knew only a few facts. Mother had deliberately checked into one of the hotels which was around the corner from the hotel in which her mother lived the day before my mother died. I didn't know if she had planned to suicide when she had checked into that hotel. If she had checked into that hotel in order to meet a man, she probably (I didn't know this for certain) wouldn't have checked into a hotel next to her mother's hotel. She could have checked into the hotel for some other reason and by chance eaten too many pills.

My mother's mother had been the family money supplier. Father was a dildo and a hanger-on. Who isn't a hanger-on of the rich? Mother's mother had adored Mother.

After Father had turned to drink to the point of death, Mother took more and more of her mother's money. Then, she stole the most valuable of the diamonds. When Grandmother had learned about this theft, a week before Mother had checked into the hotel, she had cut the economic umbilical cord. Hanger-on of the rich.

Time goes forwards and backwards. Time is only material and I'm only time, their time when a child. My older brother wanted to prostitute me. I couldn't be what I was. Time and in time.

Quentin said that when there's no solution, you can't try to find one, you have to wait.

After my brother had finished with Earl, he came up to my bedroom to talk to me. He didn't bother knocking.

I don't say useless things.

"You don't need to cry about a woman who couldn't tell her cunt from a toilet."

If I had been another person, I would have mashed his face into red. Like some girls want to become ballerinas or have babies, I hoped that one day I'd have the ability to be totally independent and then I'd never again have to be nice to anyone or see anyone. Not someone who's a creep.

Money is only one of the means (power) of freedom (for me) and I wanted the money Mother had left me which I couldn't put my hands on. Everything disappeared in that house.

If one bit of what I was feeling had appeared, I and the whole world would have exploded with it.

"I'll tell you about your mother. When she took one drink of alcohol, she turned into a bitch. Sharper than the razor blades she used on her white legs. And then she turned into a dog, on her hands and knees, and moved to the nearest man's legs. Waggling her rump."

"I never saw this."

"Women need men. As soon as she reached the man's knees, she rubbed herself against them as if she was not only a bitch but in heat."

"Father didn't fuck her."

"So if one of you doesn't get fucked, for one second, you're so hot for it that you have to crawl over to every form of man you can smell? And she complained about Father being an alcoholic."

"You murder people."

"I'm telling you about your mother. The one you keep mourning for. The bitch who gave you bitch blood and made you the whore you are."

"Who was she?" I asked. I'll ask anyone. No one including me cares whether I cry.

"She never loved you, Capitol. In fact, she hated your guts because your real father left her because she was pregnant with you and she just wanted to fuck, she didn't want a kid."

"I know," I said to the only brother who remained.

"The dead are just dead," he said.

But if there weren't any dead in our lives or our living hearts, what could life be? "I'm not Quentin. I have to remember. I want to remember."

"Then remember how much she loved you. Remember when she sat on her bed all the time, naked; talking away on the phone to her friends. And you'd come into their room, tentatively, frightened, to ask her something that meant a lot to you. Without leaving the phone, she told you to get out because you were bothering her."

I knew how to remember. "Whenever I took a shower, as soon as my eyes were blinded with liquid, she'd come into the bathroom to toss a glass of cold water over my body."

"You know who you are? Capitol. You don't know what you want or how to ask for it. All you know is the smell between your legs."

I could hear the affection in his voice. My blood is infected. I don't know why I bothered explaining to anyone. "Maybe I make up my mother in my head and what I make up keeps me alive." My blood's infected.

"Your mother was crazy and she suicided. Capitol. You can feel and believe whatever you want and it's you who lives the consequences." Rimbaud knew what those consequences were. "Since you have her blood, why don't you make some money off of it."

I fuck every boy in town.

As for leaving I didn't need to live on the streets to know what it was to live on the streets R had instructed me. It was time for dinner. My body.

Better than dog food.

There was a cocker spaniel left over from the old days. What old days nobody knew. Maybe American history. This cocker spaniel, black and white as proof of the existence of Good and Evil or morality in early American history, ate anything. He was subconsciously trying to bury his pedigree to show his superiority to the English. Ate chocolate wrappers floating in toilet bowl water; ate the white toilet paper wrapped endlessly around my used Kotex pads, presents to the Virgin, so that no man would be inflicted with or remember that carrot juice was now dripping down between my legs. Father: "Women are freaks." This dog had one flaw: an insane lust for dead meat. He couldn't forget his lust. Every night when I placed the hamburger steak or lamb chops, Father never ate anything else, on the small round dining room table, I had to guard the dead meat with my life.

We ate for a while. I love the blood that drips out of dead meat. Father always mumbled before he ate his food; Mother taught us not to listen to him. After a while, Rimbaud said, "If I'm going to maintain your support, you're going to have to do something back. You're now too old to live for free."

"I can leave."

"I'm preferable to the streets," he said.

I was beginning to learn who I was.

Rimbaud: Oh you bitch I said females can't change I said once that thing between your legs gets walking.

I knew who she was who my sister was even if no one else

did. They all wanted to sleep with her, the males, some of them thought they really loved her. But it had nothing to do with love. It was because of what she really was.

It wasn't that thing down there, it was what she had inside her that made her what she was. Build makeup on her face so her face would look and smell like what she had down there.

My regular business was trade. The main income was small arms and ammunition. We had a few stores in town which we used as outlets. But I wasn't earning enough. I couldn't figure out why. Every penny I got I saved so I could some day know I was rich. So I could have. It's not as if I disliked my own fucking sister.

The convention forbidding slavery had simply rendered this trade more lucrative.

Father was mumbling, "I've done my duty by you; I've done all that anyone can expect of me and more than most parents do; I've done my duty I don't have any more money you know I don't have endless money."

"What do you propose we do with her?" Rimbaud inquired.

"We could send her to the state loony bin," Father said.

We all ate for a while. I remembered that there had been a man, a brother, who had cared about me; I wondered how long I could remember a memory.

And what would there be when there are no memories to remember? Someone said. We would be sailors. Sailors are helpless when they're not at sea.

I knew and I didn't know why Quentin had to fuck a lot of people and he didn't care about sex. I didn't know anything anymore.

I wanted him back with sheer desperation and I didn't know if I wanted him back.

England is worse than America cause the people in England who are oppressed don't even know they're oppressed. If there's no memory, is there anything? In England, they've internalized their oppression for so long that the only revolution they can conceive is to become their oppressors. There, a populist movement is one in which the members of a poorer class defy their limits and climb into the class above them. You eat the shit you live in. The English internalized class consciousness or class torture to such a degree that their mouths no longer open naturally. Those who weren't educated properly (in torture of the body) can't *speak properly* cause they're poor. The poor don't know what art is so they hate it. And rightfully. The whole country stinks of its own prison which it keeps making smaller. "You don't eat your own shit," I said to Rimbaud, "because your mouth's too small." I didn't excuse myself. I left the dinner table.

I wasn't used to eating their blood.

I went up to my bedroom, though I wasn't being punished. I was going to run away from here. The problem of where to run wasn't a problem anymore cause my mind was made up. In order to run away, I needed to have money. Mother had left me some money. I hadn't hated her as much as she had hated me. Rimbaud had taken this money. Legally, but *legal* is *illegal* to me. It's all the fucking same. It's not my decision. Their systems. In my nation, people say "Up yours," fought for self-determination, and whether this is historically accurate or not, we believe it happened. Is. I will not give up memory. "He's also your brother," Mother had explained. "When I'm gone, he'll take care of you."

Through the one window in my bedroom, which only dirty white blinds which were now open sometimes covered, I could see through the gaps in some wire. A dying

animal lies under rubble. A small bakery sits in a white
building. There's a cake in that bakery; thirteen different
animals ride around its top. It had been my birthday and
Easter so Mother couldn't get me a real birthday cake. So the
next year, she got me the animal cake. The girls in my class at
school came to my birthday party. Each of them was given a
different animal and then there were no animals left for me. I
wanted what was remembered.

Father had said to Quentin, *because he understood him*, that
a man has two instincts, *eros* and *death*. The natural conjunc-
ture, in the male, of these two drives bends him toward
brutality and violence. Sexually and nonsexually. Is there a
difference? He asked. A man can try to kill himself, but it's
useless to try, for he'll always kill another person.

That's what he was saying before Mother suicided.

I knew I have other instincts.

Just as the desire to suicide easily slides into murder, so
my hatred of family and men also had to be hatred of
myself.

Down there, Father was giving out his rare words of
wisdom. ["If conscience had to drink, it'd be another animal. There's no difference between love of family and business like there's no difference between honesty and
dishonesty."]

"*Her*—" Rimbaud pointed at an imaginary me. "She's running around the streets and making them stink with that
thing between her legs and this family is so rotten that her
parent isn't doing anything about it. *Her*. All that I want in
life is to have a good life and raise my son and how can I do
that when this family represents an unholy cross between
hell and the abyss?"

"No man should care for a woman."

"Mother destroyed you. You know that, don't you, you

drunk? Mother despised you, looked down on your intelligence, said you didn't have a cock. She taught us to do the
same. It was the same thing as destroying herself."

"They all do it. They have something between their legs."

I would have to get to the next town's shipyards. Since I
was under eighteen, I would have to sneak aboard the ship.
Once out to sea, they couldn't send me back to my family,
then I would use my feminine or masculine charms to persuade the captain or a sailor to keep me. If I were a boy, it
would be easier.

Rimbaud. "The point is that someone has to pay. Her
upper mouth is at least as hungry and devouring as the
cavern below it. Either let the state asylum take care of these
holes or let them earn money. If blood flows out, history is
the flow of human blood."

"Do what you have to." Father explained, "Nothing matters. Women cling to that myth called *meaning* cause their
flesh's a repository for life and death. They say we're scared.
But we know the world doesn't care about us. Finally."

Maybe he was right. Maybe I had no relations to men.
Maybe that's why I could fuck so many of them at once.

I didn't remember nothing. I didn't remember Quentin.

I realized I needed R. Quentin was gone; Father as good as
dead; I needed a dream of love. Love can not exist, but if the
dreaming of it dies, there's no more love. This brother wasn't
going to abandon me. He was a creep, but he was stable. I
would hold on to him.

Rimbaud wants me to be a whore, I said. My mother was
always happy. Laughing. These are some of the things my
mother loved: clothes, books, pornography, new places,
canned kangaroo meat and chocolate-covered ants, gossip,
gambling. Her eyes were a wild cat's. She adored her own
flesh. She stuck a piece of raw chicken under the broiler until

its skin turned black. And then she ordered out for the largest, most expensive lobsters she could find. With chocolate-covered bees. The kitchen was the smallest room in the house. I don't care whether you eat or not. She knew how to use a phone who needs to cook she had a big, strong man to take care of her, a former football player. American hero. It doesn't matter what you feel about him because he's going to take care of you forever and ever. Men aren't important, she taught us. She always taught us while she was sitting naked on her bed. Father's bed, twin, sat next to hers. Like in the movies. Objects. "Look at your father," she said. "He's sleeping again." He was sleeping. "He never does anything because he's stupid. Tell him he's stupid." I always did what I was told. I told Father he was stupid and woke him up. When I was older, I learned that Father is kind and gentle. And that there's no need to laugh at kindness, gentleness. He had started trying to drink himself into death because he couldn't be what she wanted and no man could. An American hero is a man who's made American history and American history is myth.

Doomed to be unwed.

Two days before this conversation, I had been outside, not in school. Walking through some alleys that were repositories for bums' piss. Only if you're paranoid, you're scared of a bum. Rimbaud spied me.

My skirt was half over my ass and there were no underpants, just a hand, a few fingers of which had disappeared into me. It didn't matter who the guy was. I can never remember whom I've fucked. How can I be my memories? I can't remember and yet genital touching means everything.

Men told me they remembered whom they fucked: they brought out memories for display, notches cut into a belt, to name identity. Being female I didn't and don't have to prove that I don't exist. Maybe the guy who I was with looked like Quentin.

Rimbaud walked right up to us and hit the left side of my face. He told the boy or man to get out. (Of me or out of the bedless street.) (As if he didn't exist. Only Rimbaud and I existed.)

"Even if you don't have any respect for me, Cap, couldn't you remember your father and respect him?"

Before he could say anything else, I ran out to a car, dodged behind it, swiveled around up a smaller alley. The boy or man with whom I had been was waiting in his car, a beaten-up brown, at the end of the lane. I got in.

Uncle Maury was another man in my family. Was a geologist who had worked on the hydrogen bomb. Went the myth. When young, he had wed a nice Deutsch girl who went mad. Maybe because she was no longer in Deutschland. Married a second again nameless girl, and, when she hanged herself in a closet, rewed the Deutsch girl. We are German Jews. He lived on one floor of the mansion he owned near Harvard University and she lived on another. They didn't meet. There were three children. One of the males suicided; the other weighed three hundred pounds and was a violin prodigy, was about to die. The girl was a successful modern dancer. A few months before her death, Mother had begun to see Uncle Maury frequently.

Nameless at birth and already doomed to be unwed.

"Fuck me," I whispered to the bimbo in the car. "I don't like preliminaries."

But he was going down on me.

"If you touch my clit, you hurt me. Fuck."

He did what I told him cause he liked what I like. I felt good for a few moments.

Rimbaud must have found us in the car while we were

fucking. The sun was sitting inside his head so his blood felt inhuman, as if the sun had escaped humanity. Pass out. He thought the city was exploding. Just as he was about to stick his hand through the car window, the bitch's fuck having partly pulled up his pants, the car burst into speed.

"Try to convince Father that I haven't seen what I've seen."

Come was dripping down between my legs (onto the car seat). I felt good. For a few moments.

I told the bimbo to take me home. Home was a weak father and a dead mother. There is nowhere else to go. I have to go somewhere, I said to myself, therefore there has to be somewhere.

Perhaps outside where the swans are sitting are the cunts of the night. Perhaps where the heat of human flesh is a song that's being sung by the winds who will never be even slightly human.

Once-almost-red reeds crossing once-almost-blue weeds stood half upright over dark-grey water. Above them, an occasional gull was a black shape in a darkening blue sky. (The buzzing in the head comes from wanting to suicide; when you've got a bad family, you're bad. So all humans hate you.)

(Inside the apartment, Father would be sitting in his black leather chair by a semilit or unlit window. He wouldn't care.)

(I had decided to pick up a man the way men pick up, are supposed to pick up, women to show I could do it. I went out with two gay friends of mine. We met a sailor in a gay bar. Neither of my friends wanted him because they smelled trouble, but I was so determined to prove something, I forgot to smell.

(The sailor took me to his room. All I remember is a large bed. He told me he fucked men and women. The day he had married his wife, he had tied her to the kitchen table and fucked her without stopping for three days. When I gave the sailor the underpants I was wearing, he let me leave his room.

(Back in my parents' house, I looked at myself in a mirror. Black-and-blue marks stained most of my body.)

Two days later, I was up in my room and thinking about how Rimbaud wanted me to be a whore so he could make more money.

We're all how this society makes us. R, in his way, was still pure, a poet. He didn't give a damn about God. About what people thought about him. All he cared about was money. He was the only one of us fit to live in this world. *R was the last romantic,* for he had totally made himself, except for his dislike of me, so whatever I felt about him or whatever he felt about me, I looked up to him. I can't live without having someone to look up to.

Mother had suicided. I knew I had to stop needing him, but I didn't know how except by suiciding and I wasn't going to do that.

I went downstairs to inform them I was getting married so you can't talk me into white slavery I said to Rimbaud. You saw him in the car the other day. By the way.

Why?

Why what?

"Why're you getting married, Capitol, are you . . . ?" (Men can't say this word.)

"I have problems Dad [though I don't bother to speak to my father] OK you don't know anything I just slit my wrists" I showed my wrists which didn't have any marks on them. "Maybe women get married because they're in love."

I can take care of it answered Dad.

Go to the doctor said Rimbaud.

I'm suicidal I repeated.

"Don't talk about nasty things at the dinner table," Father added and took another swig just like a writer. In a sexist culture particularly threatened by its sense of its own coherence or its hypocrisy, the prostitute assumes the mythic figure, CRIMINAL. DESTROYER OF SOCIETY IN FEMALE FORM. Better dead than red, said Mom, and I was lying when I said there were razor marks on my wrists.

A prostitute is restless reckless feckless, worst of all sexually demanding, homeless like a bum only she's worse she goes from one *man's* bed to *another's*. Not even her own body. RUINER OF SOCIETY. Did my brother want to make me a criminal or a revolutionary?

"This author has concluded that prostitutes are essentially oversexed pseudomen." I reported or repeated to Father.

"Women. I guess a man like me doesn't know women because no man knows anything."

"That doesn't matter." R. *He was the only one of us fit to live in this world.*

I knew Father didn't want to make me into a prostitute cause he believed in American morality so I crumbled a biscuit I had found onto the table and asked if I could be excused cause I wanted to see the swans.

Rimbaud said we'd talk about marriage later.

When I looked at him, his eyes were those of a small animal, a ferret who's trapped and knows it and is righteous in his knowing. Every time I looked at him and bit through my lips, I made them more tender. Soon I would poison my own blood.

"Blood is thicker than water." Father before he became an alcoholic. Father didn't matter. *"Just let me go," I told Rimbaud.*

"He's taking care of us." Father.

"If I'm bad, it's because I have to be. But I won't kill

myself. You've made me so disturbed, I don't know I'm anything. You've made me hate everything. The world. Me."

"Fecund for it," Father.

I ran upstairs and slammed the door on them.

"She didn't go to school today, did she?"

I had closed the door so that I could be safe. Downstairs they could say anything about me, do anything to me. Downstairs wasn't me. ("I'm not a sadist. I don't want control over other people: I believe in love.")

Fatherless nine months before my birth, and already doomed, and knew it, to be unwed from the instant the dividing egg determined its own sex.

"How can you know?" Rimbaud answered Father. "How can you know anything that goes on even in your own family?"

"I know. My daughter." [Father was a wimp. Father was kind, gentle.] He did because he had once given me fifty dollars when I had begged him for it and the next day my mother had instructed me that if I didn't instantaneously give it back to him and apologize to him, I'd have to leave their home forever. I wish all humans were dead because they rot, but I'm never going to die.

Perhaps the feminists are right when they say that all power's evil, but don't think so because I had to fight for my power in order to live. Father had no power and he was kind, gentle.

"How can you know anything," R said, "but alcohol? How can you know your daughter's a slut?"

"I just want my children to get along."

"I followed her. Someone has to follow her. Someone has to take care of her."

"I'll take care of her," Father whined.

Rimbaud didn't bother to answer the drunk.

"Schopenhauer said. Sure Capitol wants her own way, just like her mother did, but Caddy was one of the happiest women anyone ever's seen, so wanting her own way's not . . ."

"She's dead."

"Dead?"

"Dead as that river." Pointing to the outside. "Why don't you cry more about love? Who're you going to tell me to love next?"

Father looked down at the steak fat on his plate.

Fatherless nine months before my birth.

The next heart attack would be the one that killed him. End of some American un-dynasty. "Your sister doesn't love me because she doesn't have any love in her. Just like Quentin. She and Quentin. He's no son of mine; riffraff; he's probably shooting drugs in some alley, scum. My family is decent. [Honest, American] And Capitol's taking after him. He poisoned Capitol with ideas he learned in that university [it's good you didn't go to university] and filth. He's filth. He no longer exists in this family."

"Forget about Quentin. He's not taking any money away from you."

"I won't pretend I'm anything but a weak man, but I know family matters. Quentin and Capitol never learned this. [They're sick.] Maybe if they had grown up somewhere where there's no crime."

"You've got me. That's more than most people have these days."

I could hear everything. I could hear the feathers on swans' wings brushing over each other in an orgy. Of pride.

"You've got to love Capitol for my sake."

"I'm going to take care of her," said my last brother and then I heard him call my name up the stairs.

I heard Father yell goodnight.

The key turned in the outside lock of my bedroom and someone shambled off down the upstairs hall to sleep, way past my bedroom. To whatever those who are drunk call sleep and I don't know it is hell.

A good night.

Fuck them and fuck them again because even carnage is holy. I don't know what's out there in the night because *all I will be is lonely.* Maybe swans know. Night is what is to come.

Mother didn't put her cunt around loneliness and she suicided. Loneliness isn't alienation, I said, I hate the alienation of those men downstairs, shopping malls, their city. The court. I've been a child and I've been taught and shown meaninglessness and despair, but I don't dream that.

Not emptiness, monsters sit in flesh's halls. I know monsters and loneliness and they keep me alive.

"Experience," Father said, "only reveals to a man his own folly and despair, and victory is an illusion of philosophers and fools."

But there are wonders out there. Maybe all the sailors smell my cunt. I was crying.

The last of my family. Fatherless and doomed to be unwed from the instant the dividing egg determined its own sex. Who at seventeen, on the one thousand nine hundred fifty-ninth anniversary of someone's Lord perhaps the Lord the blacks in the United States resurrected into a human caring force a discusser of freedom according to James Baldwin, opened the one stinking window in the room they had allotted to be her bedroom, implying that she had free choice in their house, her own bedroom, and climbed over its black dust sill onto a blacker iron fire escape.

But had not immediately left their household premises because she was not about to go into loneliness without a weapon. There might be right and wrong, but it certainly isn't what they teach you. Had semileaped, not just thought her way, onto the fire escape on her left so that she could clamber into R's room where she knew he wouldn't be, yet (he spent more and more time pouring over his business books in his study, figures accounts savings, every penny put away noted counted again and again, sometimes he would fall asleep over what he called *real poetry*). Wanted to get to that large pale blue and red tin box in which she knew he kept the remains of their mother's life, her will, her own father's soft grey fedora. The documents of the money and actual money.

I wanted the truth. Scared he'd catch me, but all there is to be scared of in this world is that one of your relatives will get you. Entered the window and with a chisel I had kept in my room broke up the lock of the tin which should have been filled with cookies and took her will (as evidence, unknown of what) and all the money that was there (almost $7,000), not because it was mine but because it was my method of penetrating him. Inserting myself into the only thing he cared about. You will not whore me. Which I knew he could never forgive because insertion wounds, because wounds leave scars. A child who did it in a way at one blow certainly at the end of her tether, hardly knowing what she did, not even knowing what would actually be there except something called the truth (the only truth was her action—the one thing), that her mother had left her money, and that truth is loneliness.

Let all men dream about her afterwards.

I climbed down the black fire escape in the dusk and leaped, another leap this one partly premeditated, into the car in which Rimbaud had seen me fucking. Let them all see me fuck. Leaped not quite into the arms of the car's occupant; using him to get away. Knowing he, since he was married, would be easy to leave. Using him to get what was at that time the nearest thing to love: human help. For it, loved him in return. Until I vanished. From him. Never took money from a man that wasn't mine.

Fatherless from birth and already doomed to be unwed. Afterwards vanished, but no more to myself.

THE
WILD PALMS

THE WILD ──────

HER Harlow-colored hair and men's clothes the filthy over-
alls, the kind of woman men call "a man's woman."

Smeared with grease where she wiped it with her wrist
She was now in love with all things that are male. Not
hating men, not yet, maybe never.

In order to erase.

That's what she said about her life. "This is in order to
erase my life." Ten years ago, her father the Judge about
whom she hadn't given a damn anyway had died, a marriage which wasn't a marriage lost somewhere. The kind of
woman men love, but don't want to care for.

The laws of what is named *chance* are or might simply be
laws which humans cannot name and therefore cannot
know.

Airplane liked sex as long as she wasn't being more than
physically touched. By chance, Airplane (on an airplane)
met a guy who wasn't American and drank too much. Said
something like he liked the movie *Something Wild*; she said,
she didn't. Returned with her to her apartment and there
drank everything more than five percent in sight, while

215

informing her he was in love with a beautiful German woman who was in love with him.

Casually said, to hell with him, to herself and then aloud, for he didn't seem happy when he spoke about the beautiful woman: "What's the problem?"

"It won't last."

"That's stupid." It wasn't her problem. She knew if she ever came across something like love (mutual love), she'd fight like an animal for it.

The man didn't seem about to leave her apartment. Had gone through her Guinness and now was on her sherry. Being what she considered a polite bitch, actually unsure of herself, waited until the sherry in the glass was almost gone and then, as she moved for the phone to call him a taxi, reached for her neck with his arms. He kissed her lips lightly.

Since Airplane had just come back from a three-day affair in Germany which hadn't been interesting enough to last more than two, wasn't as interested in emotionless sex as she usually was, but at the same time thought, since I'm not supposed to be back in New York, I can do whatever I want.

Cunt is perfume waft of freedom.

The man was German. His father had been bored by his mother and his mother endured, but they had remained together for the sake of the child. The happiest period of his father's life had been when he had been in the German army prior to his marriage. Was now working as a newspaper reporter.

Found herself down on the floor. The reporter taking off her clothes. It was night the windows were open. Gave a shit and didn't, but most of all, she didn't need any more rapists.

Lay on her bed, still clothed. Was naked, sitting in front of him. Inserted his second and third fingers into her cunt, then her asshole, spread the fingers until she felt pain. Then lifted her above his body, into the air, then turned her body around on his fingers.

Almost lost consciousness.

Airplane: " 'Can I ask you . . .' I ventured. I was scared to ask. My thoughts almost gone.

" 'Yes. The answer is yes.'

" 'That's not what I was going to ask you.' I wasn't sure I was presuming correctly. Now half the world was known; half, unknown. I couldn't believe either part of the world because I was being presented with my own want, though I had been taught as a child that my dreams, desires, and imaginings had no correspondence in this outside world. As if I finally an animal. As if sex is a smell, track of existence.

"I corrected him, 'I was going to ask you how far you are going to go.'

"One of his eyebrows lifted up to blond hair.

"Proceeded to tell me to do various things. Masturbate with my fingers. Then, talk. Ordered me to come. Repeated these instructions. Sometimes watched me and sometimes left my bedroom, sometimes for a long time. Felt I was entering into my privacy, my self. Penetrating and breaking my frigidity, years of erecting walls, years of refusing to show myself to others and to myself.

"Sometimes hurt me by pressing on my clit or asshole skin with fingers. While hurting me naked in front of open windows in my kitchen, asked me if I wanted him to leave, I had the choice, and I said 'No' and I was coming.

"Back in my bedroom, told him no man had ever given me so much, not sure what I meant, wanting to go to sleep, my body started shaking as if it had had too much cold. The reporter finally took off his clothes, 'It's time to go to sleep,' put his arms around my head on pillow.

"Exhaustion.

"I had been able to fuck almost any man, but never to fall asleep next to anyone before this.

"Next morning when I woke, he looking down at his cock, sucked off his cock until he came a few drops and a few minutes later, he left me.

"As if I was beginning to be an animal. Only beginning to know. Had to see him again. I had never before cared whether a man whom I had fucked fucked me again or didn't. Something in me because I was someone was as determined to see this man again as I had been determined to escape the rapist.

"The second time. As soon as opened my front door, without even entering my apartment, thrust his hand under my red skirt and underpants. Ripped the underpants. Three fingers in the cunt twisted. I fell to the ground. Reporter entered into the hall."

(As soon as had finished university, joined a newspaper staff. Now, from one police court to the next. Reporting. Then, from one newspaper rung to the next, as he had been trained and not even knowing by whom to do: Live by lying passively on his back. Do whatever is easiest avoid all but commitments so normal they're lies. Passion, whether pretended or not was hardly the question, existed only to negate fictionally the meaninglessness and boredom. Now, at the edge of his middle years, saw the years as devoid of youth because he had gone, as he put it to Airplane, immediately into work. Airplane added, "Media work." "I've never had," he explained, "what's called *adolescence*— effervescent sexual heat always to the point of explosion, a way of living called *daring*, existing on top of feelings I couldn't name, much less daren't touch, therefore uncertain to the edges of nausea. Always *the wild flesh*.")

("Men have history," Airplane replied, "carved out history, historical periods, periods, this time of war. Since women don't have history, they don't have a chance to be adolescent for just one period. We make ourselves up.")

Airplane: "Later that night after he had again hurt me and made me come, when he wanted to go to a restaurant, I thought, I can't go to a restaurant with him. For in a restaurant I have to be my usual self, not this one. Have to be self-enclosed and frigid. Asked him if we could be with each other like normal people.

" 'It's allowed.'

"Thought to myself later, that when I had lived through childhood, childhood had handled me. Since I had never known a father because the judge. Before I was born, I knew only absence. No one had made me know safety. Now, maybe now, I thought, I'm reliving childhood because now I'm strong enough to handle it.

"German is presenting me with rejection and absence; this time rejection and absence won't kill me."

(Always at least half-believing she was dead.

(Had known long ago that everyone rejects and is rejected sexually and nonsexually and that everyone dies.)

Airplane: "The last of the three nights he told me he was married."

" 'Oh.' "

" 'I thought you knew.' "

"Walking back from the restaurant down a path that was black from the night, a habit (part of me) knew all about men, a man who had a wife and a girlfriend besides me. 'Go to hell.'

"Were walking past a cinema. So late, closed.

"Shoved me up against the locked glass door, winter, thrust a hand under and up my leather coat, sweaters, down wool tights, as much as he could get in, my cunt hurt.

" 'Come.'

" 'You bastard.' "

She came.

Airplane: "Didn't want a married man. Didn't want anyone. Didn't want to be touched. For I had lived after the rapist and perhaps because not being touched. Was over with. That's how it was with me, men.

"Walked.

"Informed him of this, back in room, how much hated him, by playing whore. Being a whore and even just in the sex business has something to do with hating men but I don't understand how. Something, men are stupid.

"In bathroom to remove my contact lenses, walked into bathroom to watch everything I did. Said, 'We're lovers.'

"I wanted so much. Didn't and don't know if *so much* is *too much.*"

(In Faulkner's novels, men who are patriarchs either kill or maim by subverting their daughters. Every daughter has a father; every daughter might need a father. One result, a critic who perhaps does not like women has said, is that women have shifting identities [perhaps it is that men don't recognize the shifting nature of identity], are sluts [is a whore a slut? was the reporter a slut?], have a hankering for evil.)

Airplane had decided, after considering the facts of herself, that women don't have shifting identities today, but rather they roam. She was talking, not exactly about Faulkner, but about her own self-destructiveness and strength. We are not dead pilots, she would say, because we don't roam for the purposes of dying. Motorcycle hoods. If a man doesn't fuck me where and when I want, he can get out. Of everywhere.

Soon women will terrorize the town square, particularly the young boys who are half-innocent and half-murderers as most young boys are.

THE WILD PALMS 221

Because she had not made any public thing, history, because she wasn't a man, Airplane lived in her imagination. More precisely: Because she hated the world and the society to which her childhood and then the rapist had introduced her and because she didn't even know what society she lived in (because she hadn't made it), she had drifted into her imagination. For every human drifts, however indirectly, not into love, but into freedom.

Decided she would make an attempt to get what she wanted by arranging to see the reporter. Decided he would be at a certain news conference in Berlin (was a reporter), and persuaded (only had to ask) a girlfriend of hers to ask a homosexual friend of hers to invite her to the conference.

Upon telling the reporter that she had been invited to this conference, arranged to spend a week with her there.

As soon as they met in Berlin, informed her he had to fly to London the next day to interview Yoko Ono. Who wasn't in London.

When Airplane upset (fear covering anger), instructed her he made all the rules. On a dirty floor of the room of one of Airplane's friends (where David Bowie had once lived or done something), made fun of middle-class family life, especially middle-class wives, while he finger-fucked her ass. Her clothes were filthy. Told her not to wear pants because he couldn't immediately get at her cunt and asshole.

Asked her, do you want my children?

Outside there were three bars and more restaurants on the various corners of the street. Berlin is always decaying.

The first bar was a yuppie restaurant. As sat on high highly designed stools, ordered her to go into the bathroom and come. She could come however she wanted to come. Masturbated in front of bathroom door while listened to a woman (presumed, a woman) pissing and wondering whether woman could hear her final moans which she was embarrassed to mutter.

Mind or consciousness was going or going someplace else.

Next bar one of German hippies. Told her to come while she sat on a stool in front of him. Did.

Walked up three flights of stairs to hotel.

Airplane: "While were walking up stairs, ordered me to take off my clothes. Couldn't because of myself. (Perhaps, how I had been brought up.) Inside the hotel room, when pressed fingers into the sides of my neck, I felt as if I were being taken care of and then fainted. Since I didn't feel frightened, didn't understand when he yelled at me I mustn't let a man near that part of my body, that was my weak point. For I trusted and trust myself enough that I'll know when I'm in danger and act appropriately.

"He didn't understand that I trusted myself and am strong so strong that I find being able to act weak or cared for a luxury. The rapist had made me strong.

"Back, down, in the hippie bar. As both sat on stools, said 'Come' and I came. Again and again. Then put hand up my skirt so he could finger my cunt and said 'Come' again and again. Of course.

"Later, on the wood hotel stairs, he would say, 'I am teaching you to come whenever I just say *come.*'

"Outside the German hippie bar. The sky or something was drizzling. So the black everywhere was actually grey. A tree which looked like a New York City tree, spineless, was probably trying to grow up in dog piss. Threw me down against this tree, I don't remember if he kicked, put fingers in my asshole. Another man was watching. Wondered whether he was going to ask the other man to fuck me."

Again in the hotel room. "Do you want this?" the reporter asked the woman.

Airplane: "Told him I wanted this and was very scared. Maybe it was time to stop. Though halfheartedly said this. When tried to drag me out onto the hotel's balcony into what was now rain, *I* broke down.

"He said. 'Everybody needs somebody.' To me. And I had told him about the rapist.

"Then he fucked me for the first time and I came and he came in me he knew I wasn't using birth control protection, for I never expected us to fuck and from the moment I saw him I saw no other men, and asked me if I wanted a child.

"Next day he left, six days alone in Berlin."

(He liked to tell jokes to other reporters. Have you heard the one about the Laplanders? They eat this green and red fungus up there. After all, they don't have much to do. So it gets them high. But they can't digest much of it cause it's hard to digest or something, like poison. It comes out in their piss, they drink their own piss. That's what they do in Lapland.

("Just like the Norwegians," said the other German.

("No. You want to know about Norwegians, do you? Two Norwegians went out into the woods in order to get drunk. After drinking steadily for two days, one Norwegian said, 'I have to piss.' It was the first words that were said. 'I thought we were here for serious drinking,' replied the second Norwegian.")

Phoned Airplane from London to cry he was having a nervous breakdown. Replied, get to New York, and phoned up a girlfriend of hers in London, saying take care of the reporter until he gets on the plane.

After hurting her clit for about seven hours, fell asleep while sitting on her hall floor rug and still hurting her clit.

(He thought, perhaps as he had been trained to think, that women were those humans who wanted babies. Since she hadn't had and obviously wasn't going to have a baby, must be a man. Or she had been born complete and instantaneous, she would have said, a hero.)

Airplane: "Had never given me his phone number I thought because he's married I had to phone up the newspaper office as if I were a ticker-tape machine to find out where he was. A month later, was told he was in New York.

"To Gary: 'Come with me.'

"Gary: 'What?' "

(The loneliness. Talk about the loneliness.)

Airplane: "I said, he's in New York and he's never not called me before, when he's been in New York, and I know the hotel he's at.

" 'Richard doesn't want me to go out.'

" 'Please come with me please please I've waited five hours now for a phone call I can't wait anymore and I'm scared to go there alone.'

" 'Richard doesn't want me to go out.'

"Had decided I was going to act so I put on a disguise of a grey fedora, just like the one the judge used to wear *over the eyes* (Oedipus was blind), and a too-long navy coat, *like the ones the schoolgirls used to wear,* and black high high-heeled shoes.

"My mother had worn red lipstick.

"With forty dollars. Went to hotel. Asked for reporter. Reporter, said clerk, in hotel. Went through hotel's bars. Bought champagne. Lots of fat ugly foreign businessmen who might pay to get laid.

"Gary: 'I want to leave.'

" 'No no. We have to find him.'

"I was running out of money and running into something else which wasn't madness.

"Asked the desk clerk again, another desk clerk.

" 'He went out with his wife.'

" 'No, he never goes anywhere with his wife.'

"Wanted to go. Begged for one more drink. But ten dollars left. Slipped my cigarette lighter, I never smoke, into an envelope with the reporter's name on it gave it and five dollars to another clerk."

The next afternoon, the reporter visited her for half an hour. Then returned to wife, left New York.

(What are the uses of memories?

(Though didn't like to think about her childhood, she remembered a conversation she had had with the child of the judge and his first wife in which her half sister revealed that the judge had so terrified her, she had become frigid.

("I'm frigid too: my nymphomania's a form of frigidity." As said this aloud, realized it.

("I'm with the guy I'm with," the half sister said, "—it's the first time I've come."

("I'm so scared of men of everyone, I use my endless predilection to come to keep them at a distance.")

Had been talking about knives which scared Airplane, but she bought some. Watching her own fear. Wondering. When came back the next time, drew one of the knives down her back and didn't hurt her. More interested in frightening her than hurting her. Now. At one point, lay on his back, legs over one arm of her red couch, told her they were perfect for each other. "That's cause the power situation's right," answered coolly, not feeling cool, feeling out of her depth in love. If he leaves me, she had thought to herself, I'll die. "Don't leave me don't leave me," she had cried. "I won't ever leave you," had answered. "The situation's right," Airplane continued, "because I don't want to, never wanted to be in a couple. Couples stink." Was crazier than when he had phoned her from London. Drinking even more heavily.

Left her apartment and wandered from bar to bar. Airplane usually never drunk, now drunk.

In the apartment, held one of the knives almost in her cunt, nicked one of the full lips. Grabbed a razor blade, held it to her own wrist. (If he leaves me, I'll die.) "I can kill myself, thank you; I don't need you to kill me. Look at me. Look at me. If you want me to die, tell me right now; I can do it.

"Let's get this over with right now. Do you want me to die or live?" Said, "Live." Threw away knife. Said, no more knives, but he was already sleeping. (Airplane: "I had to take control. The judge had taught me that to love is to want to die. Or had taught me to want to die. I threw the knives away and screamed that it's stupid to kill. But he wasn't there. Perhaps, he had never been there.")

After the reporter left, wrote him he'd have to stop drinking or else stop hurting her. Disappeared. Airplane tried to decide that if he'd leave her (left her), she wouldn't die.

But something else in Airplane, another Airplane, wanted Airplane to die so that she could be born this time not as a defect. Wanted him to be gone permanently so she could learn if she'd survive, who she was.

A muscle group grows only when it's been radically broken down.

Broken only to a certain point.

Was pushing the emotive, perceptive, and rational capacities beyond their limits.

Rimbaud had said, "I am an *other*."

Airplane: "But Rimbaud wasn't a woman. Perhaps there is no other to be and that's where I'm going."

b.

It represented freedom, but why it represented freedom, she didn't know. She hadn't had shit.

It wasn't that she had repudiated anything. Anything such as sex and love, and even love for money, which was what they said women wanted. It wasn't that she had repudiated anything.

Her brothers were gone.

She had never had anything to repudiate. She had said *no* to begin with, *no* before there was anything else.

Most women, Capitol thought, once they got past the stage of equating sex and love (or sex and criminality what was somewhat the same thing) felt they had been taken in by love (men). That the entire race of men had done something to them. Capitol thought, women's interiorization of male hatred appears as women's fear especially of their own blood.

New York City was freedom not because no one cared (no one did care) about something called humanity perhaps due to the growing poverty, the streets of disease, the numbers of dead bodies lying everywhere. Not because no one cared about the things that didn't matter (revealed in an awkwardness due to a directness which seemed uncharming even desperate to Europeans, an awkwardness due to an inability or refusal to be charming in clothes or in manners, an awkwardness that above all seemed part of innocence or stupidity and a selfishness which was a necessary tool for making art). But because, for the first time, she was being given a way to be a person. To say other than *no*. Through work or the movement of the heart or of the imagination in the world. This material movement of the heart or the imagination, which is also the world, in this simultaneously angelic and rotten city, gave the worker fame (credentials) and formed a community not otherwise found in the world.

Capitol didn't hate men. Though she loved to fuck, she refused to be touched deeply. In all senses but physical, she was a virgin. (Incest.)

Men said to Capitol and about her she was like a man. According to women was the most feminine of all females.

She met Harry, at that moment not interested in sex. But she took Harry for sex and discovered he was a nice guy and she didn't know if she was a nice guy too.

Never never to be touched and doomed to be unwed.

Harry had come, as if out of Eden, from an upper-middle-class family, reporter father and psychiatrist mother. He was short, fat. Capitol liked his fatness because it made her, given her insecurity, feel secure. Since he was fat, he wouldn't try to make her into a whore.

No one was going to touch her. Except physically.

When they had met in a small town outside New York City (all small towns were equivalent to each other to New Yorkers), they had both felt lost, Capitol because she was outside the American family, Harry because he felt (even was) unattractive and in the drive-away car going back to New York, as if there were anywhere else to go, Capitol put her head on his lap simply because it was available. Or a memory of physical pleasure or, actually, a memory of what, something, she didn't want to know.

Going into dream and back, to the city.

And later when he stopped the car just off the freeway, they made it on something too minor or neglected by nature to be called a hill, so all the passersby on the freeway could have a free show if they wanted it, a form of democracy.

Like shaking hands, Capitol thought.

Years afterward she didn't remember how he had then looked she did remember plastic sheets on one of the motel's beds.

During that beginning, he hardly spoke to her and didn't help her pay for her food (there was no reason he should) even though she obviously had no money. (She had never begged Rimbaud for money.) "Poor as a dog," only rich humans take care of their dogs. Sometimes. Later he said, because he was scared. Even later, told her he had been in love with a lesbian model who had once picked up one of the Ikettes in a Californian bar.

Didn't have to say she didn't want anyone touching her more than physically because it was so obvious.

Harry was fat, but he wasn't a dog, he knew he had (wealthy parents) something called music. So he could love this woman or man without being upset by her need to be alone.

For Capitol, the main thing was money. She didn't have any. She had almost finished off the seven thousand and she wasn't going to do a straight job (higher than the level of dog) because she was married to something called art. New York City understood.

As for Harry. According to Capitol. If love is suffering, it takes a long time to learn that love is suffering and humans don't live long enough to do more than good work. "Hairy as a rat," Capitol said.

"Harry."

"I call you what I want."

Harry asked his name.

I don't want to fuck you anymore. She didn't have to say this out loud.

When, either out of fear or because he had a patience (love) Capitol didn't know much less understand, he didn't protest, she began to think he wasn't Rat the Hater of Women all men and even women were. Destroyer of her.

Maybe love is suffering but suffering is only learning. Something call it love has to force us to seek out value, a lack of meaninglessness, as anyone with no money knows, Capitol thought, (Harry wouldn't think this because he comes from an upper-middle-class family), anyone who's poor knows that everything's expensive.

"I never had any," she said to him, complaining that his family was secure, more than wealthy, whereas hers had been fodder for the loony bin. "I never had any." It was easy to use money as the sign of everything else. But that he was trying to give her everything had nothing to do with the fact, not decision, fact that she was never going to let anyone near her again.

Money's a form of absence. Capitol wasn't refusing to fuck because she didn't have money or because she didn't want to fuck for money for the sake of men's control. But there was that too. She certainly wasn't refusing to fuck because she hated to fuck because she could come just by thinking about it. She had as a child. Hot. She was only refusing to fuck Harry. She'd fuck almost any stranger, but she wouldn't get near caring.

"I do what I do to make my art."

"Art?" Harry asked. Being a musician or space-case, he usually didn't listen to most of what Capitol said. (He was working in a porn shop until he made enough money from his music nor did he mind that Capitol had stripteased and now did an occasional porn flick because she didn't know how else to make money and hated bosses' guts. Not cocks.) Harry knew that in New York only a second-rate artist announced that he did anything for art.

In New York City, second-rate artists didn't survive.

"Art?"

"No man tells me what to do." She wanted to teach Harry that she hated his guts and perhaps this was how they learned to love each other.

Said over and over, "I've never had anyone." But she knew and knew that Harry knew that she didn't give a damn. Was cold. Wasn't cold because of any childhood. When Harry returned to the walk-through they coinhabited (she lived in one seven-by-seven-foot room, he the middle smaller, and one room for visiting each other visitors eating and bathing functions), he entered into, now entering into the dream, twisted wires and bits of dried glue and wood shapes and one day the ceiling in her room had simply fallen down, and out of that plaster from she called it *war* and nail polish bottles from the days when she used silver and black and blues, were figures. Dolls she had received and made something of. Then smashed. Molded red paper and clay guts and arranged them over the carved-open stomachs. Disarranged heads.

Her eyes turned into those of a cat when she looked at her babies.

Both of them began making money out of their work. Not enough to pay, much less afford, the gigantic electric gas and rent bills of the city. Harry had connected their electricity line directly to the main in the street. But enough for real necessities: restaurants movies a thrift-store clothing item and books. Capitol worked and worked because working (making smashing dolls) was her and her had never before been.

IN SEARCH OF LOVE

a.

AIRPLANE had decided that she wasn't going to see the reporter when he came over to New York.

Over phone, ignored what she said.

While sitting with photographer after a particularly long work session, when walked in, she ignored him. Photographer left and she agreed to walk around block.

Stopped halfway up street and hugged her and hugged back. Realized she hadn't wanted to leave him to the point of doing it.

Airplane: "I'm so happy I'm drunk on happiness I can never give happiness up."

Then,

Airplane: "I saw between his stomach and my body, the white sheet. Cock appearing out of and disappearing into my skin. Red-brown hairs held beads of water. As soon as he had penetrated me, I had come.

"Then he told me to come slowly. 'Just a little; just a little.' I held back my orgasm so that the sweetness just prior to orgasm was temporarily sharp and long.

"When I've come a lot, it's impossible for me not to come. Then at that moment, told me I couldn't come. I had to.

232

"Said, 'Don't come.'

"Forced myself not to come so fell asleep like one falls asleep in the middle of a dream and then woke up again, remembering we were having sex.

"Realized that my body and that architecture which is both physical and mental is more immense, fabulous than I ever knew or imagined.

"Then.

"Woke up early the next morning, jet-lagged. Six o'clock. Am never conscious at that hour of the city. But did it for him. We started walking. Not yet for alcohol. Was relying on me as his guide.

"And so was free to look for or remember my childhood.

"Being with him made me remember that I've always looked for my childhood. Perhaps, childhood doesn't exist.

"Are memories the same things as desires?

"(The judge had told me not to exist and my mother had stopped existing.)

" 'Look,' I said.

"I hadn't grown up in this city, but I had dreamt it.

"It was the street of Jews. The street was bare on both sides. Now. On both sides buildings all alike made up of tiny square brown compartments were begging for food. Life here on came out on Saturdays. Came out from the dark brown tangles of the intellect. Having come out, clothes were sold direct from Italy at half price (half price being the same as full price in uptown department stores).

"German had no interest in this childhood. Was only interested in forgetting, though I didn't know yet how profoundly. He had never talked about his own childhood except to say that he had always been happy.

" 'The street of Jews ends in the street of pickles.' Told him. Everything was now all closed up, everything that seems to make a Jew: Store of lox, other smoked fishes, fishes softly pink like nondiseased cunts (goy, in Jewish nightmare mythology), white flour bad or good for your health depending on the mama broiled or fried in too much butter and stuffed with brown meat or white cabbage or whiter cheese or even cherries (which only the goys care about because they don't like sex, and goys don't belong in this city). All haggling and screaming. The sellers. It was early morning, still a hope of a glimpse of sun. The city doesn't open up until the sun goes down at ten in the morning.

"At the end of something.

" 'Where will we walk?' asked him. Suddenly, *suddenly* because expected him to revolve around in his own memories and dilemmas without saying them to me, the German recognized something: a center for some of the wilder artists who made no money and therefore were slightly famous for wildness and the lowest of the low. Lowest of the low artists of whom there was now no visibility crouching, perhaps crouching, in a street where no one seemed to live, Puerto Rican street, boarded-up windows, no real windows, Caddies lined up in front of the seemingly uninhabited tenements, invisible humans trying to score the royalty of objects.

"Dream because the only real currency in New York is hope and a form of hope, fame.

"Perhaps there are cities which have nothing to do with belief.

"Then.

" 'Look,' said. Was trying to point at Chinatown, but couldn't find it because I was white.

"The reporter didn't understand this, he might not have understood anything because my culture wasn't his, more probably because what he wanted to do was forget.

"Because was walking so early in the morning and seeing a light I had never before seen or because wasn't alone and with him, I was lost. But there was in me the region to which I was going. I'm going to find my childhood. Have been saying this to myself for a long time. Now am finding childhood somewhere.

"('When there's nothing left,' Quentin had said, 'you're an artist.' I've seen people who have nothing.)

"Didn't know who he was only his news stories maybe that makes a reporter. Fell in love with every news story or other or freak whom he met. Love usually lasted five days. Most recently had been fascinated by or loved a tattoo artist who used his tattooing studio as a front and ran two girls. 'Look,' I said to him. 'Look.' It was dead water. (It was my home. The death of my parents.) Dead grey water in that bright morning sunlight. The water was someone's hair shining, must be rats. Garbage lay on and just under the surface of the dead, grey water; it, the garbage, was a giver of beauty. Bottles, half a milk carton, an indecipherable conglomeration like dead wood logs condoms plastic blue trucks, the dead wood logs also on top of the sharp declivity from the parking lot in which we were squatting to the river. Down. Two-foot declivity composed of something like dirt but not. Down, to dead liquid steel.

"In back of us, in the narrow streets, at night, cats prowled for the fish the fishermen who worked out of this neighborhood left behind. The skeletons of dead fish found under cars.

"Fish like cunts.

"To the right of the parking lot, a bright and clean white yuppie bar stood over the remains of another place. Inside had been all wood, long mirrors against two walls, a bar that ran from one end of the room to its other, sawdust on the floor. The fishermen would start their work at midnight. Behind this bar, a fifty-year-old blonde who had perhaps walked out of a film noir and developed a taste for girls would give every man the drink he wanted before he asked. All the neighborhood dykes, cats and fish, had been after her, but only to worship, not to touch.

"Outside, the cats in heat sounded like babies who were screaming.

"Didn't want to leave my home. Hart Crane, sailors. Gulls eat the dead (life) and the nondead (no life).

"The reporter said, 'Let's go.' It was after ten in the morning and still wanted a drink.

"Finally found Chinatown, but no one was there.

"Then.

"Entered it. Then there were tiny women dragging green and white shopping bags larger than themselves and these women were haggling with men not much larger than them over long white dirty roots and greens as wrinkled as lizard skin. Dead fish stunk.

"He wanted a beer and I wanted to run to one of the cappuccinos in my memory, but what I had remembered, memory had closed down.

"Then walked through the city of the rich. Their buildings appeared normal, like other buildings, decaying walls, colorful words and filth smeared across walls and windows. Piss stunk. But empty. Childhood I didn't want. Get out of here. Here stinks.

"Bought two wads of bubble gum out of machine, spat them out.

"Could smell the liquor the way I could smell trouble—any hope of my frigidity being penetrated—but it was still too early in the morning for a bar to be open. Were out of the arena of the rich.

"Sat down at an Italian café where there was a kind of liquor.

"Asked him if he wanted me.

"Said he wasn't sure.

"Didn't know of what. Unsurety, because it hinted rejection, made me panic. The judge. Persuaded him, at that moment, he wanted me though he said he didn't know who he was.

"For days wandered through the city.

"One day, found a roof. Told me he wanted to be with me for the rest of his life. Answered he was my life. Though my belief that he was deeply indifferent to me made me hesitate. If close my eyes, there is no end to these days.

"Look.

"Whenever someone touches them, my nipples're hard.

"Were also friends because I would disappear with my friends and he would wander and later would tell each other.

"Then.

"When had fucked, used to watch me coming and that way had come. Now I was coming all the time. Our last night together walked through the homes of the Mafia. Walking back again, a drunk told us we belonged together. Back in my apartment, I handed him a knife too dull to cut anything, not because I wanted a knife in my flesh, but because I was as happy as I was going to be.

"Was angry.

"The next morning woke up before the sun and left. Thought to myself, it's over. Returned, told me he loved me. I quarreled. Knew what my real childhood was.

Quarreled back.

At the airport, he fingered me in front of fat businessmen, gave me a tiny robot warrior. I put one of my fingers in my cunt, then on his lips.

b.

Harry *drawn by the idea of the doomed and isolated against the world*. Maybe she was too. Only in those few moments she wasn't either scared to death of starving or determined to make her dolls.

Since Capitol wouldn't fuck him, Harry must have been getting something besides just the realization of his ideal ("love") (he thinks "love," Capitol thought, because he's straight). Capitol didn't know what, nor did she ask.

She slept with lots of guys. Actually, there was no standard by which to measure. Many of her friends slept with more. Many of them Harry's friends, but then that's whom she'd meet, and she'd sleep with almost anyone with whom she wasn't friends. But not with any woman because she liked women too much. Not with Harry because he had become a person to her rather than a whore-maker.

Sex mattered immeasurably to Capitol and it didn't matter at all. At the same time. "Freedom," Capitol said. "They can have it."

We don't know what love is. Harry had some understanding. That she must live in solitude and that, since she didn't know this and needed to be touched, she was fighting herself. So all she needed was that innocent form of war called *wildness*. Maybe here's love, Harry thought.

He was now supporting both of them. By showing his upper-middle-class parents he would work so his parents were willing and supported both him and Capitol. Capitol would no longer strip for money because it made her hate men.

Worked by selling books in a porn shop and something else in its upstairs booths. Booths where one of their best friends, Gaylord, gave twelve blowjobs a night. Gaylord had come from American aristocracy, whatever that is, and had an aristocratic tongue.

Gaylord's best friend, Gil, and Capitol had once made out on a bed. Kissed, touched nipples, taken off their clothes. Confused that he didn't want to fuck her, she said, "You're gay," whereupon Gil replied that sexuality has nothing to do with names. Words. Capitol was learning.

Two months ago, Gil, part-time taxi driver, picked up a guy at Kennedy. When they were almost in the city, the guy exclaimed, "Oh dear! Mama forgot to enclose my credit cards and I don't have any change!"

"Sure, honey."

For some unknown reason, Gil took the stranger home with him and kept him, sans money, for a month. But didn't touch him. Gil had a habit of fucking anything. This was before the disaster of AIDS. The guy turned out to be a prince, Prince Michael of Somewhere or a princely friend of Prince Michael of Somewhere, the title meant nothing to Gaylord, and took Gil away to England and no one ever hears from him again except for one letter which says, "They're all gay over here."

Harry worked in the porn hangers-on victims of gun knife wounds and Capitol stole one of each of the porn titles in the shop in order to get inspiration for the smashing of dolls.

Harry wanted to earn all his money from playing and composing his music and later he did.

In a joint people called "The Rat," a dump and restaurant on Third Avenue, Rhy, a tall redhead who had been a Jehovah's Witness when a kid, worked as short-order cook and waiter. Having become friendly by necessity with a large rat in the kitchen, Rhy would inform the few customers who ventured in that there was an addition to their menu. Fried.

Capitol was always hungry.

The Rat's absent owner allowed Rhy and friends to use the joint once a week for performances. During some of the performances, Capitol's smashed dolls would make speeches, even enact scenes out of real-life personal dramas, while Rhy or someone else did something musical or even once, a beautiful girl showed a movie about high school and sex.

One of the smashed dolls was a Quixote, not the usual Quixote looking for love and purity in a society in which there weren't. In a society where language (the expressions of ideals) and acts had no relation to each other. But a Quixote writhing, like one of Capitol's guts, into thinness from anger. A Quixote hating everything that he knew, *not out of loneliness,* but in a world in which love and community had been so forgotten that the absence of love no longer occurred, was known. It wasn't actually anger, but a longing unto hunger which had eaten up all but the bones. The bare bones resembled bestiality.

Was Quixote's lover. Not someone who loved him or someone who had any idea what love was. Someone from this society. Someone he had once loved and after a pain unto death realized his love was useless. Three colors of nail polish covered this plastic doll; some of the nail polish lay glopped over chewed gum. Her eyes were composed of dried vomit.

Was a publisher. This publisher, who was of course English and who was rather faceless, was crawling and scurrying under every covering he could find, just as if he were a rat or worse a mouse, because everywhere he was seeing possibilities threats lawsuits that five pence out of each category of his enormous earnings might, just might be taken away from him and worse, the respectability which he had never accorded any of his writers except those who won prizes and made big bucks.

The agents who darted around this publisher were one-fifth the size of the publisher and composed of Silly Putty.

There was one beautiful doll who was shaped like a woman, but was all eyes.

"She doesn't even know what it is to hope." He thought that he had to know for the two of them. There were times when she yelled, nothing else for hours, just screeched, and he, though he had his upper-middle-class parents and because, held on. Held her. He wasn't angry; his jazz might keep fading into disco, but knew how to hold.

Then, their problem wasn't the lack of sex, it never is; it was business. Harry knew this knew Capitol was the more successful artist (at the moment, he thought) (and didn't want to think) and because the only value in this city is fame or success, if they stayed in this city, they would never love each other. He persuaded her for the sake of something called *love*, which she didn't know, to leave.

To go outside the city was to go nowhere.

a cheap place, a cottage on the New Jersey coast where they could develop their work in isolation ("In my childhood, New Jersey was rotting eggs").

In her own room, Capitol made one final doll, a harmless foolish sort of misshapen putty man. "It's not a man," she said to her girlfriend. "It's not a man.

"Otherwise there are only animals and all animals have the strength of desire."

"Hold me," she screamed at that end, "hold me."

"She couldn't work as a stripper anymore because it was making her sick," Harry said. "She doesn't want to make people, she said, people make her sick, she wants only the process of making. 'Everything,' she said, 'is time.'"

Harry: " 'Hold me,' she said. 'Hold me.' But I didn't know how to do anything else but hold her.

"I didn't know how to, if anyone could, if God could, kill her childhood for her, destroy her memories, her. I tried earning and receiving the money from my parents so she didn't have to strip for men anymore, and I decided to take her away when I knew that there was no way to hold her because I didn't know how.

"I began to give up: I knew I was ignorant and she was older than me, so now I tried listening to all that she said and doing what she said.

" 'Don't hold me,' she ordered. 'Get the fuck away from me. All men want to do is own me and they don't want me to be me and do my work.' The anger in her could have burned down the world.

"But she was clinging to me and I was clinging to her in that I loved her.

"I think that she kept on screaming, through time, when we were together, of course because she had been hurt or hurt and because no one had ever slapped the shit out of her, no one had brought her up to do other than be a whore. If that. Taught or demonstrated to her she was a wild animal untrained to wisdom, that she would have to fuck with pain in order to see the world. She was howling and howling and she didn't see me nor give a damn that I was through something like patience giving up my life to her.

"We loved each other and she was reducing me to nothing. 'Rat-hair,' she said. 'Rat,' and she despised my music because it wasn't wild enough.

"We had to get out, but maybe it wasn't New York we had to get out of, maybe it was the world.

"Had no money.

"As soon as we had left the city, she wanted to break up, not because she had lost New York City, but because I had to leave her alone there, in isolation, every time I had to gig with my band, so she said, 'I can't fuck with you again [even though we weren't fucking] because if I fuck with you and also we're living together, we'll become too close and then when you leave me again, you'll hurt me because you're the only one I've ever had.'

"It didn't matter that we weren't fucking. It was isolation."

So they went back to the uninhabitable city because Capitol loved that city as if it or that love was her. *Because she had to get rid of all isolation.*

In a passivity of despair Harry was doing whatever she wanted and Capitol fucked a man to get away from Harry and Harry and the man, another musician, became best friends.

Nothing seemed to have changed though now they both had their own lovers so maybe, in the impossibility, something had changed in Harry. Something called *hope* had given way. Despair turned into action. He was making money from his music now, no longer selling books at a porn store, though Capitol still acted in an occasional sex flick for quick cash. Between brothers and sisters, she stated, incest is forbidden. He had one girlfriend who told him Capitol was treating him as if she didn't care about him and the girlfriend was right. But Capitol had never stopped holding on to Harry, howling, "Hold me. Hold me."

Perhaps she never would. Until memory has died.

Just as Harry used to pick Capitol up at the strip club and take her away from the sailors who informed Harry they were envious of him, now he was ensuring that Capitol had her own space in which to work. And Capitol did (offend the few art critics who saw her work, offend anybody without trying) make her work, not principally because she wanted to succeed or be anyone, but because every animal needs water.

ABORTIONS

a.

A FEW days after had left New York, phoned Airplane and told her he loved her, then didn't phone or visit again.

As had been determined to get away from the rapist, now was determined to keep him in her life even though he seemed to be outside.

Had always spoken in war terms: "You'll win; I'll lose." Airplane hadn't understood what he meant. Lincoln, the great American egalitarian, suspended habeas corpus and moved around other civil rights issues only for the purpose of promoting the success of his Union. During war is democracy possible and, if so, to what extent democracy?

Though it no longer mattered returned to her life which was mainly work and some friends. (As if she had ever left.) By returning to a reality which no longer mattered or existed for her, work or art criticism (the old New York art world was dead) and friends (who had become totally desperate to be famous because, approaching middle age, it was their last chance), she was actually building a new life. Not in terms of content, but form. Fiction. Realized that fiction, only as reality, must work: life begins in nothingness.

The world of nothingness.

Due to feminist and, probably more, to yuppie landlord intervention, the German sex business was about to become illegal, die. Was asked by a reputable art magazine more as journalist than as art critic to investigate sex shows in Hamburg.

Airplane: "I'm being sent back to my childhood."

"Again."

Expected to like the sex shows because she both respected and felt sorry for (identified with and didn't want to identify with) the women who worked in them.

A week before left, the reporter phoned and asked if she would spend the rest of her life with him. Said, yes.

Phoned him the next morning to ask if he had meant what he said or had been drunk. Said, the former. "It's like Christmas."

"It's my Christmas present to you."

Expecting. That night, the night before flying to Germany, stomach blew outward, immense pain in right side of stomach, fever. Knew why. Decided to go to Hamburg because work must be her life.

The end of a Hamburg sex show: girl naked except for black leather straps crisscrossing her chest not obscuring her nipples and black leather strap around her thighs above cunt hair so "nothing" is obscured crawls like dog through curtains on stage floor to an edge. There (in what is supposedly the most "chic" sex joint in Hamburg), motions at a fat man in the front row. All men are fat. Here. Fat man wiggles his head, "No."

A second girl, naked except for very high-heeled plastic black boots, walks onto the stage. Holds a black seemingly leather dildo at cunt lips. Moves dildo circularly a few times, hand holding dildo moves away from cunt, walks up to first

girl who's still in dog position and motioning at men. Together, they motion at men. Trying to get one. On the stage.
Finally they get a young sausage who doesn't seem to know
what sex is. He does whatever they say. Get the blubber
down on his back. Wiggle off his light blue pants. Wearing
white boxer shorts. They don't look dirty. Kneeling girl puts
the black leather dildo slightly up his asshole. Standing
woman wiggles a white plastic dildo across his lips. Perhaps
a comedy routine, for the man can't get his cock up. Workers
need decent working conditions, Airplane thinks. The
standing girl shows the audience a condom so the audience
knows what a condom is and that they use them in this sex
show. Shows how to take a condom out of its package, then
expertly rolls it around a cock that's trying to disappear from
everything and everyone. Bends her body over the plastic
bump and her mouth more precisely over. Jesus Christ died
for somebody's sins, not mine. The cock can think for itself
and grows up. As soon as it has, grown up, the mouth
releases it and the second woman sits on it.

"What's this childhood to which I'm returning?"

Now the center of the stage reveals itself as a turning
circle. Spectacle! To the music of Kurt Weill, fake velvet
curtains open onto a tableau of four heterosexual couples.
Around, around. Four men or studs, heavy, probably
heavily muscled, disdainfully eyeing the audience, appearing bored, sit or lean on high wood stools. The schoolroom.
Below the studs, four kneeling women repeat the condom
lesson to make sure the audience understands, place the
four condoms over four cocks which are immeasurably
stiffer and larger than the white man's. Place their lips over
condoms.

Watched the mouths moving back and forth.

Curtains closed. Curtains opened.

Same four couples after same condom lesson started fucking. Watched the genitals move back and forth into each other. Studs were still bored.

While fucking, two more women at each end of stage walked onto stage. Wearing science-fiction clothes and holding tremendous white plastic dildos.

Airplane thought, perhaps it's the white race.

Every time phoned reporter from Hamburg, he sounded increasingly unfriendly. The more unfriendly sounded, the more her fever increased, the more she begged him to love her. Hated her goddamn childhood and adolescence.

The closer rejection came, the more wanted love or was able to love.

At the very end of Hamburg, desperate to do anything to halt what was growing, informed the journalist over phone they shouldn't meet as they had planned. Repeated this once, he agreed. Hung up phone. Immediately phoned again and begged to see him. Said he was in bad shape and had to be with his child. Said he was with his child all the time. Asked why couldn't she be his child, why couldn't she be anybody's child?

Didn't see reporter and wrote her article. Learned that when you feel pain you don't feel's bearable, then you feel worse pain.

Christmas.

And the ice of the blood will melt however it has to melt.

"Society," Faulkner said and I don't remember where, "should rest on generosity, that is to say, on the disposition to consider itself as being of a noble race, of a race heroic and even divine."

b.

Capitol couldn't remember what she had used when she had gone with the musician who later became both hers and

Harry's friend, but after she had gotten pregnant and had had an abortion without his knowing either, for they had broken up prior to the abortion and she had gone back to Harry (had helped her through the abortion, again watching out for her), she told the musician the day after the abortion and his white face became red and he said, "I was going to name him Jesus Christ."

Capitol thought, Jesus Christ.

"No," she said to Harry. "No." When they thought they were home free, had figured out the mechanics of their relationship or needs and were beyond surviving. "I don't like what men and women do together. Rather what happens when they do it: lose their honesty and integrity. Try to take away each other's pride. They stop being human. This is why you're my brother."

Then became pregnant again, not because she had ever wanted to, or now wanted to, or even out of forgetfulness, but because she was that age. When a woman's body turns into a baby-wanting machine and if the woman doesn't want a baby, she has to wage war against herself. Her best girl-friend the same. Both of them had three abortions in one year.

Capitol thought smashing dolls was good for her. Art: she was frightened she'd lost, would have to find anger. Actually she had too much for one body.

(As Harry had supported the stripping, he supported these abortions.)

Had a bad internal infection. It's not abortions: Capitol thought, it's poverty. Always damn poverty. I never have any choice because I'm poor; all I can do is struggle to survive. I have to take whatever I can get if I can get it. On the seventh day of the infection, dragged herself like a cat in heat out of the hospital so she could be the star in a friend's film which no one would ever see and which was more fun.

Now in her work she smashed up dolls and remade the pieces, as one must remake oneself, into the most hideous abstract nonunderstandable conglomerations possible which certain people saw as beautiful.

Then it was clear that she no longer had to punish herself (Rimbaud) or train for invisible Olympics, that the abortions had hurt her, for a lump in her right breast was cancerous. Doctor said. Two months later, she and Harry got married, not because they were sleeping together, but because she wanted someone to come to her grave.

"A good reason for marriage," she told Harry.

Something like when you're on a run, you're on a run, she only wanted to work and that meant going out as far as possible with her self, body and life (for who knows what the soul is, she thought).

It was the last day according to their license they could marry and neither she nor Harry yet knew. Two hours before she had to be at the unemployment office. She was crying.

Harry had a witness but no ring, so he gave the Town Hall judge Capitol's skull ring and the judge blenched but there were people waiting in line. Afterwards, they couldn't figure out if they should sleep together again because now they were married and Harry didn't want to so, perhaps not because, Capitol went off with another man, doomed to more than to be unwed,

The lump wasn't cancerous.

Went off,

"For freedom," Capitol said, "no man is going to tell me what to do nor woman. Sometimes women are the worst of all. Smash all the goddamn dolls again and again that's what my beauty is."

And later when all the business people would be after her obscenity judges bloodsuckers born-agains mealymouths her own dealers who had picked her up because she was famous but didn't really know what her work was would turn around and say, "You're foul. You make our decency and decent society into something black. Stripper nympho- maniac. If you want, you can still join us the tea party of those who are known in even control this world, but if not, you are doomed," Capitol could and would reply, "I had training in puking and in saying *no* even before I was born."

And Harry agreed—though might not have totally agreed with not fucking her and thus, never really marry- ing her.

"Right now, there's no memory of love in this society so we have to construct our own memory. But it's not exactly love that matters. Red meat and dead meat too," Capitol said to Harry, "stink up the whole place and that stink is life. Since life and death are inextricably mixed, you can't condemn abortion. Maybe that's why I had so many abortions."

AN END TO CHILDHOOD

AIRPLANE: "I decided I was going to make my life. I wasn't going to let this relationship just die, without a goodbye. Wasn't going to let die.

"Decided to return to Germany. Did.

"Was hesitant about seeing me. In a sleazy Italian restaurant in the soldier section in which I was staying, in a friend's unheated room, shook as if he was on the edge of a nervous breakdown. 'You're shaking.'

" 'I'm either going to buy a co-op development for my wife and son which will take all my money or I'm going to get my own room.' "

Airplane: "Said, that's some choice.

" 'Do you know anything about real estate? Do you want to get into real estate?

" 'My wife wants.' "

Airplane: "I asked why.

" 'Money.' "

Airplane: "I asked him why he needed so much money since he must have a good salary. Perhaps, said hesitantly, should figure out where he stood with his marriage and then figure out about buying and selling property.

251

"When departed, shaking less. Had arranged to meet for drink that night.

"In bar probably owned by Arab Mafia, said he was too tired for dinner. Alternately made out and discussed which of us could sleep with the woman behind the bar.

"Next day walked into my friend's apartment while I was finishing work (doing a minor article with photographer to pay for trip). Sat down on red couch, motioned me over to him, informed me he made my rules, not me.

"Took me to a fairy-tale Lebanese restaurant. To the sex section of town. To the bar of boxers. Told me to masturbate. Young woman sitting alone at next table departed. To street where threw me on top of car, shoved his fingers into cunt, then asshole. Sheer black pantyhose down around feet. Picked me up by cunt and asshole, turned me upside down. Screaming. No one noticed. Took me to bar of bums. We talked with a bum who looked like he had been a retiring middle-aged gentleman. Only other humans were woman with large breasts behind bar and two young black kids.

" 'You don't understand bums because you think you're better than other people. I'm a bum.'

"Drunk.

"When went to toilet, I talked to bum. When returned, when gave me white roses, gave them to bum.

"Drunkenly down wide street of hotel where I had made reservation. Walked into another hotel.

"No rooms with double beds were left. 'Which room would you like?' asked manager.

" 'Which room would you like?' asked reporter.

"I didn't know.

"Told me to try out all the beds.

"Did.

"In room. Took off my clothes.

" 'Now go downstairs and fuck the manager. And get me some cigarettes.'

"Have always been unable to make my sexuality public. Did always what he told me.

"Put on underpants. Fuck him. Left room on third floor. Walked down two floors. Shivered. (Can't even ask a friend to fuck me.) Crawled back up flight of stairs. Many dark brown old bureaus and tables cluttered up hall. Decided cigarettes might be in one of these drawers and, if so, could lie that I had fucked manager. None. Crawled up next flight of stairs. Wiggled like baby across red fake Persian rug, still searching for cigarettes, less quiet, shivering into giggles. Made bang closing one drawer with teeth. Lay back on rug like cat being petted and laughed. Opened door, saw my head peeking around a bureau. Took me up in his arms into room. Now shaking. For hadn't done what he had ordered. Held me held me. Then, hurt my clit a little, 'I'm making it easy for you,' turned me over, fucked me in my asshole without lubrication; both came hard.

"Bleeding a bit.

"Saw him looking out window as first light of day coming through, his cock jutting out. Wasn't usually hard; now always hard.

"When asked me to sleep in bed other than his, begged him to let me sleep with him, if only on floor, because am rarely with him. (Have become a person who begs.) Allowed me to stay, curled as small as I could into corner of wall and bed, then pushed me down so face slept on cock.

"Next full morning, in café of dead philosophers. 'I have to spend the day finding my own apartment. Then, I'm going to take my child on a trip. So I won't see you again I'll phone you.'

"Since I couldn't change the date of departure, spent my

next few days in the city, trying to trace where he lived. Didn't find.

"Our relationship had changed. It was no longer about my childhood. It was now my purpose to understand him.

"Weeks passed. For months, had been telling reporter about an artist, a friend, whose work had put him in jeopardy from several governments.

"For months, replied, 'That's not a story.'

"The day the artist went into hiding, phoned to ask for his address. Replied, no. Flew to New York as fast as possible. To find out address. Replied, no. Tried to force it out. Felt torn and hated media, media people. Imagined him tying me up, forcing me at point of death to tell him. Nothing happened. Didn't have sex. The next morning, said he had had a good night and left me.

"A week later, returned, now not on business, for two nights. Can't remember what. Remembered only he wasn't there. Over phone told me could never come to Germany, for Germans would never accept me. (The Judge.)

"Became hysterical. Replied, I had work in Germany.

"Replied, I'd lose my work if I came to Germany.

" 'My work is my decision. I know what's best for my work. I've always known what's best for my work.'

"What's the use of remembering?"

It was a week before Airplane's birthday. Was always excited about her birthday even though the Judge had taught her not to want to be.

When phoned was coming to New York, Airplane was excited and because thought it was for her birthday. Simultaneously felt from the phone call that their relation had changed a third time: now no longer needed her.

Asked over phone if he still cared about her.

Replied that everything is the same.

Dependent upon memory.

Airplane in person showed him she wasn't as physically or emotionally open to him, because no longer trusted him as had trusted him, by telling him he could no longer hurt her. Actually, was defying the rejection she thought would come or was frightened was making.

Walked to a bar. Mentioned was back with his wife.

Said had never left his wife.

"Do you have any room in your life for me?"

Shrugged. Replied that he loved Airplane.

Walked to second bar. "OK. Can I be your second wife?" and gave him her Hell's Angels ring which she didn't really love and didn't fit him. Pushed it halfway up his finger; looked at it for a long time; gave it back to Airplane. Wanted to return to Airplane's apartment and Airplane to cook. About New York. Were holding hands. Airplane asked, "Do you want wildness?" and ran in front of cars. Pulled her back. Pulled down in doorway of dead grocery store under spotlight in well-lit street and pulled her wool pants down to her knees. "Come," as put fingers on her clit. Half came. Decided to eat at cheap Indian restaurant next door, whose waiters wanted to be posh. Five times during meal during which he only drank, she ate lightly, told her to come and she half came five times. Trembling growing. Told her to come slipped his fingers under her ass to cunt lips, and publicly, very strongly, came. Told her to come.

In apartment, naked except for her white man's undershirt over her head. Hit her lightly with belt. Hit head. Hit the corner of eye, knicked the skin there. End of sex. Knew she had been sexually tight because no longer trusted him.

Next day, said alternately he loved her and didn't know if he wanted her. Airplane alternately cold and desperate for his life.

Had to leave her to review a huge Broadway musical and wanted to be with him because it was her birthday. Arranged to meet after play in her apartment; didn't want to meet her uptown.

When didn't return, drank as much red wine as she could, (usually didn't drink). When returned three hours later, pretended to be drunk and rolled on study floor. "A fake drunk can't fool a real drunk" and pocketed her tiny stuffed mouse as a present for his kid.

At six o'clock in the morning, left to see doctor in Germany to learn whether dying from drink, but wasn't.

To write is not to record or represent a given action, but to lose one's capacity to be the subject or initiator of that action. I lose myself, in putting down memories, in writing, but I don't escape the fatality of the events, their weight and their irreversibility, merely because I cannot claim them for myself. What happens to me happens to no one, because what happens is my exclusion from what is happening. I am no longer able to participate in transformation: Stuck; stuck in prison; pain.

Airplane cried, "Does this pain have any good? Does memory which is painful have any good?"

Had never told Airplane his private phone number. Had phoned Airplane between once and three times a week for the past eighteen months. Now, stopped phoning Airplane.

When phoned his office, informed he was on vacation.

Though had previously arranged to take motorcycle trip, because the German had done exactly what he had promised never to do (reject her), decided had to force herself not to see him again.

When phoned day before arranged trip, told him to go to hell.

When arrived in front of her apartment building on tremendous motorcycle, the image of desire drawn from her flesh, she wanted him and wanted him to disappear so she wouldn't be hurt again.

Told him.

Touched her breasts lightly. More on fire than had ever been.

Told him didn't want to be hurt again.

Led by hand into bedroom then fucked in ass with lubricant until they both came.

Softly smiled at her.

Half died for that smile; half hated him for feelinglessly refusing to be with her.

Though refused to cook for anyone, made dinner for him.

Airplane: "I wanted to love him as I used to but I thought he didn't love me.

"Next day, drove on his motorcycle out of city into trees so unused to I hallucinated, down winding, narrow roads. This had been my actual dream. Always had made my actual dreams real.

"Sitting on his bike, felt the dream was a nightmare because wasn't touching me anymore. Begged him to touch me.

"Asked me, what's the matter?

"Had attended university in America. Was now driving into his adolescence.

"Went to make phone call, then looked around, he wasn't there. Thought, deserting me.

"With him, went to the bar of his adolescence. There, told me he had been fucking the beautiful woman about whom he had told me the first time we met until the breakup of his marriage. He and beautiful woman had had a symbiotic relationship. A *symbiotic relationship* is when two people want to join, become a new person. Explained. When she had touched a glass, that glass was sacred to him. Had had to reject the beautiful woman because never happy. Had tried to suicide right before both breakups. He and beautiful woman had wanted to suicide together so they could be reborn.

"Didn't want to be.

"Said, 'Let's go.'

"Sat down on doorstep and said, 'Drop me at train station.'

" 'Do you want to say *goodbye* like this?'

" 'No.'

" 'Airplane, let's go home.'

"Sitting on his motorcycle, I thought I could jump off like he had wanted to. Told him at filling station, I've decided I'm terrific and if you don't want me, you're stupid and you're going to regret it for the rest of your life. Said, agreed.

"For the first time, on motorcycle, put my arms hard around his body and relaxed.

"That night, fucked me while watching me fuck and come.

"Next morning, blew him and came together my mouth from blowing him. Said, I'm a natural.

"In kitchen, right before leaving. 'I thought we had agreed you'd decide whether wanted anything to do with me.'

"Said, no, though he might disappear for four or five months. 'I always return.'

IN MEMORIAM TO IDENTITY

b.

Harry determined not to let Capitol (out of love) make him into nothing.

After Capitol partially, not totally, ran away with the film-maker, he started composing a cycle of almost classical songs dedicated to her. When she returned to their apartment, for the first time in their relationship, he became or acted jealous and broke a chair on the wood floor. Now, the opposite of the beginning, he was violent and Capitol appeared emotionless.

Capitol knew that she couldn't live with the film-maker for more than a few weeks because she had to give herself (work) up to him in order to live with him. For, to make his films, avant-garde in form and pro–working class via art world in content, he let every piece of riffraff into the loft so they could watch his footage over and over. Footage rarely made it into film as anyone in the loft did into sleep, except that sleep which was total exhaustion.

About one in the morning, would go off with his buddy to the local artist bar. About five in the morning, returned to room, ate two fried eggs and steak, threw the meat bones on the floor for the dog who never existed, and fell dead over Capitol. Sometimes she woke up, rolled his shoes and smelling socks off.

Some nights when the party wouldn't end, he didn't go to the bar, but passed out over whoever was in the bed at the time. When everyone had gone or, at least, disappeared into some loft space defined by long sticks of wood and stray bricks (he used to be a sculptor), Capitol would try to take off all his clothes.

She liked the energy of this life as inspiration, but couldn't maintain living in such frenzy without hurting her working. Three weeks later when the film-maker left the country, which she had always known would happen, she was glad to be able to return to Harry.

Only now shut him more and more out of her life. (When

Harry had given the concert of his romantic cycle, had brought the film-maker. In defiance of what? Something called *marriage* which [(she said)] she didn't recognize? Her own welfare, for she knew she needed Harry, which that part of her that had to do with art had to defy?) When abandoned her, she didn't know that anything had been wrong. Now realizing that she'd been mistaken to shut him out (though always wanting to put herself to the ultimate test), begged him to reconsider. Though she would do anything for a second chance, he wouldn't give her one, and that was that between them.

She learned she must be several, if not numberless, parts because there was a black hole dividing these parts.

No memory.

But afterwards remembered pain, so destruction of memory is no cure for the wounds of pain.

The black hole was dividing both her parts and the world, apart. Then, over months, she learned, not how, but just to be a person again and a person for whom there was no one to beg to be held by.

But all this—Capitol always knew this is the point—doesn't matter. No love can cause suicide in the way work can. What matters, Capitol didn't have to learn, and she could have been condemning not her own sexuality but her own conjunction of sexuality need and heart, is what perhaps according to actuality cannot ever be said, "I will not be nothing."

Doomed to be unwed.

(Perhaps there are only stories and perhaps there aren't.)

From then on, she didn't have to promise herself celibacy just as she had never had to promise herself to work (make art). Simply and naturally refused to place her sexuality next to anyone or anything again besides the simple doing of it.

Afterwards lived in a room in New York whose windows

never opened to sunlight which wasn't there and whose one door had several locks, as did all the doors. There. No friends, there were some, penetrated hers.

Worked alone here, no longer smashing her dolls, older, calmer, or so she thought, at least older, here in her jail, redoing dolls with paint and garbage, now dolls bigger than any possible human being always the dolls under a growing surface of artistry, now aware of every other New York artist's work.

Sometimes even putting their work crudely into hers as if all the world (making) were now freedom.

Whatever, and she found out one day, was the legality of plagiarism. The law. The judge. Another artist, a big fat pig Capitol later thought who is old and rich and doesn't even make his own work because he's so old, but she didn't think this when she used his work, who made a sort of soft-core pornography which had had a left-wing bias when he had still been young and made his own work (but many artists don't make their own work), sued Capitol for, he said, *replicating* not *using* a tiny one of his pieces. If it had been any artist other than Capitol, known to be a troublemaker, the fat pig's lawyers and dealers, who surrounded him to such an extent that the fat man like a Hollywood movie star didn't exist, might have asked the perfunctory hundred dollars for breach of copyright. Ownership. If anything. Ownership is money. Capitol learned. The lawmakers of this world (lawyers, judges, dealers) who were the rich sculptor demanded that Capitol not only destroy this doll, but also publicly apologize for using a rich famous person's work, for hating ownership, for finding postcapitalist and Newtonian identity a fraud, for all her years of not only publicly hating an ignorant therefore unjust society but also of trying to make someone of herself. ("I am an *other*.")

And remembered.

Work, like the room, was a window through which, a safe method of seeing the city, the society in which she was living. Her own dealer had signed the public apology for her without her permission and published it in a prominent art magazine. I've lost, she thought. I had already lost my body. What's going to happen to my work?

Now, nothing.

Harry and I had love, didn't we?

She took out a cigarette because she didn't want to go near the despair, not yet. Since her hands were shaking, the cigarette calmed her because to light it her hands would have to stop convulsing. So a cigarette went between two lips and hung there because it took two hands to light it. A single lance of fire. Left a track of smoke. The smoke, moving into the throat, hurt there. Tasted something like rancid. Put the cigarette away.

We had love, didn't we?

I can't forget love because I can't forget the pain, all that he taught me, that a human being can lie to another human being and know full well that he's or she's lying. Love dies. Like that. He left me. *Lie* like *leave*. Reject. Therefore judge. My whole life is not touching and being touched, but my memory of how I have failed in what is most important of all.

Is the memory of love enough?

(In the face of death.)

Sure I remember every fucking detail the smell of the flesh on his shoulders the smell of his flesh's sweat when he was lying next to me on a bed, looking away, a night, not thinking about or even noticing me. Then. If I don't remember the details, I make them up, and what's the difference?

I could live in memories of him, what I have made up, as if they are a castle. A desolate castle. But (not only do I not know what I'm making up), there is nothing to hold on to.

On reversed. That's probably the saddest, not death, but the nothingness everybody now seems to want.

I could be talking about the disappearance of history, our public memory, because they're trying. Money instead of history.

But memory is not enough.

All memory can do is a scream to be touched. And I need to. There has to be meat; meat stinks. And without memory, the meat, my cunt, rots.

Capitol thought, so it isn't these memories that know. It's something else.

She walked out of her apartment into the daylight which she didn't like unless she was on her motorcycle. Had all of her dolls' hair bleached.

Then, returning, sat them in appropriate positions for a court.

"This won't do," said the first doll, "this won't do at all of course."

"What won't do, Your Honor?" said, while the clerk doll kept reading out, ". . . against the peace and dignity of the nation. Manslaughter."

"We believe we can prove murder," the district attorney interposed.

"This person is not indicted for murder," the Judge mentioned.

Capitol hadn't decided if the accused (doll) was a man or a woman.

"Doesn't matter. Doesn't matter," said the D.A. "Arraign the accused."

A plump and young bleached-blond lawyer rose up. "Guilty, Your Honor."

The doll who was being accused sighed. She knew she had to get out of this country fast only here was no country.

"Is the accused trying to throw himself on the mercy of the court?" asked the judge.

"Guilty," the accused stated.

The judge was hammering his in this case croquet mallet. "No one asked your opinion." A strand of his bleached hair died and, falling on the table, broke into two pieces.

"There's no need to make a case," the judge further instructed the lawyers. "The case is closed. I will instruct the jury."

Capitol left her dolls in order to make a sandwich. She placed raw cabbage and pepper simply because it looked pretty on top of smelly white goat cheese on top of black German bread and brought it back to her Nazi dolls.

The judge had become very angry. "The case is closed," he said. "The accused is guilty."

"No," a tall spectator doll cried out. "I want to make a plea for the accused."

"What? A plea? For this woman? For a murderer?"

All the other dolls stood up and beheaded the doll who tried to make a plea.

Capitol beheaded her dolls. It was five years since Harry had left her. She knew that since she had killed their love, she ought to suicide. She had fought this for nothing. So. It's time to suicide. It's time to lop off the consciousness of memory. Memory is deathless and inescapable as long as alive.

"Fuck you," said aloud. "The waste isn't just me. It's not waste. It's as if there's a territory. The roads carved in the territory, the only known, are memories. Carved again and again into ruts like wounds that don't heal when you touch them but grow. Since all the rest is unknown, throw what is known away.

"Sexuality," she said, "sexuality."

Note: All the preceding has been taken from the poems of Arthur Rimbaud, the novels of William Faulkner, and biographical texts on Arthur Rimbaud and William Faulkner.